Ben Lawrence—Ever since landing in this sorry excuse for a town, he's been beset by woman problems. His two daughters hardly talk to him, his ex-wife resents him and his newest law client is a crotchety old woman who's determined to make life difficult for her neighbor's cat.

Eve Kearny—The cat's owner. She's been hiding out in this town for two years now. But it's time to get on with her life, time to put her failure as a wife and a woman behind her. She's not about to let a handsome lawyer change her plans.

Kate, Matthew and Jenny Lawrence—Ages fifteen, eleven and five, respectively, they hate their new home and their parents' divorce. And while they may be stuck with a stepfather, they sure don't want a stepmother.

Ben's moved halfway across the country so he can be with his kids. He's got a resentful ex-wife and a nonexistent law practice. But he's just met the woman of his dreams. Problem is, she's determined to leave town. *Can he tempt her to stay?*

ABOUT THE AUTHOR

Ever since winning a national short-story contest when she was in high school, Ellen James has wanted a writing career. As *Tempting Eve*, Ellen's first Superromance title, is actually her tenth romance novel, Ellen obviously has her wish. (Be sure to look for *The Confirmed Bachelor*, available this month, from Harlequin Romance.) Ellen and her husband, also a writer, love to travel and share an interest in wildlife photography and American history.

Ellen James

Tempting Eve

Harlequin Books

TORONTO • NEW YORK • LONDON
AMSTERDAM • PARIS • SYDNEY • HAMBURG
STOCKHOLM • ATHENS • TOKYO • MILAN
MADRID • WARSAW • BUDAPEST • AUCKLAND

ISBN 0-373-70613-8

TEMPTING EVE

Tempting Eve

CHAPTER ONE

BEN LAWRENCE was certain he'd landed in hell. He looked around the dried-out town of Cobb, New Mexico, its squat adobe houses scorched a dull brown in the sun, its drab streets laid out like a ticktacktoe game scratched into the dirt. As Ben drove down Central Avenue in his shiny new Jeep, he marveled at the battered, rusted pickups most of the residents seemed to favor. But this was home now, Ben reminded himself. Forget Boston. Forget corporate law, that was for damn sure. Cobb, New Mexico, wasn't the kind of place where corporations flourished on every street corner—or on any street corner, for that matter. The market for lawyers in Cobb was just a tad different than in Boston—just a tad nonexistent. But he'd stay in this town and practice whatever kind of law he could. He'd damn well stay. He wasn't going to lose his kids—not again. Never again.

Ben wheeled onto Alameda Road and steered the Jeep between a double row of sickly poplars. He'd only been in Cobb a few days, but already the town had lost its novelty. There were no surprises left. By now he knew to stay well clear of the "specials" at the Rio Diner, and he knew that Dixon's Bar served lukewarm beer. He knew that the projector at Cobb's only movie theater was perpetually out of focus and that the local teenagers hung out at the strip mall because there wasn't anything better to do. He also knew that Silas T. Cobb Community College was the town's one faint hope of urban sophistication.

Ben slowed to a halt in front of the college, a long, low-slung stucco building, and then he climbed out of the Jeep, bringing his briefcase with him. In spite of the heat of this September afternoon, he'd chosen to wear a tie and one of his dark suits, remnants of the days when he'd been a full partner in Wexter, Hollis and Greene. Might as well look the part of a bigwig lawyer, even if he'd forced his own career into a sharp and unexpected nosedive. He didn't feel comfortable in this suit anymore, but what the hell did you wear when you were a professional on your way down?

Ben strode up the walk toward the school, noting that the waist of his pants was starting to fit just a little too snugly; not a good sign. Unfortunately the men in his family had a tendency to spread around the middle, a trait that until now Ben had battled successfully on the racquetball court. He'd have to find some other way to work off the pounds. He doubted the folks of Cobb were into racquetball. He wondered if they'd even heard of it.

He pushed open the front door of Silas T. Cobb Community College, finding the air surprisingly cool inside. The building was a rectangle of classrooms that opened onto an inner courtyard, where a scrawny cactus garden struggled for life. One spindly plant had valiantly produced a single red bloom. The flower seemed out of place, startling in its vividness against the bleached green of the cactus.

Several students milling about glanced at him with curiosity, but it only took him a moment to find the office he was seeking. He knocked on the open door and poked his head inside.

"Ms. Kearny? Eveline Kearny?"

A woman was kneeling on the floor, rummaging through the piles of books strewn around her. She didn't seem to hear Ben, and from this angle he caught only a quick impression of tumbled red hair and a well-shaped posterior.

"Eveline Kearny," he said a little louder. This time the woman glanced over her shoulder.

"Yes—come on in," she said. "I just have to find a book. I know the darn thing's here somewhere...."

Ben looked around. Books covered almost every available space, stacks upon stacks. This was the room of someone who loved books, someone who loved them to intriguing excess. The place even smelled of books: that musty pungent scent of paper pressed between bindings.

"Need any help?" Ben asked.

"I'm reorganizing," the woman said. "That's why everything is such a mess." She straightened and turned to face him. "It's Eve, by the way. Eve Kearny. No one calls me Eveline, thank goodness. What can I do for you?"

Ben hesitated, studying Eve Kearny. Her skin was pale, as if she spent too much time cooped up in this office. But she was pretty, with vivid blue eyes and a capricious mouth that curled intriguingly. A kissable mouth, the thought struck him. Ben was relieved that after his divorce he still had enough sex drive left to appreciate an attractive woman—or maybe he was just relieved to discover any attractive women at all in Cobb, New Mexico.

She was gazing at him expectantly, and he motioned toward the shelves. "Go on looking," he said. "Don't let me stop you."

"Hmm..." She stared at the shelves. "Just drives me crazy when I can't get my hands on something I need, that's all. I wanted a particular quote to use in one of my classes tomorrow." She gave a shrug, and he noticed that one of the middle buttons of her blouse had come undone, revealing a glimpse of pale white skin. Obviously she didn't know the button had come free, a fact that made her seem somehow...vulnerable. Ben looked quickly back to her face, feeling as if he'd intruded on her privacy. But that enticing glimpse remained with him.

"Ms. Kearny, I'm Ben Lawrence. Josephine Scott's attorney."

Eve frowned a little. "Josie's hired herself a lawyer? I guess I shouldn't be surprised. She's been threatening to ever since I've known her. What did she do, drag you here all the way from Albuquerque?"

"I've just moved to Cobb."

"No one just moves to Cobb," Eve remarked, sounding matter-of-fact. She went behind her desk and plunked herself down in a squeaky swivel chair. Then she surveyed Ben with an air of resignation. "Might as well tell me the worst of it, Mr. Lawrence. Josie's decided to sue me. She wants me hauled into court and tossed into jail, not necessarily in that order."

"Something like that." Ben tried to keep his gaze off Eve, but it wasn't easy. Now that she was sitting down, her blouse had rumpled open a little further, a scrap of lace visible next to her pale skin. Ben averted his eyes, feeling like some damn voyeur.

The day seemed to have grown just a little warmer. Ben sat down in a stern, straight-backed chair across from Eve. Trying to concentrate on anything but her wayward blouse, he balanced his ankle on his knee and clicked open his briefcase. The one file inside was slim, containing only a page or two of jotted notes. Ben was used to having big meaty files on his clients. He removed Josephine's paltry folder and snapped the briefcase shut again.

"You aren't taking this case seriously, are you?" Eve asked, swiveling back and forth in her squeaky chair.

Ben grimaced. He'd gone from devising tax shelters for multi-million-dollar firms to playing mediator in neighborhood squabbles. But hell, yes, he'd take Josephine's case seriously. A good lawyer always took his client seriously, even if the client happened to be an old lady bent on causing trouble. Ben opened the file folder and scanned his notes as if he actually needed to read them again.

"Ms. Kearny, I believe the two of us can clear this up before Josephine decides to proceed any further. It seems her principal complaint is the fact that your, uh, cat—"

"Oscar," said Eve. "Did Josie tell you that my cat's name is Oscar?" She craned her neck as if to read the notes in his file.

"No, Ms. Kearny. The plaintiff never mentioned the defendant by name. Josephine referred only to a certain 'blasted furball' that's been harassing her chickens. So here's the deal, Ms. Kearny. All you have to do is shut the cat in your house. Then Josephine can go find something else to complain about, and I can go find myself a cold beer. Fair enough?"

Eve leaned back and swiveled her chair in a thoughtful manner. "No, Mr. Lawrence, it's not fair enough," she said after a moment. "Oscar hates being locked in the house. It makes him nervous, and he tends to shred the curtains, things like that. Oscar is a Siamese, you see, and he's a bit high-strung. If you ask me, Josephine could solve the whole problem very easily by tacking up more chicken wire in her yard. But she won't do that because she wants a fight with me. I think she has to fight somebody just to prove to herself she's still alive and kicking. Why *did* you take this ridiculous case, Mr. Lawrence?"

He had to admit it was a good question. Why, indeed? But Josephine was his first client in this scrubby town. She'd shown up at his office practically the moment he'd hung out his shingle—Cobb's small-town grapevine at its most efficient.

"Let's just say I took the case, Ms. Kearny, and leave it at that. I have to warn you, Josephine's getting all worked up about legal conferences and depositions and court hearings...."

"Why would someone like you move to Cobb?" Eve said bluntly. "It just doesn't make sense."

"Someone like me," he echoed, keeping his tone wry

"This isn't a place where anyone usually comes to start a new life. It's a place most people leave so they can start a life somewhere else. My students, Mr. Lawrence—they take my classes to give themselves the hope of leaving."

Ben gazed out the window toward the courtyard. He could see that one stubborn cactus bloom. "My ex-wife came here," he said. "She packed her bags and dragged the kids along. She's starting all over again. Which means I'm starting all over again, too."

"You followed your ex-wife to Cobb?"

Ben went on staring out the window. Eve Kearny had helped to put him in a contemplative mood. "I woke up one morning, Ms. Kearny, and realized the people that mattered most to me were gone. I decided to get them back—even if it meant coming all the way to this forgotten town."

Eve began rustling through the papers on her desk, and he saw an oddly troubled expression flicker across her face.

"I'm sorry, Mr. Lawrence. I've been prying. That's one of the hazards of living in Cobb. When you meet someone new, well, curiosity just flares, I suppose."

Ben was undergoing his own battle with curiosity. Before he could stop himself, his gaze dropped and lingered on that carefree middle button of Eve's blouse. With an effort, he looked into his file folder again, peering at his notes as if they would tell him something of great importance. But it was too late to act disinterested. He could tell that Eve had just noticed the button herself.

Her face went from pale to pink. Ben had never seen a woman flush with embarrassment in quite the pleasing way Eve Kearny did. A warm rose color suffused her skin. Obviously trying to be nonchalant, she inched her hand toward the offending opening and tried to cover it. Ben made one last heroic effort to study his notes, but then he gave up and studied Eve instead. By now her face was a bright rose, and she swiveled her chair rather too forcefully. "I don't think we have anything more to talk about, Mr. Lawrence," she said in a stiff voice. "You can tell Josie I think this whole thing is nonsense."

"A lot of legal work is nonsense, Ms. Kearny."

"I refuse to get involved. I have more important things to do. Teach my classes, counsel my students." Eve gave her chair one particularly impressive swivel—so impressive, in fact, that it whipped sharply around until her back confronted Ben. The chair paused for a brief significant moment and then swiveled forward again. When she faced Ben this time, she was still pink, but her middle button was firmly fastened.

It had been a masterful move. Ben felt a mixture of admiration and regret. He put the file folder back into his briefcase, stood up and reached across Eve's desk to shake her hand.

"Ms. Kearny, this meeting has been . . . informative. It looks like we'll be seeing each other again."

She withdrew her hand from his. "Mr. Lawrence, I'm sure that if you wished, you could persuade Josie to be sensible."

Sure, maybe he could persuade Josephine to be sensible. But if he did that, he wouldn't have an excuse to see Eve Kearny again. Ben smiled. It felt good to smile; these past months he'd gotten too much out of the habit.

"I'll see you and your cat in court, Ms. Kearny."

"Are Josie's chickens going to testify?" she asked caustically.

"Something tells me anything could happen in this case." Ignoring Eve Kearny's sour look, Ben took his briefcase, stepped around a pile of books and strode out the door of her office. He was still smiling as he climbed into his Jeep and wheeled away from Silas T. Cobb Community College.

"JOSIE, OPEN UP. I know you're in there." Eve knocked on her neighbor's door, listened for a moment and knocked again. Dammit, she wasn't going to allow Josie to harass her with a lawyer. That one visit today from Ben Lawrence had been quite enough.

Eve knocked again, then sank into the wicker chair on Josie's porch. Evening sunlight slanted across the floorboards, warming her toes. She slid off her sandals and slipped her heavy carryall from her shoulder. She could wait Josie out. She had time. It wasn't as if she had a date tonight. She hadn't gone out with any man since her divorce, which added up to twenty-six months of strict celibacy.

Eve shifted uneasily in the wicker chair, bringing her legs up and wrapping her arms around them. Usually she didn't dwell on her lack of romantic preoccupations. She could only assume that her encounter with Ben Lawrence had stirred these uncomfortable thoughts. It was no consolation that she'd made a complete fool of herself with the man. Her blouse had been hanging half-open the entire time she'd talked to him, and she'd blatantly poked her nose into his personal affairs. Somehow it had seemed important to learn certain facts about him. Was he single, married, divorced?

Divorced, it turned out, just like she was. Except that Ben Lawrence had followed his ex-wife to Cobb from who knew where. Surely you didn't follow an ex-wife unless you were intent on patching things up with her. And could any ex-wife resist a man who looked like Ben Lawrence? He wore his hair just a little longer than you'd expect for a lawyer, and it was a rich shade of golden brown, a color that reminded Eve of the autumn grasses that would soon soften the banks of the Rio Grande. And Ben Lawrence's eyes were so dark they seemed almost black, quizzical lines etched at the corners as if he looked out at the world in perplexed amusement....

Cursing her photographic memory, Eve scrambled from the chair and went to bang on the door again. "Josie, I'm not leaving until you talk to me," she called. She paced the warped floorboards, hands crammed into the pockets of her skirt. This afternoon she'd challenged Ben Lawrence, asked him why he'd come to a town like Cobb. But maybe she didn't want to admit *she'd* been hiding out in Cobb for two years now.

The day Eve's divorce had become final, she'd abandoned everything: the university career that had once seemed so promising, the house in Albuquerque where she and Ted had lived together and dreamed of the family they'd raise someday. She'd given up and run just as hard as she could. She'd run from all the memories of her marriage, all the memories of her two babies, each one born so small and still....

No. She wouldn't think about it. What was there to think about, after all? It was over. A part of her life completely finished. A wall came up in Eve's mind, a wall solid and strong enough that memories couldn't breach it. She went to pound on Josie's door again, her knuckles scraping against the splintered wood.

At last the door opened a crack, and Josie Scott's thin face scowled out at her. "Go away," Josie said. "I can't talk to you without my lawyer present."

Eve stifled a groan. "You're being plain silly about all this, and you know it. Oscar has never once hurt your chickens. He just likes to look at them."

"That beast torments my hens till they won't lay. He's a menace to the neighborhood. You talk to my lawyer. He'll tell you."

"Josie, I did talk to your lawyer. Mr. Lawrence came to see me today at school."

The door opened a crack wider, and Josie's expression changed to avid interest. "That boy works fast. Now you know I'm not someone you can push around just because you're a college teacher."

Eve had never pushed Josie around in any way, but she let that pass. She struggled to remain patient. "I thought you and I were starting to be neighborly. I know we can solve this problem without a lawyer. What do you say, Josie?"

The old woman marched out onto the porch. Josie never seemed to go much of anywhere, but she always dressed as if momentarily expecting a big event. Today, as usual, her square-toed shoes were carefully polished, every elaborate pleat of her broomstick skirt crisply ironed, her sparse gray hair set into rigid curls. A scent of clove sachet wafted around her, as if Josie kept her entire self neatly folded in a bureau drawer while she waited for life to happen.

"You'll be a little more respectful now that I have a lawyer," Josie proclaimed. "A lawyer from Boston."

Eve examined this tidbit. Ben Lawrence certainly looked like someone from a big cosmopolitan city. He had a certain natural elegance, something that went beyond his well-tailored clothes. He seemed like the kind of person who'd been bred on concerts and plays and classes at a good school somewhere, not a place like Cobb Community. Eve realized his sophistication had brought out a defensiveness in her she couldn't seem to shake. But it was time to try another tactic with Josie.

"Have you really thought this through?" Eve asked gently. "I don't see how you can afford a lawyer, especially one like Mr. Lawrence."

Josie stared loftily back at Eve. "Maybe I don't teach college, but I am still a person of means. Remove yourself from the premises, Miss Kearny, or I'll have my lawyer begin proceedings for a restraining order."

Now Eve did groan out loud. "I'm asking you one last time. Let's be rational about this."

Josie's eyes seemed to glitter with excitement. "I'm a very rational person, Miss Kearny. Rational people hire lawyers to protect their rights. That's what they do. Goodbye." Josie marched back into the house and exuberantly slammed her door shut.

It was hopeless. Eve suspected Josie was having a wonderful time. She'd practically glowed when she'd mentioned a restraining order. She would no doubt be terribly disappointed if Eve took the simple measure of locking her cat inside, away from the chickens. Then Josie would have to find another excuse to keep Ben Lawrence busy.

Grumbling to herself, Eve scooped up her carryall and sandals, stalking barefoot to her own house. The homes along this quiet road were simple and unimaginative, clapboard boxes with tarred roofs and rickety chimneys. But they possessed generous yards shaded by cotton-woods, and that was why Eve had chosen the neighbor-hood. Her cat needed a good yard on a street with little traffic. Poor Oscar. The Siamese was one of the few remnants of Eve's old life that she'd dragged with her from Albuquerque. She'd hoped to provide him with a peaceful happy existence, but now he was embroiled in a lawsuit, of all things.

As Eve pushed open her front door, Oscar materialized from under the hydrangea bush and streaked into the house like a flash of silver. Eve followed him and quickly checked his mouth for telltale chicken feathers. The cat gazed at her with wide turquoise eyes. He looked innocent enough.

"Watch your step, Oscar," Eve warned. "I think the two of us are in for it with Josie and her big-city lawyer."

Oscar sprang up onto the kitchen counter and then strolled toward the sink. Eve made a halfhearted effort to spritz the cat with a water bottle, her only means of discipline. Oscar looked offended, but refused to remove himself from the counter. He knew he ruled the house, and so did Eve.

She tossed her carryall onto the couch, unwilling at the moment to think about the English papers she'd lugged home for grading. Filled with a vague dissatisfaction, she glanced around her living room. Except for the bookshelves she'd had built when she first moved in, she hadn't done much in the way of decorating. The walls were still painted an uninspiring tan, she had yet to hang any pictures, and she'd neglected to buy throw rugs for the bare wooden floors.

For the first time in a long while, Eve admitted to herself how temporary her living arrangements appeared. In the beginning, she had meant them to be temporary. She'd simply needed a time-out to think about new directions for her life. But she'd been here two years now. Did she, after all, want to commit herself to this town?

She didn't know the answer yet. Cobb Community College might be an academic backwater, but Eve enjoyed teaching her students. They were so intense, so full of dreams about other places, so eager to gain the knowledge that would take them to a broader world. At one time Eve had been full of those dreams herself. She'd envisioned herself teaching at a large university somewhere. Perhaps in a city like Boston, Ben Lawrence's town....

Eve wondered if those dreams still mattered. Sometimes longings did stir in her, desires to apply for a position somewhere more cosmopolitan, more exciting. But didn't her students in Cobb need her in a way more privileged students never would? That was something she had to consider. One way or another, she had to make a decision soon. Her life couldn't go on feeling temporary like this.

Eve went to her bedroom to change clothes. She caught sight of herself in the bureau mirror, wincing at her disheveled appearance. She hadn't brushed her hair since this morning, and it fell in unruly waves to her shoulders. Worst of all, that darn button had come undone again.

She examined her blouse and found a frayed buttonhole to be the culprit. Before she wore the blouse again, she'd be sure to mend it.

As Eve undressed, she turned automatically away from the mirror, not wanting to see any of the marks left by her two ill-fated pregnancies. *Stop,* she told herself. *Don't think about it.* Quickly she slipped into jeans and a T-shirt, padding back out to the kitchen to feed Oscar.

She opened a can of his gourmet chicken-and-liver cat food, stood by warily while he sniffed it, then relaxed when he finally started nibbling. Oscar was a picky eater, and Eve was always trying to tempt him with some new delicacy.

"Spoiled creature," she told him without malice. Feeding herself was a much easier proposition. She heated up a can of vegetable soup, took a whole-wheat roll from the breadbox and sat down with a book at the kitchen table. It was rather a large book, a rambling eighteenth-century novel about the adventures of a plucky servant girl. Eve managed to balance the book in one hand so she could eat and read at the same time.

She had grown used to these simple solitary meals. She had actually come to enjoy them. But this evening she set down her spoon before she'd quite finished, and she stared across at her cat with a frown. For some reason she could picture Ben Lawrence looking at her with that perplexed amusement of his. And she could picture him pointing out that she was becoming a bit too much like her neighbor Josie, hiding herself away in this little house, this little town. Hiding from life....

She couldn't finish the soup, after all. Rinsing her bowl, she was now grateful to have all those English papers confronting her. She spread them out on the kitchen table and got to work.

But even as she marked decisively with her red pen, the image of Ben Lawrence hovered in her mind, his dark brown eyes mocking her.

CHAPTER TWO

WHEN SHE ARRIVED home late the next afternoon, Eve immediately took a hammer and began tapping along the wall of her living room. That was a hollow spot, so it wouldn't do...hollow again...ah, that sounded like she'd hit a stud. Positioning a nail, Eve banged it in forcefully. She rustled through the large sack she'd brought home with her, took out a framed print, hung it, and then stood back to examine the results.

The picture was attractive enough, although cheaply framed, showing a country maid talking shyly to a gentleman in knee breeches and a tricorn hat. Eve possessed a weakness for anything even remotely eighteenth century. She'd just spent the last hour or so browsing through the home-decorating section down at Cobb's Discount Mart on the highway. Granted, the home-decorating section at the mart was a bit limited in scope: a selection of preframed prints, a few throw pillows on special, and several sets of salt and pepper shakers shaped like chili peppers. Eve had passed on the salt and pepper shakers, but now she lobbed two ruffled pillows onto her couch. She supposed things did look a little cozier in here in a chintzy sort of way. But somehow that didn't make Eve's life in Cobb seem any more permanent. And it didn't help her decide if she really wanted to stay in this town.

With a sigh, she plopped herself on the couch. Oscar jumped up beside her, sniffing fastidiously at the new throw pillows. Although an aristocrat at heart, Oscar curled up next to one of the plebeian pillows. Eve rubbed his head. In Albuquerque, she and Ted had furnished their home with expensively framed prints and well-chosen finds from antique stores. Being extravagant now and then hadn't been a problem; Ted's salary as an engineer at the government labs had more than compensated for Eve's paltry earnings as a teaching assistant while she completed her doctorate. She and Ted had been happy then, in love with each other and with the life they'd planned together....

Eve stood abruptly, grabbed the hammer again and went to work locating another stud. She had one more print to hang, this one showing a girl in a high-waisted Empire dress, flirting with two dandies. It occurred to Eve that she'd chosen two particularly romantic scenes while browsing at the mart. She wasn't a romantic—not anymore—so she didn't understand her choices. She should have bought pictures of flowers, instead.

Someone knocked at the front door and she went to answer it, swinging her hammer. When she opened the door, she was surprised to see Ben Lawrence standing on her porch. Today he was dressed casually, in jeans and a cotton shirt with the sleeves rolled up, but still he carried a briefcase. He looked attractive, and Eve allowed her gaze to linger on him. Meanwhile, Ben contemplated the hammer in her hand.

"I know you don't like lawyers, but are you planning to attack me with that?"

"Mr. Lawrence. Let me guess. You're here to subpoena my cat."

He smiled. "It does seem that another legal conference is in order, Ms. Kearny. I've just been to see my client, and there've been new complications in the case."

Eve didn't want to let him in, even though he seemed to expect an invitation. "What new complications?" she asked distrustfully.

"It's complicated, Ms. Kearny."

"I see," she murmured. "Complicated complications."

His smile broadened. "Like I say, I just had a meeting with Josephine. Can't tell you what was discussed—client confidentiality—but I can hint that a certain feline was mentioned several times in a derogatory manner."

Ben Lawrence seemed to be actually enjoying this silly case. It didn't help that Eve felt compelled to glance furtively down at the buttons of her blouse—all of them firmly fastened, thank goodness. When she glanced up again, she saw the unmistakable amusement in Ben's eyes.

"We do have legal matters to discuss, Ms. Kearny."

"Oh . . . come on in, then," she said grouchily.

Ben walked into her living room and glanced around. He didn't say anything, but Eve couldn't help feeling defensive again. She doubted Ben Lawrence would ever shop at a discount store for home furnishings, or for anything else. Even his jeans looked subtly expensive, made of soft faded denim, so unlike the ones favored by Cobb cowboys. And Ben's cotton shirt wasn't just any old cotton shirt. With generous flap pockets, it was a natural shade of khaki that seemed weathered by years in the sun, yet it was touched by discreet elegance, too, the type of shirt you'd expect an upper-crust Britisher to wear on safari. Eve tried to tell herself she looked smart and sophisticated in her tailored skirt and striped silk vest, but it wasn't any use. She didn't feel smart and sophisticated at all. She just felt somehow unsure, and that bothered her. Oscar stretched from his place on the sofa, gave Ben a supercilious glance, then loped from the room as if seeking privacy from unwanted guests.

"You can tell my cat is hardly a vicious animal," Eve pointed out.

"I'll take note of the fact for my case file."

"Well . . . I suppose you'd better sit down." Eve motioned toward the boxy sofa. She perched stiffly at one end while Ben attempted to settle at the other end. Eve knew the overstuffed cushions were uncomfortable, but, as with most of her furniture, she'd hurriedly purchased the couch in Albuquerque and had it shipped to Cobb once she knew she'd be teaching here. She hadn't paid attention to style or comfort, but had simply chosen the first thing that looked serviceable. She'd allowed herself no luxurious forays to the antique shops she'd once loved.

"More books," Ben observed, glancing at all the shelves lining the room. "Most people have a few books tucked here and there, a few shelves maybe, but you . . ."

"I *am* an English teacher," she reminded him. "Books are my stock in trade."

"It's more than that," he said, his tone musing. "I'd say this place is barricaded in books."

"Is that how you picture me—the staid teacher who's hiding from the world?"

"Not exactly. I wouldn't use the word 'staid.'" His gaze lingered on her now, making her feel uncomfortably warm.

"I thought you had legal matters to discuss," she said with an effort.

"Right. I do." He snapped open his briefcase and took out a single sheet of paper. "I tried something with Josephine that has often worked well with corporate clients. I asked her to write down her complaint in her own words. Sometimes people get so tied up having their attorneys turn everything into obscure legalese, they forget what the case is really all about. They need to think it through for themselves.''

"Hmm...imagine that, a lawyer who doesn't object to plain English."

"Only as a last resort. But you'd be surprised how many cases I've been able to keep out of court this way. It cools people down when they have to write what they're feeling. It clarifies their thoughts, at least."

Eve considered this. She'd once kept a journal, and writing in it had, indeed, clarified her thoughts and emotions through some bad times. But she hadn't written in it for three years or so. Ever since her marriage had started to crumble, somehow the journal had remained closed. Maybe some things shouldn't be written about.

She took the sheet of paper from Ben and studied Josie Scott's laborious uneven handwriting. Josie had left a forceful imprint on the page, and she had a tendency to use short staccato sentences: "Cat howls. Keeps me awake. Can't sleep."

People revealed so much of themselves when they put pen to paper—more, perhaps, than they intended. Eve shook her head. "Ben, my cat doesn't howl. If Josie can't sleep at night, I suspect she's lonely, or frightened about something. It's not Oscar keeping her awake."

"She won't budge on her statement. Writing things down can have another effect on clients—hardening their initial resolve. It can make them determined to go ahead with the case no matter how rough it gets. I remember one particular patent dispute between two brothers who'd been business partners..." Ben got a nostalgic look. "It was more dramatic than any play you'd see on stage, believe me. Family betrayal, the works."

"And you help the drama along by having clients delve into their psyches with a pen and a piece of paper."

"Like I say, sometimes it quiets things down. Josephine did have a choice. She could've crumpled up that paper and thrown it away. Instead, she told me to come over here and present it to you as a formal complaint."

Eve stared at the arduous and oddly valiant handwriting. "I know what you're thinking. You're thinking I'll look at this and decide to be kind to my poor elderly neighbor."

"You could keep the cat shut inside."

"Oscar does stay inside at night, and he doesn't howl!"

"I guess we're at an impasse, then." Ben didn't sound particularly perturbed. He closed his briefcase and set it at his feet. He made no move to leave and didn't seem to mind when a silence stretched out between them. Eve gazed into his dark eyes, and she felt her skin heating up, as if the weather had suddenly turned . . . tropical.

She took one of her recently acquired throw pillows and smoothed its ridiculous ruffle. "Ben . . . can't you find another case to occupy yourself? Maybe something to do with dogs or cows this time. Forget cats and chickens."

He shrugged. "Believe me, I'd like to work my way up the animal kingdom. I'm available for more clients, but so far Cobb hasn't exactly been a hotbed of legal activity. Something tells me it isn't a hotbed of anything."

For some reason she couldn't fathom, Eve felt compelled to defend the little town. "Cobb has a great deal to offer, if you know what to look for."

"Such as?"

Eve thought hard. "For entertainment, you can always take down a few pins at E-Z Bowl. And I suppose you can go dancing at the Red Carpet Saloon. The owner of the Red Carpet has a brother who plays in a country-western band, so I hear there's even live music."

"You hear?" Ben echoed. "You've never gone dancing there yourself?"

This conversation was making her edgy, and she was sorry she'd gotten involved in it. "I'm a busy person. Papers to grade, faculty meetings... You needn't look so skeptical. I suppose I *could* have a rollicking social life if I really wanted one. After my divorce...let's just say I'm out of practice." An understatement, if ever there was one. Right now she had a good-looking lawyer lounging on her sofa, and she didn't know what to do with him. Instead of flirting, she was trying to steer him out of her house and down to the local bowling alley.

Ben stretched his legs as if settling in for an even longer stay. "We have something in common, then, because I'm out of practice, too. Dating, the whole thing. I'll bet you and I could share a few war stories about life after divorce." He kept his tone light as if to imply they would only discuss the humorous superficial stories, not the grim ones. But Eve didn't want to share any tales from the trenches with Ben. She didn't want to have anything in common with him. Besides, at thirty-seven she was more than out of practice. She was darn near fossilized when it came to dating rituals. What amusing stories could she possibly tell Ben Lawrence? She tossed her pillow aside.

"I'm sure our situations are quite different. For one thing, I got the impression that you and your ex-wife... well, you *did* follow her all the way to Cobb."

This made him straighten up. "You think Rachael and I still have something going? You're way off base, Eve. My divorce from Rachael's been final six months now. She came all the way out here because she suddenly married Phil Marcus. You know—Phil of Phil's Hardware store. And I didn't follow her. I followed my kids. Maybe I wasn't much of a father to them in Boston, but I'll sure as hell be one now."

"I did hear about Phil getting married," Eve said. "Some of my more romantic female students were quite taken with the story. Phil going back East on vacation and then unexpectedly coming home with a bride after all his years of bachelorhood."

"Romantic. Right." Ben's tone was sardonic. "A real whirlwind courtship." He didn't seem very enthusiastic about the love story of Phil and Rachael. His life certainly sounded like a jumble—kids, ex-wife, ex-wife's new husband.

Eve stood. "I can tell you have your hands full in this town, and I sure don't want to keep you from anything."

"I get the message, Ms. Kearny." Ben stood also and picked up his briefcase. "So, before I leave, let me get this straight. For a good time, you recommend E-Z Bowl and the Red Carpet Saloon?"

"I didn't say I recommend them. I just wanted you to know that Cobb has alternatives to offer. I've been here two years, and I can honestly tell you I've never been bored with the place."

"You like this town?"

"I didn't say that, either," she hedged. "Cobb is a sort of way station for me, I suppose. It's been a good stopping place for a while, and I won't complain about it."

Ben studied her. "Eve..." He seemed about to say something else, but then he shrugged and walked to her front door. He glanced over his shoulder at her. "Maybe I will go knock down a few pins. Bowling could be the beginning of a whole new life for me—who knows? By the way, be nice to Josephine's chickens."

Eve watched as he strode down the walk and climbed into a bright blue Jeep. He pulled out of the drive and waved at her before disappearing up the street.

Once again, because of Ben Lawrence, Eve felt like a fool. She'd let him know about her nonexistent romantic life—her nonexistent sex life, for that matter. And she'd overreacted to his presence: even now she felt as if her temperature had shot up a few degrees.

Oscar came slinking back into the room, peering around as if to make sure all intruders had been evicted. Eve realized she'd become as cautious as her cat, shutting out unwelcome guests like Ben Lawrence. She swung the front door shut. Her cat was happy, at least.

"Oscar, I need to get out more," she muttered. "And you need to do something besides harass a bunch of chickens in the neighbor's yard."

Oscar jumped back onto the couch, settled down next to a pillow and gazed at Eve with pitying superiority. Then he batted a paw at the sheet of paper that lay on the couch beside him—the page detailing Josie's complaints, hand-delivered by Ben Lawrence.

Eve experienced a sudden and unaccountable urge to leave her cat at home and meander on down to the bowling alley. If Ben actually did show up there, she could always tell him she was a closet bowler and simply hadn't been able to stay away.

"Ninny," she chided herself. Restless again, she surveyed the shelves, which still weren't enough to hold all her books. Ben Lawrence had gone so far as to imply that she hid behind books.

Her thoughts kept returning to Ben. Sure, he was attractive, but maybe she was dwelling on him so much because he reminded her of the wider world she'd left behind two years ago—a world that had once seemed full of wonderful promise. Of course, she didn't have to leave that world behind forever. She could apply for another job in a city somewhere. She could simply pack up her cat and go fulfill some of that wonderful promise. The choice was entirely hers. Suddenly Eve was seized by a mixture of hopefulness and fear. Lately she'd forgotten how many choices she truly had.

Maybe it was time for a new choice. Maybe just about time....

EARLY SATURDAY MORNING, Ben parked in front of the home of Rachael and Phil Marcus, recent newlyweds, as well as mother and stepfather to Jenny Lawrence, Kate Lawrence and Matthew Lawrence.

His kids had a stepfather. Ben still couldn't get used to the idea. He didn't like it, that was for sure. He didn't want his kids going to the roller-skating rink or to a ball game with some other guy pretending to be their dad. Okay, so back in Boston Ben had never taken his kids roller-skating and somehow he'd always been too busy at the office for any of the ball games at Fenway Park. But he'd changed since then. The divorce and losing his family had changed him. These days he was determined to be the one who took his kids roller-skating—even if the metropolis of Cobb, New Mexico, did not boast a skating rink. That was beside the point.

Ben climbed out of the Jeep and stood for a moment observing the Marcus house. It was a two-story brown stucco job, a little run-down at the edges, but still impressive by Cobb standards. The wide front lawn had plenty of room for a heap of bikes, a plastic wading pool and the collection of monster trucks that five-year-old Jenny dragged with her everywhere. Ben smiled a little. It was only recently he'd learned that Jenny preferred trucks

to dolls, that fifteen-year-old Kate loved to write stories
although she'd never admit it, and eleven-year-old Matthew dreamed of someday being a seven-foot basketball
pro even though he'd always been small for his age. In
Boston Ben had devoted most of his time to building a
crackerjack law career, letting Rachael raise the kids. But
it was different now. Everything was different.

He cut across the lawn and went to ring the doorbell.
No one answered, the silence seeming to taunt him. He
punched the bell again, then tried the door. It was unlocked, a small-town grace note. No one seemed to worry
much about robbery in Cobb; no burglar with any self-
respect would waste his time here.

"Hello—Rachael?" Ben called down the hallway.

"In here," came his ex-wife's voice from the kitchen,
her tone brusque, the way it usually was when she spoke
to him these days. Ben went to lean in the doorway of the
kitchen, watching as Rachael pulled a tray of lumpy
cookies from the oven. She cursed as she burned her finger on the rack. Rachael claimed to enjoy domesticity, but
she was a rotten cook. Ben hadn't yet lost the reflexes
learned during fifteen years of marriage, and he stepped
forward automatically.

"Let me have a look at that burn."

"No," Rachael said sharply. She turned to the sink and
ran cold water over her hand. "I'm just making some
treats for Jenny's Sunday-school class tomorrow."

"You never used to take the kids to church," Ben said.

"I like Phil's church. The kids like it, too."

"Great," Ben said lamely. He didn't have anything
against organized religion. It was just another of those
things he'd never taken time for in Boston. But maybe
Cobb was the kind of place where you got together with
a group and started to examine your immortal soul, for

lack of anything better to do. "So...where is everybody? The kids—good old Phil."

Rachael twisted around with a frown. She was combative by nature. "I hate the way you call him 'good old Phil.' It's patronizing. It's demeaning. Don't do it anymore."

Rachael was a wiry woman, athletic, her dark hair perpetually cropped short because she'd rather be playing tennis or riding a horse than messing with a new hairstyle. She always seemed to need some physical activity to vent her energy, but today Ben sensed an unusual tension in her.

"Rachael...anything you want to talk about?" he asked. "Are the kids adjusting okay? Are you, uh, happy here?"

"Of course the children are adjusting. Of course I'm happy." Rachael took a spatula and began slapping cookies from the tray onto a plate. She was wound up, all right.

"Listen, Rachael, I just wish for this thing to work out for all of—"

"If you want to talk about wishing, I wish you hadn't decided to move here!" she burst out. "It's making everything a whole lot more complicated." She thumped her spatula down on the counter. "The kids still could've seen you for summer vacations and at Christmas. We could've worked it out."

Long ago, when they'd first been married, Ben had known how to comfort Rachael. He'd known her tendency to pick a fight when what she really wanted was to have Ben cajole her into revealing her fears and problems. He'd known how to prod her into long talks, how to joke a little until she smiled, and then he'd end up making love to her. But over the years, he'd gradually lost the talent for cheering Rachael up. He'd grown impatient with her skittishness, her unwillingness to be straightforward about her own feelings and needs. Now she was married to another man. He could tell something was bothering her, something more than his inconvenient presence in Cobb, but it was no longer his place to coax Rachael's troubles out into the open. Regret stirred in him, but just as quickly died.

"I want to be a real father," he said now, the litany of his new life. "You know that's why I moved here. I'm willing to give you and good old Phil—I'm willing to give you and Phil a break. Do the same for me, Rachael."

She hesitated, then slapped more of her lumpy brown cookies onto the plate. "The kids are out jogging with Phil. They'll be back in a few minutes. And don't start getting sarcastic about the jogging, Ben—just don't. It was my idea, and everyone was more than happy to go along with it. I know Phil isn't in the best of shape, but he wants to trim down a little and that's the important thing. He also realizes how essential it is to exercise with your children."

They weren't Phil's kids, so why the hell did he need to exercise with them? Rachael was full of unsettling surprises today—first group religion and now group jogging.

For some reason, an image of Eve Kearny flashed into Ben's mind. Maybe it was because she seemed so different from his ex-wife. Eve looked like the kind of person who'd rather surround herself with a pile of books than go out and smack a tennis ball. She was aloof rather than combative, and he found it hard to picture her with the turbulent emotions that always seemed to churn in Rachel. He'd been spending a little too much time lately thinking about Eve Kearny. But there was an elusive quality about her that seemed to tantalize him even when she wasn't around. Not to mention that she was beautiful. And damn sexy.

"Ben, I don't understand you, I really don't," Rachael said, staring at him disapprovingly. "All those years you never understood what having a family meant. Now you act like you can turn around and make up for everything you missed. You think it's that easy?"

"Hell, it's not easy. That's one thing I know." Ben rubbed his neck, aware of the absurdity of his situation. He'd been daydreaming about Eve Kearny when he already had enough females in his life—two daughters who needed all the attention he could give, as well as an ex-wife who resented his very existence.

He heard the front door bang open down the hall and the sound of his children's voices: Jenny's low and thoughtful even at five, Matthew's charging ahead as if his words were chasing each other, fifteen-year-old Kate's no more than a reluctant mutter. The three of them seemed to be arguing about the latest film showing at Cobb's movie theater. From their conversation, Ben gathered they'd already seen it twice. Heck, he'd take them to see it again—whatever they wanted. He had a lot of lost time to make up for.

And here they were at last, trooping into the kitchen, sweaty and healthy, hair plastered damply to their foreheads, the three kids Ben loved fiercely. The three kids who in many ways were still strangers to him.

CHAPTER THREE

"YOUR FATHER'S HERE," Rachael said brightly, and unnecessarily. Obviously his kids could see that he was standing here in the kitchen, large as life. Problem was, they didn't seem to know what to do about him.

During the week or so he'd been in Cobb, they'd treated Ben cautiously, like someone they couldn't quite recognize outside the usual surroundings. He realized that all those years in Boston they'd come to expect certain things from him: arriving home late from the office after they were all already in bed, missing school plays and concerts and games because he was meeting with clients, never taking them to the doctor or dentist, never sitting up with them when they were sick. In sum, he'd been known more for his absence in their lives than anything else. He supposed it would take them a while to understand he'd changed.

Five-year-old Jenny gazed at him solemnly. "Hello, Pop," she said.

"Hi there, princess." He reached out to rumple her blond hair, but she whisked by him, taking the glass of orange juice her mother offered.

"Hey, Dad," Matthew said carelessly on the way to the refrigerator. Kate didn't say anything at all, pointedly ignoring Ben as she took her own glass of juice and slouched into a chair at the table. Jenny and Matthew began arguing over some Popsicles in the freezer, Matthew grabbed the plate of cookies, and Rachael scolded all three children.

"We're having omelets for breakfast, not Popsicles and cookies."

"I hate omelets," Jenny said.

"Phil likes omelets, so we're having omelets. Made from egg substitute, of course. Phil's watching his cholesterol. Matthew Benjamin Lawrence, stay away from those cookies!"

"They taste funny, Mom. What'd you put in 'em?"

"They do not taste funny. Oh, here . . . let me try one."

Ben felt the life of the room eddy around him, as if he were a boulder stuck in the middle of a fast-moving stream. Nothing for it but to jump in. He took a seat beside his oldest daughter. Kate had long dark hair she often swung in front of her face like a veil. This curtain of hair dropped efficiently into place the moment Ben pulled out the chair next to her and sat down.

"Have a good run?" he asked.

"Really, Dad, you don't have to make conversation with me," Kate muttered in a long-suffering tone. She stared morosely into her juice glass. "But for your information, it was a boring run, and this is a boring town, in case you haven't figured it out yet. Anything else you want to know?"

Ben couldn't decide whether to be pleased or dismayed that his daughter had inherited his tendency to sarcasm. Meanwhile, Rachael nibbled on one of her cookies, looking distressed.

"Maybe I put in too much baking soda," she fussed. "Where *is* Phil, anyway? Why didn't he come in with you?"

"He kind of, uh, lagged behind," Matthew said diplomatically. "Phil isn't used to jogging, Mom. I don't think you should've sent him out there."

"For goodness' sake, you were supposed to monitor him. What if he collapsed? What if—"

The front door banged open again, and Phil's heavy tread could be heard moving down the hall. He appeared in the kitchen doorway, red-faced, sweat trickling down his forehead, his breath coming hard. He didn't look happy. Without a word to anyone, he stalked to the fridge, yanked it open and pulled out a can of beer. Popping the lid, he took a large gulp.

"Phil," said Rachael, "wouldn't you rather have orange juice, instead?"

"No," said Phil between labored breaths. He took another swig and glared at Ben. "Lawrence. What are you doing here?"

"It's his day with the children," Rachael cut in quickly, rummaging through the fridge herself.

"Mom, I don't want an omelet," said Jenny.

"We're having omelets, and that's all there is to it. Phil specifically requested omelets, and I listen to all requests in this house. Matthew, no Popsicles!"

"I'm starving, Mom. How come you're making those weird cookies, instead of breakfast?"

"They are not weird. And I was in the *mood* to make cookies. Is that such a crime? You'll get your omelet in a minute."

"I hate omelets," said Jenny.

"We're having omelets!" Rachael clattered a frying pan down on the stove and glanced around belligerently, as if ready for all comers.

Ben felt a familiar longing kick in, an urgent desire to be down at his office, elbow-deep in contracts. Unfortunately Josephine Scott was his only client in town, and his books and papers were still packed in boxes at his new office on Central Avenue. But he'd always been better at handling legal disputes than family altercations. Rachael had a way of stirring up the kids. She seemed eager to leap into any conflict, thriving on the turmoil she helped to create. Throw in Phil Marcus, and the family really got lively.

Ben pushed back his chair and stood. "Tell you what," he said to Rachael. "I'll take the kids out for breakfast at the pancake house, and the two of you can eat those egg-free omelets on your own."

"Pancakes," said Jenny, gazing at Ben with enthusiasm for the first time.

Rachael frowned. "You really are disrupting everything, Ben. You shouldn't have shown up until after breakfast."

"What does he mean, egg-free omelets?" Phil asked. "There's no such thing as an egg-free omelet."

"These will be the best omelets you've ever had. Trust me, honey." Rachael turned to the kids and snapped her fingers. "Okay, upstairs, the three of you. Change clothes so you can go for pancakes with your father. I mean *now*, Kate."

Jenny and Matthew tore out of the kitchen, Kate stalking resentfully after them. Rachael started mixing some concoction in a bowl, and Phil retreated to the living room. It seemed to Ben that both Rachael and Phil were making a concerted effort to ignore him. He decided to go bug Phil.

Phil's living room was...interesting. A couch and a few armchairs were pressed up against one wall, but the rest of the room had been converted into an office, with file cabinets, a wall covered in corkboard, a bulky metal desk and an ancient computer. It looked as if no one but a solitary bachelor had lived here in quite some time. Phil, the bachelor turned husband overnight, sat down in front of the computer screen and punched the keyboard as if he'd rather be punching Ben's face, instead.

"Rich hotshot lawyer," he muttered. "You should've stayed back East, Lawrence. There's nothing for you here."

"My kids are here," Ben said as he wandered impatiently around the room. Sure, his career in Boston had given him money, but that hadn't been the point of it. The point had been that he liked being a lawyer. He liked unraveling intricate puzzles, guiding his clients through a legal maze and coming out triumphant on the other side. He also liked the human aspect that could emerge in even the driest and most straightforward of cases. That was it. More than anything, he liked the unexpected humanness that had infiltrated the elaborate structure of the law.

Ben missed immersing himself in all that. It was one thing to finally acknowledge that too many years of twelve-hour days had helped to wreck his personal life. It was another thing entirely to stop working those twelve-hour days, cutting back to spend time with his kids. Sometimes, when it came to work, Ben felt like a recovering alcoholic still in need of a drink.

With relief he heard Jenny and Matthew come tramping down the stairs toward him. He even felt relief at the sound of Kate's reluctant tread a few moments later. He'd learned almost too late that fatherhood was more important than his career. This would be his first full day with the kids in a very long while. In fact, he couldn't remember ever devoting an entire day to his children. It would be something new, a real adventure.

It might even be fun.

BEN GLANCED DOWN the length of Cobb's shopping mall,
and that was when he saw her. Eve Kearny, wandering
along with a few bags swinging from her hands, gazing at
storefronts—window-shopping, the very activity Ben had
suggested to his kids after lunch. Eve wore a skirt of some
soft material that swirled enticingly in the breeze. Her
loose hair fluttered in the breeze, too, shining like a glossy
ribbon of copper. She looked bright and cool at the same
time, reminding him of some cinnamon ice cream he'd
once tasted, all frosty spice. Without thinking about what
he intended to do, he shepherded his three kids toward
her.

"I need to say hello to someone, guys. I'd like to intro-
duce you, too."

"Spare us, Dad," muttered Kate, who seemed obses-
sively shy about meeting strangers.

"Who's that lady?" Matthew asked with at least a
show of interest.

"I want to go home," Jenny mumbled. Ben took his
youngest daughter's hand and gave it a reassuring
squeeze. She didn't look reassured, but he tried to ignore
that small detail.

Ben kept on heading purposefully toward lovely Eve
Kearny, who at the moment seemed like an oasis of
adulthood. He hated to admit it, but his kids were starting to wear on his nerves after only one morning. It
amazed him how imaginative and persistent they were in
the art of complaining. Kate objected to the hot weather
and the New Mexico dust that tickled her nose. Every half
hour or so Jenny asked for something to drink, then insisted they find a bathroom. And Matthew had a stone in
his shoe that couldn't be located no matter how many
times they unlaced the shoe, shook it out and laced it up
again.

Were all kids this cranky? Was it just *his* offspring? Maybe it was simply that his children didn't feel at home yet in this tumbleweed of a town. Ben supposed he couldn't blame them for that, because he didn't feel at home, either.

He hauled all three of them along Cobb's one excuse for a mall: a narrow strip of connecting storefronts on Central Avenue that included Phil's Hardware. Ben had run out of amusing activities, and this was the only place left in town where he hadn't taken the kids yet. By now Eve had seen him, and an expression he couldn't decipher flitted across her face. Wariness, perhaps? Certainly a hint of the aloofness he had sensed in her before. Ben found himself smiling. Eve Kearny probably wouldn't be too happy if she knew that her air of remoteness only challenged him.

"Ms. Kearny," he said with exaggerated formality when he reached her.

"Mr. Lawrence," she returned, subtly mocking his tone. She glanced at his children, and now he was certain he sensed a wariness in her. Hell, three kids all at once were enough to make anyone wary.

"Ms. Kearny, this is my family—Kate, Matthew, Jenny. Gang, Ms. Kearny is . . . a business associate of mine."

"It might be more accurate to call me a legal adversary," Eve said with a faint smile, nodding at each of the children in turn. Only Matthew acknowledged Eve, giving her a self-conscious nod of his own. Ben wondered if he should apologize for his daughters, then quickly decided against it. He gave Eve a regretful shrug that he hoped would carry enough of an apology for now.

"So . . . this is what you do on your day off," he said.

She jiggled the bags she was carrying. "I've been on a regular shopping spree. New light bulbs, pliers, tile adhesive—the works."

"I take it you're into home repair."

"Not really. But my landlord isn't into home repair, either, so..."

"You have a landlord. That's something. I'm still looking for a place to rent or buy. Until I find one, it's a room at the Cactus Inn."

"I didn't realize anyone was actually brave enough to stay at the Cactus Inn," Eve remarked.

Ben grinned ruefully. "If I'm not brave, at least I'm foolhardy."

He could tell his children were less than enthralled with this sparkling dialogue. He sensed their restlessness, as if any moment they would take off like a flock of agitated sparrows.

"Look," he said to Eve on the spur of the moment, "how about joining me and the kids for ice cream? There must be someplace that sells ice cream around here."

Eve was clearly not enthusiastic about his invitation. "I really do have to go home and, uh, put in my new light bulbs. Besides..."

"Let me guess. You think it would be a conflict of interest."

Eve seemed to consider this, and then she surprised him. "I don't suppose one ice cream will jeopardize the case. The drugstore over there has a soda fountain."

Ben felt things were proceeding just fine until he glanced at his daughters. Both of them wore betrayed expressions as they stared back at him. Anyone looking on would think he'd just asked Eve Kearny to marry him, not share an ice cream. All morning long the kids had been so fidgety he'd started to think they wanted to be somewhere else. But maybe this day was more important to them than he'd realized. He'd promised to spend it with them—with Kate, Jenny and Matthew, and no one else. Was his invitation to Eve Kearny therefore a betrayal of sorts?

Eve was starting to look as if she was about to change her mind. She glanced at her watch a couple of times. Matthew, however, decided the final outcome of the moment. Clearly unaware of the undercurrents his two sisters sent out, he marched toward the drugstore.

"I want triple-fudge chocolate-chip," he announced as he pulled open the door, causing a bell to jingle overhead!

Ben ushered Eve inside and finally prodded his daughters into the store, as well. All of them formed a row at the soda fountain, which was old-fashioned: a chipped counter lined with crusty sugar jars that looked as if they'd been around since the fifties, menus encased in yellowed plastic, a gold-flecked mirror behind the counter that made their reflections waver. No one else was there, and Ben could see a film of dust on several of the shelves. Maybe nobody *had* wandered in here since the fifties.

Somehow Jenny ended up perched on a stool between Ben and Eve, effectively separating them, while Kate slouched on Ben's other side. Matthew sat next to Eve, entertaining himself by swiveling around on his stool. Watching their reflections in the cloudy mirror, Ben imagined they could pass for a family: perturbed father, reluctant mother, glum daughters, energetic son. Ben glanced at Eve over Jenny's head, but Eve was examining one of the menus, and he couldn't even guess what she might be thinking. He could only study the decisive lines of her profile and note the smattering of freckles across her otherwise pale skin.

At last a man appeared from the back of the store. He had a wispy fringe of hair that straggled over his collar as if to make up for his bald spot, and he wore a baggy druggist's coat a few sizes too large. He seemed rather startled to see the row of people at his soda fountain until he focused on Eve.

"Miss Kearny—how's it going?"

"Just fine, Ray. These are the Lawrences, and they'd like some of your famous ice cream."

"Triple-fudge chocolate-chip," said Matthew, with all the faith of an eleven-year-old.

Ray scratched his chin. "Would you settle for vanilla with extra chocolate syrup?"

Matthew pondered this alternative. "Okay. But lots of extra syrup."

It didn't take Ray long to serve Matthew, then everyone else with large bowls of vanilla ice cream, this being the only flavor available. Ray leaned his elbow on the counter and surveyed his younger customers.

"Lawrence...Lawrence... So, this is Phil's new brood. Imagine that. A ready-made family. Never thought Phil'd get married. It was enough of a surprise when he upped and took that vacation back East. Next thing you know, he comes home with a wife and a passel of kids."

"Yeah, well, this is actually my passel of kids," Ben said.

"You don't say," remarked Ray. "So you're the fellow who followed Phil's wife out here."

Ben wished the townsfolk of Cobb would get their rumors straight. He noted that Eve was giving him a bland perusal as she spooned her ice cream. He returned her gaze. "I followed my kids out here, not my ex-wife."

"That so," said Ray, not sounding convinced as he leaned his other elbow on the counter. Eve didn't look convinced, either, but she smoothly changed the subject.

"Ray, did they ever get around to digging that irrigation ditch behind your cousin's farm?"

Ben half listened to the ensuing discussion of Ray's cousin Hank's alfalfa fields. Eve Kearny might give the impression of being reserved, but she seemed to know people in this town pretty well. Maybe she'd just decided to be aloof with Ben.

A short while later, Ben and his troop filed out of the drugstore, borne along by Ray's promise that he'd see about adding another flavor to the ice-cream selection—possibly butterscotch; triple-fudge chocolate-chip seemed too daring for Ray at the moment. Eve came along with her shopping bags, but she was brisk.

"I really do have to get home now. Thanks for...well, thanks for the ice cream, Ben. And it was good to meet all of you—Kate, Matthew, Jenny."

Ben wasn't ready to let her go yet. "Kate's a writer. Maybe you could look at her stories sometime." He turned to Kate. "Eve's an English teacher at the community college, just the kind of expert you need for advice."

Too late he realized his blunder. Kate looked stricken, as if he'd exposed her deepest secret. Chances were he had. He cursed his clumsiness. He should've known she'd be sensitive on the subject.

Eve, however, seemed to know exactly what to do. "Come to my office," she said to Kate with just the right note of carelessness, in the manner of one adult addressing another. "I might have time to read something."

Kate didn't answer, but she looked slightly less appalled. Eve turned toward Ben.

"Well, goodbye," she said.

"Goodbye for now," he amended.

She gave him an ironic glance. "Goodbye," she repeated firmly. And then she crossed the street, swinging her shopping bags, her skirt swirling once again in the breeze. Ben watched her until Jenny tugged on his hand.

"Is that lady your girlfriend, Pop?"

"Of *course* she's not his girlfriend," Kate said sharply. "She didn't act like his girlfriend, did she?"

"No, she didn't," Ben agreed in a wry tone of voice. He gazed after Eve, watching the breeze lift strands of her vivid red hair. He wasn't in the market for a "girlfriend," that word with all its connotations of innocent devotion. He could imagine only having a lover in his life—the type of woman who would understand that he had his hands full with his family and that he couldn't take on any other commitments.

He smiled a little. He had a feeling Eve Kearny would laugh in his face at the idea of being either his girlfriend *or* his lover.

CHAPTER FOUR

EVE FOUND HERSELF thinking about Ben Lawrence again. Late Monday afternoon she sat in a faculty meeting, and instead of listening to Professor Halford maunder on about homecoming festivities, she thought about Ben. She pictured him with his three kids. He'd looked different, somehow, surrounded by those kids. Anchored. Steady. A man who had found his place and a man who perhaps had also seemed a bit harried.

Eve allowed herself a slight smile and doodled on the notepad in front of her. It had been an awkward situation, sharing ice cream with Ben and his children. She'd felt like an intruder, yet she'd unaccountably wanted to linger. It had taken an effort of will to say goodbye to Ben, to go home to her solitude—

"Eve, what do you think?" Professor Halford asked earnestly, and she gave a guilty start. She searched her mind for clues as to what he'd been saying. Homecoming. Something about refreshments...

"The arrangements we had last year worked very well," she hazarded. "Why don't we just do the same thing this year?"

Professor Halford nodded, considering her words earnestly. "I do believe you're right. You and Angela will be in charge of refreshments again, and Sal will coordinate athletic events with the science department."

Now Eve grimaced. If her mind hadn't been wandering, she could've shaken things up a little—suggested that Sal handle refreshments, while *she* organized the annual Cobb Community football game. Homecoming at the school was a rather pathetic affair. Few alumni returned for the festivities; the celebration was mostly to inspire some semblance of school spirit among current students.

Eve glanced around the table. The others appeared so solemn, so intent, as if homecoming at Cobb Community College was an event of supreme importance. And what the heck—maybe it was. Eve felt an unexpected stirring of affection for these colleagues of hers. Angela Thornton, the school's one history teacher, was a fiftyish woman who always looked vaguely worried, as if trying to remember snippets of information she'd forgotten to give her students. Sitting next to Angela was Sal Lucero, soccer coach and journalism instructor. Sal was a young teacher, barely out of college himself, his enthusiasm resolute and at times wearing on the other teachers. Then there was venerable Professor James Halford, dean of humanities. Professor Halford always wore the same tweed jacket, an ancient item of clothing that was fraying at the seams. Rumor had it he'd been wearing that jacket for more than twenty years, steadfastly objecting to the new coats his wife kept buying him. Professor Halford refused to retire his tweed jacket—and, at seventy-five, he refused to retire himself. For that matter, teachers at Cobb Community were simply too hard to come by, and so were never asked to step down.

Eve herself rounded out the meager faculty of the humanities department. Little by little, without realizing it, she'd formed a quiet camaraderie with these people. Perhaps she only noted the camaraderie today because she'd started to consider the possibility of leaving.

"I believe we've finished our business," Professor Halford intoned, gravely rubbing his salt-and-pepper beard. "The meeting is adjourned."

Eve gathered up her notepad and books, and headed back down the corridor. Then she saw Ben Lawrence leaning in the doorway of her office, waiting for her. Her first reaction was a simple unquestioning pleasure. Maybe it was because he looked so good: golden brown hair curling at his shirt collar, a silk tie loosened casually at his throat, his dark eyes seeming to hold their own pleasure as he watched her approach. Eve had only a few seconds to put up her guard, a few seconds to retreat behind her usual cool demeanor.

"Mr. Lawrence," she said, brushing past him to go into her office. "We just keep running into each other, don't we?"

"It's a small world, Ms. Kearny."

She deposited her books on the desk, sat down and surveyed him. "What can I do for you, Ben?"

He settled himself into a chair in front of the desk, snapping open his briefcase and extracting a file folder. He was all business. "I'm here to take a deposition from you," he said, his tone all business, too.

She glanced at him suspiciously. "You're not serious, are you?"

"We're at the discovery stage of this case, you know. I'm here to discover everything I can." He almost remained solemn, but then his smile showed he was teasing.

Ben Lawrence had a good smile. It came on slow and thoughtful, as if he gave amusement time to grow. Eve drew her eyebrows together, not wanting that smile of his to get to her.

"All right, so you've had your joke," she said. "All you have to do now is tell Josie to go find a hobby. She ought to be too busy with life to think about my cat."

Ben nodded with a judicious air. "Speaking of your cat, Eve. Arnold, I believe you said his name was—"

"Oscar. His name is Oscar."

"Has Oscar had any past run-ins with the law?"

Now Eve's glance was sharp. Ben sat there calmly, flipping through his file folder, behaving as if he had nothing more pressing to do than discuss Eve's cat.

"This time you're really being ridiculous," she said.

"Not necessarily. If my client and I can prove that Oscar has any previous tendency to rowdiness, I think we'll have a real case here."

Ben was enjoying himself, no doubt about it. Eve leaned back in her chair and went along for the moment. "If this is a deposition, shouldn't I have my own lawyer present?"

"By all means."

"Actually," Eve said after quick consideration, "I've decided to represent myself. And for your information, my cat has never been in trouble before. He didn't have a chance. When I lived in Albuquerque, there certainly weren't any chickens in the neighbor's yard."

"So . . . you're from Albuquerque," Ben commented.

"Not originally. I moved there from Colorado to work on my doctorate."

"I should've been calling you Dr. Kearny all this time."

Now she was the one who smiled, a bit ruefully. "I think that would almost be as bad as you calling me Eveline. Anyway, I moved to Albuquerque, started graduate school, met Ted, and—" She broke off. "I thought this was supposed to be about my cat, not me."

"You don't have to talk about your ex-husband if you don't want to."

The conversation was making Eve uncomfortable. "How did you know I meant my ex-husband?"

"There's a certain tone people use when they mention their ex. A certain resignation, I guess you'd call it. I hear it in my own voice when I talk about my ex-wife." He turned reflective. "As a matter of fact, I hear the same tone in Rachael's voice whenever she talks to *me*. She always acts like I'm a meteorite that fell in her backyard. She's not happy about the crater I've made, but she knows there's nothing she can do about it."

Now Eve's smile was genuine. "That was almost poetic, in a perverse sort of way."

"Yeah, well, apparently my daughter Kate's not the only one who has a talent with words. Not that she ever lets me read her stories." Ben rattled his file folder, looking bemused. "Where was I, anyway?"

"You were talking about your ex-wife. Rachael." Eve tried the name out again, silently. Rachael. She hadn't seen the woman around town yet and wondered what she was like.

"On second thought, let's not talk about my ex," Ben grumbled. "That gets to be a very complicated subject."

"Your kids, then," Eve said. "I've intended to tell you . . . all three of them seem delightful."

He studied her, that leisurely smile playing around his mouth again. "I took you to be an honest person, Dr. Kearny."

"I am being honest. They all seem like wonderful kids. If your oldest daughter was a little reserved, well, I understand that. I remember being a teenager myself."

"'Reserved' is a polite way of putting it, and I suppose I appreciate your diplomacy."

Neither one of them said anything for a moment, twilight beginning to drift down around them. Eve was reluctant to turn on the lights. For some reason, she wanted to go on sitting here in the gathering dusk with Ben. She didn't feel particularly at ease with him, but still she wanted to go on, prolonging this odd tension between them.

It was Ben who spoke at last. "So, you and Oscar lived in Albuquerque."

"Yes. Oscar and I—and Ted, of course. I'm sorry to say that my cat and my husband never got along well. I adopted Oscar when he was a kitten. Ted came on the scene afterward, and my cat disapproved heartily." Eve didn't normally talk about her ex-husband to anyone. She finally did stand up to switch on the light, as if banishing ghosts. "Are we finished with your so-called deposition?" she asked.

"Not quite. I thought maybe we could continue over a drink. If you're free, that is." Ben made it sound so casual, so unpremeditated, this suggestion of his. Eve knew her own answer ought to be just as casual, but somehow she couldn't manage it.

"Ben, I really don't know. It doesn't seem right..."

"Maybe it's time you checked out the Red Carpet Saloon. I'd be glad to go along for the ride."

Eve hesitated. She knew she was reading too much into Ben's invitation. They'd already shared ice cream. A drink certainly wasn't all that different.

"All right," she said reluctantly. "I suppose it couldn't hurt."

"Only one way to find out."

They exchanged a glance, and Eve realized just how much Ben Lawrence unsettled her. She was too attracted to him, for one thing. As they walked outside together, she found herself savoring his nearness. A ripple of warmth went through her as he took her elbow to help her into the Jeep. The contact was very brief, but still . . .

Soon they were headed toward the center of town, silence between them all the while.

"This is some vehicle," Eve said at last, searching for conversation. "I bet your kids love it."

"I bought it with that in mind. When I saw it in the showroom, I pictured myself taking the kids all over New Mexico, the mountains, the desert. I didn't count on their hating the mountains. They hate the desert, too."

"They'll adjust," Eve said, knowing how inadequate that sounded.

"Yeah, but will I adjust? That's the question."

She glanced at him, unable to read his expression. "Do you think you'll go back to Boston? I suppose that's an option for you."

"No, it's not. It's true I miss Boston already, but I'm not going back. My kids are here, and I'm staying. I'll damn well figure out how to be a real father for once." He sounded almost grim, and she tried to lighten the mood.

"Parenthood is that bad?" she asked.

"It isn't bad. It's just frustrating, confusing, aggravating—but satisfying, too, if I ever get the hang of it."

"At least you're trying. There's a lot to be said for that."

"Trying's not good enough," he muttered. "I like to see results when I put my mind to something."

Eve didn't say anything to that, but she wondered at the word he'd chosen—results. Was such a thing possible? Surely a child was never a "result." As a parent, you simply invited another person into your life, a person who would be part of your life forever . . .

"Damn," Eve said to herself in a low voice—but not low enough.

"Something wrong?" Ben asked as he turned down Central Avenue.

"Oh, I was just thinking how we all seem to have a picture in our minds, a vision of the perfect family we'd like to have someday. But one way or another, the vision never translates exactly the way we thought it would. Sometimes we don't get the family at all...."

Ben was silent for a moment, and then he asked quietly, "Did you and Ted want to have kids?"

"Yes. We wanted them." Eve's throat was tight, and she had to force the words. Ben said nothing more, and she was grateful for that. He seemed like a nice man, a sensitive man who knew when to let a subject drop. But Eve's ex-husband had been a nice man, too, in his own way. She'd already learned that being with someone nice didn't necessarily solve any problems in life.

Eve took a deep breath. "I think I should mention something," she said. "I'm considering moving on from Cobb. Applying for a job somewhere else, at a larger school. Possibly in the very near future."

She wondered if that was a flash of disappointment on Ben's face. She couldn't tell for certain; it was gone too quickly, replaced by his usual quizzical expression.

"There's nothing to keep me here," she added.

"Too bad," he remarked. "You're leaving Cobb—and I'm staying."

Eve lapsed into silence again, battling a melancholy she couldn't explain. She told herself that the fall season always made her feel this way. But she knew it was something more. Something to do with Ben.

A few minutes later they pulled into the dirt parking lot of the Red Carpet Saloon. Killing the engine, he faced her.

"Would you still like a drink?" he asked.

He was giving her another chance to turn him down. Not that she could blame him. She hadn't offered him a great deal of enthusiasm so far. Maybe it would be best to say no, after all.

Instead she surprised herself by nodding. "Yes. Let's have that drink."

THE RED CARPET SALOON was murky, and Ben supposed that counted for atmosphere in a place like this, where the dance floor was a scrap of linoleum laid down like an afterthought. He stood by the door with Eve, glancing around. The country-western band played in a cramped space to one side. The drummer was good, but the singer sounded slightly off-key. Maybe he'd warm up in a while. It was early yet, and no one was dancing. Ben glanced at Eve in the dark smoky air. She didn't look like an English teacher right now. There was something a bit untamed about her, with her red hair tumbling free to her shoulders. Yet she held herself stiffly, as if she longed to turn and hurry out the door again. She looked like a woman trying to decide whether or not to be reckless.

He escorted her to the stools at the bar and they ordered a couple of beers. Eve wrapped both hands around her bottle and said something he couldn't quite hear over the music. He had to lean closer to her. He caught the scent of her perfume, something sultry, something musky. Something sexy.

She turned to him. "So, what are we going to do about Josie?"

Ben felt dissatisfied. At the moment he didn't want to discuss Josephine Scott.

"Maybe you should invite her to dinner," he said. "It might soften her up."

"I seriously doubt that." Eve tapped her fingers on the bar and glanced toward the door. Ben sensed that he needed to distract her.

"Would you like to dance?" he asked. Before she had time to say no, he took her hand and escorted her to the patch of linoleum. Two other couples were dancing now, which amounted to a crowd in this limited space. Ben drew Eve toward him, holding her close. At first she was rigid in his arms, but gradually she relaxed. She felt good. She felt damn good. Ben didn't question his response to her. He just went on holding her close, moving to the music.

Eventually Eve started to pull away. "Ben..." She gazed at him, her eyes shadowed in the dim light. He waited for whatever else she wanted to say, but then, with a shrug almost of defeat, she came back into his arms.

Ben liked the slow song. The singer in the band was starting to warm up, after all, voice mellowing. Ben drew Eve just a little closer, and she didn't resist. It was dangerous to start desiring a woman like Eve Kearny, and he knew it. He sensed too well the vulnerability in her, hidden underneath her aura of aloof self-possession. Someone had hurt her badly—no doubt the ex-husband. Ben suspected she was still hurting, and she was therefore a woman to be treated gently, carefully. It was inconvenient as hell to feel this desire for her.

When the band stopped for a break and Eve stepped away from him, she looked a little disoriented. Ben felt more than a little disoriented himself, unwilling to relinquish Eve's soft warmth. But they both made their way back to the bar.

Eve started to look tense again. "This is an awfully small town," she said. "People will start speculating about us...."

"Do you mind if they do? I don't."

She swiveled toward him on her stool. "I guess what bothers me is the fact that *I'm* speculating, Ben. I'm not sure what's going on here."

"I'm not sure, either," he admitted. "But it sounds like you're going to leave town before we have a chance to find out."

Now she turned away from him and gazed at her beer with a frown. "There are some good opportunities out there. I'm thinking of applying at a university in Santa Barbara and another one in Denver."

Ben took a swallow of beer. He wanted to ask her not to go. That didn't make any sense, of course. If she had a chance to get out of this town, she ought to take it. He couldn't very well ask her to stay behind because he liked slow-dancing with her at the Red Carpet Saloon.

The band started playing again, and he drew her back out to the floor. This time Eve's hands traveled up over his shoulders and she linked her fingers behind his neck. She leaned against him, and Ben rested his own hands above the flare of her hips, moving gently with the music. Forget speculation. Forget questions that couldn't be answered. He was just going to hold her while he still had the chance.

Ben lost track of the time, and he suspected that Eve did, too. The music wrapped itself plaintively around them, keeping them locked together. Song after song. As long as the music continued, Ben had an excuse to hold her. Silently he commanded the band to keep on playing.

The band, unfortunately, took another break. And this time Eve, looking determined, headed straight to the door of the saloon. Ben had to quicken his pace to catch up to her.

"I need a little air," she muttered, walking out to the parking lot. Then she turned to face Ben. "Listen," she began, "this just isn't working out—"

He didn't wait to hear any more. He simply drew her into his arms and kissed her, capturing her before she eluded him. Her lips were soft, pliable under his, and he discovered that he'd been right all along—she had a very kissable mouth. She tasted sweetly of beer, and Ben smiled against her lips. But then he deepened the kiss, Eve opening her mouth to him with a gentle sigh.

He knew she'd pull away sooner or later, but she took her time. Eventually she did extract herself from his arms, striding the few feet to the Jeep. She rubbed her arms distractedly.

"Cold?" Ben murmured, already thinking of a remedy for that. Eve's wary stance, however, warned him not to proceed.

"Listen," she said again, more forcefully this time, "I made a mistake coming here tonight."

"Eve, my only crime is that I find you attractive."

She hesitated, then sounded even more determined. "I happen to find you attractive, too, Ben, but that's not the point. I'm really considering leaving Cobb, and I'm sure neither one of us needs this complication."

"Something more than that is bothering you, isn't it?" he asked quietly. "Something to do with your ex-husband, I'd guess. Maybe you haven't really recovered yet."

"It's been over two years," she said, her own voice sharp. "Of course I've recovered. Why does everyone talk about divorce as if it's a disease?"

"Because for a while there it can make you feel like you're sick. During my own divorce, it seemed there were weeks when my stomach clenched so tight I couldn't eat. It takes a while to get your appetite back."

Eve seemed to relax a little. "All right, so it's a sort of disease. But I *am* recovered. All that's left is the anger about failing."

"Maybe you didn't fail," he suggested. "Maybe your ex-husband did."

She gazed at him in the starlight. "Is that how you feel about your own marriage—that you were the only one to blame?"

"Not the only one. But I can't help thinking that if I'd put more time into the relationship over the years, I'd still be with Rachael. And I'd be an in-house father, instead of always knocking on Phil's door asking to see my own kids."

Eve gazed off into the distance. "If you want to know the truth, my husband put plenty of time into our marriage. He was—he *is*—a good man. In the end he just couldn't handle the stress any more than I could. We both failed."

Ben didn't say anything, nor did he attempt to touch Eve. He just waited, sensing there was something more she needed to say. The music of the band drifted out to them from the saloon. Those musicians seemed to have a fondness for sad country ballads about lost love, lost chances.

At last Eve spoke again, her voice expressionless. "You asked me if Ted and I wanted kids. We wanted them, all right. Having two or three children was part of the picture we had in our minds—the picture of the perfect family. It took me a while to get pregnant, but finally I did and we were ecstatic." Eve's voice was still impassive, as if she were describing distant acquaintances. "Everything went along fine until I was almost seven months pregnant. And then, without any warning, I lost the baby."

"I'm sorry, Eve."

She made a restless gesture, as if intent on finishing. "We were both heartbroken, especially when the doctor told us it could happen again. Because of me... because of my body. Congenital incompetence—oh, the doctor had more technical terms than that, but it all came down to my incompetent body. Ted and I refused to listen. We tried again, and this time the pregnancy lasted all of six months."

"Lord, Eve, I am sorry—"

She made another impatient gesture. "I don't want you to be sorry. I'm just telling you this so you'll understand. Ted and I had a very good marriage. We should've been able to handle what happened. But we *didn't* handle it. We started blaming each other. We drew apart. And if a good relationship can be so quickly destroyed, I don't want to imagine a bad relationship."

Ben thought about his own children—how easily, carelessly, he and Rachael had become parents. Their first two kids hadn't even been planned. The arrival of Jenny, the youngest, had been: an attempt on both their parts to salvage their floundering marriage. The marriage hadn't survived, of course, but they still had their kids. In spite of all the problems, Ben couldn't imagine not having those kids. Now he did reach out to Eve, but she stiffened.

"Don't," she said, her voice brittle. "The problem is, I don't seem to have it in me anymore. The knack of being... casual. I'd like to have it, believe me. But there it is. I just don't." Eve swung open the passenger door of the Jeep. She was going to elude him, after all, and there didn't seem to be a damn thing he could do about it.

"Eve...maybe we could just take this a step at a time."

"Don't you understand? I'm not even good at the first step. The stage where you go out for drinks and share life stories and all the rest of it."

"I thought you were doing a great job."

Eve surprised him by actually returning his smile. Her expression was almost wistful. "It's just not going to work, Ben."

For a long moment, she and Ben gazed at each other. The music went on drifting out of the saloon, still plaintive, still lamenting lost chances. And that was how Ben felt right now—as if he'd lost a chance with Eve Kearny. He'd lost her before he'd even had an opportunity to know her. He'd never met a woman more prickly and more lovely all at once. He felt oddly depressed, thinking about it.

A truck pulled up in front of the Red Carpet and two women climbed out. They were both wearing cowboy hats, they were both pretty, and one of them glanced over at Ben with unabashed interest. Maybe, in some other lifetime, he would've shrugged off his defeat with Eve. He would've returned to the saloon and whirled some pretty girl in a cowboy hat onto the scrap of dance floor. But he couldn't do it now. He couldn't do it tonight.

Ben climbed into the Jeep beside Eve. The silence was heavy between them as he wheeled onto the street and headed back to the college so Eve could pick up her car. They didn't speak at all, and the thought struck Ben: maybe he, too, had lost the ability to be casual with a woman somewhere along the way.

CHAPTER FIVE

EVE SET DOWN the telephone receiver and made another checkmark on her list. So far, two of her former professors in Albuquerque had agreed to supply letters of recommendation. Both had been pleased to hear from her—and they'd seemed relieved that she was starting to apply for a new job. "You've buried yourself down there," one of them had chided her. "You're capable of so much more, Eve. Welcome back to the real world."

The real world. The phrase annoyed her with its implication that her past two years of teaching somehow didn't even exist. Cobb, New Mexico, might be a very small town, but it *was* real enough. Her students were real, and so were her fellow teachers.

Eve pushed the phone away and glanced around her office. It was an agreeable room, with a window that looked out on the cactus garden. She enjoyed the continual process of organizing all her books in here, never quite finishing the job. But as soon as she landed another teaching post, she'd have to pack them up and find a new home for them. The prospect didn't thrill her.

Did she want to leave...or didn't she? Eve propped her elbows on her desk and wearily rubbed her temples. She was going through all the motions of applying for a new position. But that was just it. She was going through the outward process, while inside her feelings were a hopeless jumble. They'd been a jumble ever since the day she'd first met Ben Lawrence.

Eve pressed her fingers over her eyes as she remembered what a fool she'd made of herself last night at the Red Carpet Saloon. First off, she'd practically twined herself around Ben on the dance floor, her body's reactions to him startling and much too pleasing. Kissing him had been rather too pleasing, also. Apparently two years of celibacy had done nothing to dampen her libido.

Then, after she'd regained her common sense, she'd actually blurted out the whole sorry mess of her marriage. She'd let all those memories come spilling out, the memories she'd tried so hard to deny these past few years. And so she'd really laid it on Ben. In one breath, she'd admitted that she found him appealing, and in the next she'd declared that she couldn't see him anymore. The worst had been telling him about her two miscarriages. But maybe that, after all, was the real reason she couldn't see him. Somehow, Ben Lawrence made her think of the two babies she'd lost, and she simply couldn't tolerate thinking about those losses. It was supposed to be finished, all of it.

Eve pressed her fingers harder against her eyes, trying to obliterate the images in her mind. Surely, in spite of her confusion, she was making the right decision about leaving Cobb.

A slight rustling noise made her straighten and open her eyes. Someone was hovering at the doorway to her office. One of Eve's more shy students, no doubt. She caught a glimpse of dark hair and plaid skirt.

"Door's open," she called, making her tone as welcoming as possible. Even that didn't do the trick at first. Whoever was out there ducked completely from sight. Eve was about to push back her chair and go investigate when she caught another glimpse of plaid.

"Come in," Eve said gently, as if enticing a frightened bird. A slight figure appeared in the doorway, face almost hidden behind a cascade of dark hair. It took Eve a moment to realize it was Ben's daughter.

"Kate," she said, "do come in." Eve began to think the girl would dart away for good, but at last she came slinking into the office. Clearly nervous and ill at ease, Kate tucked her hair behind her ear and frowned as if she'd been dragged in here forcibly.

"Miss Kearny?" she mumbled.

"Yes. But you can call me Eve. Please—sit down." Eve was intrigued by this visit. She'd never imagined that Kate would actually show up at her office. Eve had rejected the father, and now the daughter had appeared. How ironic.

Kate sat down in front of the desk, shoulders immediately hunched. She carried a folder clasped protectively to her chest. Eve studied the girl without being too obvious about it. Kate looked strikingly like her father: same strong features, same deep brown eyes that almost seemed black. Perhaps she'd inherited the dark hair from her mother. Kate had a dramatic look to her, and maybe someday she'd have the confidence to appreciate her distinctiveness. At the moment, she only looked awkward and miserable. Some poignant memory stirred in Eve, some remembrance of her own painful adolescence.

"I'm glad you took me up on my offer to drop by," she said, trying to sound both encouraging and offhand. "I hope you brought some stories for me to look at."

The cascade of hair fell over Kate's face again, and she fumbled with her folder. "Are you a writer, too?" she asked dubiously.

"Yes, I am," Eve said. "At least, I was. I didn't write fiction, though. I liked writing about storytellers, not telling stories myself."

Kate looked skeptical as she considered this information. "Do you know... I mean... can you tell if someone's any good?"

Eve realized she had to proceed carefully here. "I'm a teacher, Kate, and I do consider myself a fairly competent authority on what makes decent literature. I'll be glad to look at any writing you've done—and I'll be honest with you about it, if that's what you'd like. But I have to warn you, it's very difficult when someone's honest about your writing. Usually you end up listening to things you'd rather not hear."

Kate bent her head as if in concentration. She didn't say anything at first, but then her head came up again, her expression intense as she gazed at Eve.

"I have to find out," she said. "I have to *know* if I'm any good. So I want you to be honest. I'd want you to be *brutal*." Kate uttered this last word with a sort of tortured zeal. She really did have a flair for the dramatic, whether or not she realized it.

"How long have you been writing?" Eve asked, curious about this daughter of Ben's.

"I started last year. My parents were getting divorced and it was awful. I had to do something—" Kate stopped abruptly and stared at Eve. "You're a friend of my father's, aren't you?" she demanded after a moment, almost accusingly.

Eve had to think that one over. Nothing was simple where Ben Lawrence was concerned. "I'm not sure, Kate. I'm not sure if I am his friend," she said at last, battling regret.

Kate seemed relieved. "Anyway, that's when I started writing—when my parents broke up. And I've just reached the point where I need to find out if I'm any good."

"Hasn't anyone else read your work? Surely your teachers—"

"No." Kate spoke emphatically. "That would be too horrible. I need to be private about this." She tightened her grip on the folder, and she still looked as if any moment she'd bolt from the room. Eve suspected it had taken a lot of courage for Kate to venture here today.

"Listen, why don't you just leave your stories with me," Eve said gently. "I'll read them, and you can come talk to me again sometime next week." She saw the disappointment on Kate's expressive face and realized that next week probably seemed an eternity away to her. "On second thought," Eve amended, "why don't you come back tomorrow afternoon when you get out of school? We'll talk about your work then."

Kate nodded, getting to her feet. She laid her folder tentatively on the desk and hurried to the door, pausing for only a second to glance back at Eve. "Goodbye," she mumbled, and then she was gone. Eve heard her running all the way down the corridor.

Sitting back in her comfortable old swivel chair, Eve smiled to herself. What a delightful, contradictory child— no, not exactly a child. What was Kate—fifteen, sixteen? A girl on the agonizing brink of womanhood. A girl, nonetheless, young enough to be Eve's daughter.

Eve shook that thought away and picked up the folder. Kate had held the thing so tightly that it still bore the imprints of her fingers. Eve opened the folder and found three stories inside, each one typed but with many words crossed out and revised in ink. Kate had gone to a great

deal of work here, and Eve felt rather honored to be the
first to see it. She glanced at her watch, thinking of the
tasks she still had left to do. She needed to modify her
lecture notes for tomorrow's class in American literature,
as well as grade the weekly papers for her composition
class—but Kate's stories beckoned, and Eve couldn't resist. She pulled out the first story and began to read.

IT WAS AN HOUR before Eve glanced up again. She'd read
each story twice, jotting notes in the margins, her interest
growing as she made the discovery that Kate Lawrence
was a very good young writer—a very good one, indeed.
She might be raw and uncontrolled, but the talent was
there.

The subject matter Kate chose was something else
again. Two of the stories were melodramatic wanderings
about twenty-year-old heroines involved in wild soulful
love affairs. All Eve could deduce from these was that
Kate longed to be twenty and have wild soulful love affairs of her own. Eve remembered much the same wish
when *she'd* been a teenager. But Kate's third story was
something special, something unique. And it was almost
disturbing in a way. Written with a mordant, bleak sense
of humor, it described a girl sitting at the dinner table and
listening to the icy politeness between her parents, knowing that divorce was imminent—even though neither parent had spoken of it.

Feeling almost as if she'd been spying on Ben, Eve
gathered up Kate's papers and tucked them in her carryall, along with the compositions she still had to grade. She
was deep in thought as she went out to her car and began
the short drive home. She was still deep in thought as she
turned down her street, cruised past her neighbor's
house—and saw Ben Lawrence sitting on Josie's front

porch, Josie herself arrayed regally beside him. Ben waved nonchalantly to Eve as she drove past.

She pulled into her driveway, silently delivering an oath. It was very difficult to reject a man and then find him right next door. Eve climbed out of the car, bringing her carryall along. She now had several options. She could dash into her house along with her cat and lock the door, she could turn and wave at Ben with her own nonchalance and then saunter into her house, or she could simply walk over and say hello like a rational adult.

Eve forced herself to take the rational-adult route. She crossed the yard, raising her eyebrows at Oscar, who peered out at her from under the hydrangea bush. Then she went up the walk to Josie's house, climbing the porch steps.

"Hello, Josie . . . hello, Ben," she said.

Josie scowled at Eve. "Miss Kearny, I'm having a private conference with my attorney. Please don't interrupt."

"That's okay," Ben said easily. "Josephine, maybe Eve would like to try some of your apple cider, too."

Josie pursed her lips, accentuating the wrinkles on her face. She looked shriveled and discontented, like someone who spent too much of life brooding on misfortunes, and Eve couldn't help feeling sorry for her. But at last Josie stood and went into the house, banging the door behind her. Ben nodded at the mug he held.

"It really is good cider," he said.

Eve leaned against the porch railing, wishing Ben didn't look so attractive this afternoon. Lately he seemed to be going for less lawyerly attire. Instead of a suit, he wore a nubby wool jacket with informal slacks. The tie was in place, but once again knotted loosely. No matter what he wore, though, he still carried that subtle air of elegance, bringing a hint of Boston to New Mexico. Eve tried to think of something to say, something superficial. The problem was she'd already gone way beyond superficial with Ben. She gazed at him and he gazed back. They might just as well have been on the dance floor again, only this time they closed the distance between them with their eyes, not their bodies.

Josie came banging out the door and thrust a mug into Eve's hand. Eve welcomed the opportunity to glance away from Ben, and she sipped the apple cider.

"It's delicious," she said sincerely.

This seemed to do nothing to mollify Josie. The old woman sat down in the wicker chair beside Ben's, spreading out the starched pleats of her skirt. Ben, however, ignored his client's inhospitable mood.

"Josephine," he said, "Eve wants to be neighborly. She'd like to invite you to dinner some evening. What do you say?"

Eve glared at Ben. Inviting Josie to dinner was *his* idea, not hers.

"Dinner, huh," Josie said. She pursed her lips again, and this time she appeared almost cunning. "Fine. I'll do it. I'll go to dinner—but on one condition. My lawyer has to be there, too."

After Josie's pronouncement, Eve sipped some more cider. She tried to picture sophisticated Ben and sour old Josie sharing her dinner table. Ben himself did not seem very happy at the prospect.

"Josephine," he began, "I'm your lawyer, not—"

"You want us to try to get along, don't you?" Josie asserted. "At least that seems like what you're after. And my terms are nonnegotiable."

Ben frowned. "A lawyer shouldn't get this involved in his case. He should maintain a certain . . . distance."

"It's a little late for that," Eve murmured, and found her gaze locked with Ben's again. He set down his mug and stood.

"Eve, you and I need to talk." He began escorting her down the porch steps and across the yard.

"Nonnegotiable," Josie called after them.

Ben didn't speak until they'd reached Eve's porch, and then he surveyed her gravely. "Don't worry, I'll be able to talk some sense into Josephine. You can have her over for dinner, but I'll stay well clear. After all, last night you made it pretty obvious you don't want me hanging around."

Eve turned her key in the lock and opened the front door. "About last night—it was nothing personal, Ben."

"Nothing personal?" he echoed. "I'd say it was just the opposite."

She wondered why this had to be so difficult and tried again. "Ben, the truth is I think you're a very nice man— and, yes, I *am* attracted to you. I just don't want to get involved with anyone yet. I don't know when I'll be ready for that. It may be a long time."

He leaned against the doorjamb, studying her. "What if I told you I'm not looking for involvement, either? I've got enough on my hands as it is."

"Then I'd say we both agree on this. We shouldn't get involved. It wouldn't work out for either one of us." She stepped through the doorway and turned to face him. "Well, we've cleared that up," she said, making an unsuccessful attempt at lightheartedness. "I don't see what the problem is."

"This is the problem," Ben murmured. He, too, stepped through the doorway, and took Eve in his arms. He lowered his mouth to hers, and last night's magic began all over again. With a soft moan, Eve gave herself to his kiss. She moved her hands up over his shoulders to the back of his neck, pressing him closer to deepen the contact between them. His hair was silky underneath her fingers, his body wonderfully solid and masculine next to hers. A sensual heat went through her, bringing with it feelings she'd almost forgotten. With Ben, she seemed to be relearning a great many sensations. . . .

Something brushed against her leg, making her start and pull away. Glancing down, she saw her cat streak past, tail held high in affront. Eve pushed a hand through her hair, her breath coming unevenly.

"Yes . . . we do have a problem," she said.

"The fact that your cat doesn't like me—or the fact that I can't even look at you without wanting you?" Ben's voice was warm and husky, and his eyes were very dark as he gazed at her. Eve turned away, struggling to regain some composure.

"Dammit, Ben, I don't want this to happen."

"But it is happening."

"I'm still planning to leave Cobb."

"I know you are."

"Dammit," she muttered again. In another second or two, she might not be able to resist going straight back into his arms, and then she'd really be lost.

Ben, however, didn't give her the chance to find out. He stepped out onto the porch. "Goodbye, Eve. I'll straighten out the situation with Josephine, by the way."

"Oh . . . just come to dinner, will you?" Eve said grouchily. "Friday night, eight o'clock. You and I and Josie will sit down and try to reach some sort of agreement. Maybe then we can be finished with this ridiculous case."

He looked at her wryly. "You want it finished so you and I won't spend so much time bumping into each other.

If you could, Eve, you'd probably duck out of town right now, wouldn't you?''

She heard his unmistakable challenge, and it angered her. "I'm not trying to leave town so I can run away from you. I just want a better opportunity for myself."

"No one can blame you for that." He studied her for a few more moments, and then left. Eve crossed into the living room and sank onto her couch, cradling one of her silly throw pillows. Oscar came out of hiding and settled down beside her, purring because he finally had her all to himself. Eve rubbed her cat's head. Only now would she admit the truth: she did want to run away from Ben Lawrence. She damn well wanted to run.

CHAPTER SIX

BEN WALKED DOWN one of the corridors of Silas T. Cobb Community College. Most of the students had left for the day, giving the place a forlorn deserted air. He glanced out to the courtyard and saw that the single red cactus bloom was still holding its own, even if beginning to look a little scraggly.

The corridor was silent, although Ben heard a lively conversation in progress as he approached Eve's office. He paused just outside, recognizing his daughter's intent voice. He was surprised—yet pleased, too. It seemed Kate had actually heeded his suggestion that she talk to Eve about her writing.

"...but it *does* have a plot," Kate was saying. "The girl leaves and her boyfriend never sees her again and he's miserable."

"I'm just suggesting you make your heroine a little more dynamic," came Eve's voice in a patient tone. "Why don't you have her confront her boyfriend, work out a solution?"

"There *isn't* any solution," Kate said stubbornly. "And I want the story to have a tragic ending."

Ben winced as he listened, not sure he wanted to hear any more. For that matter, he didn't like eavesdropping. He moved to knock on the open door.

"Hello, Kate," he said cheerfully. "Imagine seeing you here."

As always with his oldest daughter, he seemed to say the wrong thing. Kate twisted around in her chair to stare at him, looking distressed.

"What are *you* doing here?" she demanded. Ben thought longingly of the days when Kate had been a small child and had run eagerly into his arms whenever he appeared. She certainly wasn't eager to see him now.

"I dropped by for a legal conference with Eve," he improvised.

"An unscheduled conference," Eve said lightly. She glanced at her watch and stood. "I suppose I can fit you in. Kate and I got carried away, talking about... literature."

Kate stood also, holding her arms against her body as she glanced from Ben to Eve. "I thought you said— I thought you and my dad weren't—"

"We do have a legal case to resolve," Eve said. "Your father is the prosecuting attorney, and I'm the defendant."

Kate looked even more perturbed. She grabbed some papers from Eve's desk and slid by Ben without even glancing at him again.

"Are you going straight home?" he asked.

"Of course," she muttered. "You don't need to check up on me, Dad. It's not like I *know* anybody in this stupid town." And with that, she left.

Ben rubbed the back of his neck, feeling an ache he couldn't quite seem to reach. "I'd ask what that was all about, but I'm afraid I already know. I shouldn't have come in when I did. Without meaning to, I've invaded Kate's privacy."

"No, it's better this way—everything aboveboard. I'm glad you're here."

Ben wondered how he should interpret that last remark. It probably wasn't something he should get too enthused about; today Eve seemed to have retreated into that coolness of hers. He wondered if she would respond coolly to his touch, and he wanted to reach out and run his fingers over her skin. She was alluring, her hair a bright splash of color against her pale complexion as if to hint at passions underneath her restraint. It seemed to him he hadn't stopped thinking about her since the night they'd danced together at the saloon. Something had happened that night, something he still couldn't define. But always Eve retreated from him, not giving him a chance to find out what was between them.

Now she busied herself at her desk, piling books together. "Kate has let me read a few stories of hers. She shows talent—her writing has a great deal of potential. I thought you'd be interested to know that."

"I am." Ben felt a mingled pride and regret. "Kate and I don't seem to get along very well. She doesn't share a whole lot with me, and everything I say seems to rankle her. Just to have a glimpse of what's really going on with her..."

"Kate asked me yesterday if you and I were friends. I told her I wasn't sure, but I thought we weren't. That seemed to be what she wanted to hear. She loves you very much, Ben, and she doesn't want to share you with anyone."

"She acts more as if she hates me."

"Oh, but she doesn't. The way she writes about you—" Eve stopped, looking chagrined.

"It's too late—you've already said too much. You might as well tell me the rest of it. What *does* Kate write?"

Eve piled more books together. "It won't be fair to Kate if I tell you anything else. And if I don't tell you... I guess I'm not being fair to you, Ben."

He moved restlessly. "So just tell me a little," he said. "Just tell me anything that will help me get close to my daughter."

Eve seemed to think this over, but at last she spoke. "I suppose I can tell you a few things. From Kate's writing, I gather she's still very upset about your divorce. She describes you and your ex-wife with a great deal of... insight. She loves both of you—but at the same time she's furious at you. Don't you see? Kate has that picture in her mind, too, the picture of the perfect family. But it's been destroyed for her, and she doesn't know what to do about it. She blames you and Rachael. I suspect she also blames herself, the way many children do when things go wrong between their parents."

"None of that helps me, Eve. I've already guessed as much about Kate. I want to reassure her, tell her she's not to blame in any way, but whenever I try to talk to her, she acts like she's horrified at the very fact of my existence."

Eve shook her head. "I'll tell you what *I* think. I think that what really horrifies Kate is that she still needs you so much. She wants desperately to be an adult, and at the same time you're the center of her world, Ben. That scares her."

Now Eve had given him something to consider. "I'd like to believe that what you're saying is true," he murmured. "Because that would mean I could still reach Kate, and make a difference for her."

"You can," Eve said, sounding confident. "I know you can."

"Thanks."

She busied herself with a stack of books. "I know I'm no authority on relationships between parents and children, but I am a teacher. I constantly deal with students not all that much older than Kate. I suppose that's what makes me think I can tell you anything...."

"Eve, you don't have to explain yourself. I trust your judgment." He went to stand beside her. "Tell me—do you always stack books when you're nervous?"

"What makes you think I'm nervous?" she countered.

"You keep trying to avoid what's between us. Only you can't avoid it, and I'd say that makes you nervous." Ben watched a rosy color suffuse Eve's face, and it made him think of a beautiful ivory cameo touched with an artist's paintbrush. Eve *did* make him turn poetic.

"I've already told you how I feel," she said. "I don't want this to go any further."

"Are you afraid we'll end up like that story Kate was talking about? You walk away, I never see you again, I end up miserable...."

"Your daughter has a very melodramatic turn of mind. I don't plan on anyone being miserable."

Now he did reach out to touch her, trailing his fingers over her cheek. The rose color of her skin deepened, and she turned away from him.

"Don't start," she said. "Please ... don't start."

He didn't know what he was trying to start. He wanted Eve Kearny, wanted her badly—that was certain. As for the rest of it, he sure as hell didn't know.

"You said you came for a legal conference," Eve reminded him with some asperity.

"Right. Josephine's involved in counternegotiations now. She wants you to serve dinner on Saturday night, not Friday."

"I see. It's a power play. She's making sure I know she has the upper hand."

"Something like that."

Eve gazed at him with a slight frown. "Ben, you could've called and told me this. You didn't have to come all the way over here."

"I wanted to see you. I was glad to have an excuse." He didn't mind admitting the truth, even knowing it wouldn't go over particularly well with Eve. He watched her frown deepen as she picked up a few books and headed out of her office.

Ben walked with her to the parking lot. Glancing behind him at the school building, he saw where the stucco had chipped away here and there to reveal the adobe bricks underneath. Someone had once planted grass around the building, but now it was being overtaken by scrubby weeds.

"I can see why you want to go somewhere else," Ben said reluctantly. "I imagine Cobb Community College isn't exactly a place that's open to new ideas."

Immediately Eve seemed to grow defensive. "It's only that the school has had to fight so hard just to maintain any position at all. Over the years, it's continually been on the verge of closing down for lack of funds and lack of interest. When you're up against that, it's understandable you'd become a little insular."

She spoke about the school almost as if it were a person, at the same time regarding Ben defiantly.

"So maybe you should stay here and help, then," he said, knowing he wanted Eve to stay.

She took a deep breath. "Cobb Community has its limits, and I can't deny them. Especially now that I've really started to investigate a new job in Denver. I grew up there, and I know some people at the university where I'd be applying. It's a small private school, but very progressive. I think I could be happy there. . . ." Her voice trailed off, and she looked uncertain.

"Who are you trying to convince?" Ben asked gently. "Me—or yourself?"

"I think I *would* be happy in Denver," she said, her voice carrying more conviction now. "My roots are there. I already have friends waiting for me. Maybe it's time I came out of hiding."

"That's what you've been doing here—hiding?"

"I don't know what else you'd call it. Tomorrow I'm sending out my résumé. It's the right step for me to take."

"Yes, of course." The worst of it was he couldn't argue with her. If his kids weren't here, he'd be out of Cobb in a second. Who was he to hold Eve back?

The New Mexico sky arched over them, brilliant blue and limitless. That was the irony of Cobb—all this clear splendid sky, but nothing else to offer. No reason for Eve to stay, no reason Ben could give her. . . .

"You and I won't have much of a chance to know each other," he said at last. "I'm sorry about that."

"Believe it or not, Ben, I'm sorry, too. I really am. But you'll come to dinner with Josie Saturday night, won't you?"

"Somehow it's not what I had in mind for the two of us, sharing dinner with Josephine."

"What *did* you have in mind?" she asked, surprising him with her directness.

"I was hoping we'd have time to find that out—together."

Eve shifted the books she was holding. "I guess our timing's off—your coming to town just as I'm planning to leave."

"You're right, our timing's rotten," he acknowledged dryly. He wasn't ready to let Eve go yet. He lingered a moment longer, even though he had nothing left to tell her.

"Well," she said at last, "I'll see you Saturday evening."

"Right. Saturday evening."

He watched as Eve climbed into her car and left the parking lot, gravel churning under her wheels as she accelerated just a little too quickly. It seemed to Ben he was always running out of time with Eve, always saying goodbye to her in parking lots, watching her on her way to somewhere else.

He climbed into his Jeep, realizing there was no place he had to be in a hurry tonight. He had plenty of time on his hands. And so he sat there, without turning the key in the ignition, without doing anything at all. He sat there for a long while and thought about Eve Kearny.

IT WAS SATURDAY evening, and Ben had just spent the day with his kids. Another full day of trying to entertain them, make them happy, get close to them. A full day of trying, a full day of failing. All three kids had gone stir-crazy cooped up in his room at the Cactus Inn, and he'd finally taken them to a double feature at the movie theater. They'd already seen both shows, however, and fidgeted the entire time. Afterward they'd visited the soda fountain, but Ray the druggist still hadn't stocked any butterscotch ice cream. Ben's kids had eaten the vanilla without enthusiasm, and now Ben had no alternative but to take them home—home to Phil's house.

The one thing cheering up Ben at all was knowing that he'd have dinner with Eve later this evening—dinner with Eve and Josephine, of course. Lord, he was in a bad state if he was looking forward to seeing a woman in the company of his ill-tempered client. But it seemed he looked forward to seeing Eve in any circumstances, no matter how the rest of his life was going.

Ben drove down Central Avenue, tension making the back of his neck ache again. He'd been getting that ache more and more around his kids.

"I've decided to buy a house," he announced to them. "Enough of that lousy hotel room, don't you think? I want a big house with a big yard, someplace where I can put up a basketball hoop, someplace where you can invite friends over."

For the first time all day, he had their unqualified attention. Matthew, sitting in the front seat beside him, went through the motions of slam-dunking a basketball. "How soon you gonna put up the hoop, Dad?"

"As soon as I get a house," Ben promised solemnly. "That has to come first, I think."

"A house," Jenny echoed from the back seat. "And my friends can come over?"

"You don't have any friends," muttered Kate.

"I do so!"

Ben intervened. "Kate, don't tease your sister." The words sounded useless even as he spoke them. It was a little like being a judge, telling the jury to disregard someone's testimony after the testimony had already been given, the damage already done.

"Who's your friend in this stupid town?" Kate taunted Jenny, suddenly sounding much younger than fifteen. "Name just one."

Poor Jenny couldn't seem to come up with any names. "I do have friends! I do!" was all she could say, close to tears.

Matthew spoke up again. "I want to sleep over at your house, Dad. That way I won't have to listen when Mom and Phil fight. They fight a lot now."

Immediately Ben was wary, thinking of his children's welfare—Rachael's welfare, too, he had to admit. "When you say they fight, what do you mean? Is Phil ever violent?"

"It's not like that," Kate said scornfully. "He doesn't hit Mom, or anything. They try to be really quiet when they're bickering with each other. Just like you and Mom used to do. You always told Mom to keep her voice down, but we could hear both of you, clear as anything."

"Ouch," Ben said. "You know how to find your mark, Katie."

"Don't call me that," she muttered. "And I was just making an observation, that's all."

Ben wondered how Kate could sound one minute like a six year-old and the next sound like thirty. He turned off Central Avenue and a few moments later pulled up in front of Phil's house. The kids piled out and went straggling up the walk, Jenny hauling along her knapsack of monster trucks. Ben went along, too. He never liked to leave the kids at the door; he insisted on personally delivering them inside. It was one of the few ways he knew to make a claim on his own kids.

As Ben shepherded his children through the door, Rachael called a greeting from the kitchen. Kate instantly disappeared upstairs as if she could abide neither one of her parents at the moment, and Ben ushered the other two kids into the kitchen. Rachael proceeded to ignore him, fussing over the children with a forced enthusiasm.

"Matt, Jenny—I missed you guys! I'm making hamburgers. Doesn't that sound good? Vegetarian hamburgers, of course."

"We already had ice cream. And how can you make hamburgers out of vegetables?" Matthew asked.

"They're not made out of vegetables. They're made out of soybeans. Sit down and try one. I'm sure your father would never have fed you ice cream if he'd realized how close it was to dinnertime. Jenny, you sit down and eat, too. Where on earth is the catsup? And mustard—we need mustard." Once again Rachael created a frantic sort of bustling in the kitchen, seeming to expend even more energy than the kids. This was the awkward moment for Ben, when he delivered the children yet didn't know how to bid them goodbye. Today the moment was made even more difficult by the turmoil he sensed in Rachael. He wanted to leave his kids in a peaceful atmosphere; he didn't want to abandon them to Rachael's barely controlled agitation.

"Where's Phil?" he asked.

"It's his night out with friends. Saturday-night poker, to be exact. I want Phil to still have his friends. Marriage shouldn't change that. Any more questions?" Rachael was definitely on edge, explaining too much even while ready to pick a fight.

"Just asking," Ben said mildly.

"You never just ask, Ben. I'm sure you always have some ulterior motive where Phil's concerned. Matthew Benjamin Lawrence, do not dissect your meal. Just eat it."

"My hamburger has spots," said Jenny.

"All food has spots," said Rachael.

"I don't like spots," said Jenny.

"Children, eat your hamburgers!"

Ben recognized the despair threading its way through Rachael's voice. Apparently the kids recognized it, too. They both stared at their mother, wide-eyed, as if waiting for a pressure cooker to explode. And that was how it had always been with Rachael; now and then, when something was really bothering her, she would simply explode. This seemed like one of those times.

"Matthew, Jenny, why don't you go upstairs and let me talk to your mother for a few minutes," Ben said.

For once the kids obeyed with alacrity, no doubt happy to give up their soybean hamburgers. As soon as Ben heard them pounding up the stairs, he turned to his ex-wife.

"I think you'd better tell me what's wrong," he said.

"Nothing's wrong." Rachael thumped a pan down on the stove. "No—something *is* wrong. It's you, Ben. I really hate the way you come in here and undermine my authority with the children. They're supposed to eat their dinner. First you spoil their appetites with ice cream, and then you give them permission to leave the table."

"Rachael, this is me you're talking to. Something else is going on here."

She stared at him. "It isn't really your concern anymore, is it?"

"I think it is. My kids live in this house. If you're having problems of any kind, it affects them. And that means it affects me, too."

Rachael grabbed the catsup bottle and twisted the lid on tight. "I hate when you get so damn logical. Point A leads to point B, and that leads to point C. I really do hate that." She ducked behind the refrigerator door and rummaged around. When she emerged into view again, she seemed unnaturally calm.

"I wish you'd leave now, Ben. I have only one problem—and that's you. How can I start a new life when you're always intruding?"

Ben didn't trust her calmness, but he'd already confronted her directly. If she wouldn't talk, what else could he do?

He turned to go, struggling with his lack of power in this house. He was almost out of the kitchen when Rachael spoke again.

"You're wearing a suit and tie—very fancy. Going someplace special tonight?"

He thought about the peculiar evening he would no doubt spend at Eve's. Then he nodded. "Yes, I think you could call it someplace special."

He walked down the hall and out the door. His life was getting too damn complicated. It frustrated the hell out of him not being able to help his children with the problems here. And he was convinced that there *was* a problem. And yet, knowing he'd see Eve tonight somehow made him feel better. Ben ignored the fact that Eve Kearny had only added more complications to his life.

He just wanted to see her.

CHAPTER SEVEN

BEN COULD TELL it was a big evening for Josephine because the old woman was wearing a hat. Not just any hat. This was something special, a sort of straw bowl turned upside down and adorned with a tuft of paper flowers. At first the hat almost made Josephine seem endearing, but then she turned into her usual cantankerous self. She sat on the sofa in Eve's house and complained about cat hair.

"Cat hair makes me sneeze," she said. "I don't know if I should have come over here tonight. I really don't."

"I locked Oscar in the bedroom," Eve said. She sat on the sofa, also, and Ben had appropriated an armchair across from her. He and Eve exchanged glances, and he suspected that they were both thinking the same thing about Josephine's hat. It seemed they were becoming adept at silent communication. He switched his thoughts to an image of kissing Eve and saw a slow pink flush coming over her face, as if she had caught the image—and responded.

Eve stood up hastily. "I'll go check on the lasagna. It should be done by now."

A few moments later all three sat around Eve's dinette table. Everything was simple and spare. No fussy tablecloth or place mats, no useless knickknacks to get in the way. Ben liked that. He liked the spareness of Eve's life, her only excess seeming to be one of books. Unfortunately the very simplicity of her life made it clear how easily she could pick up and move. How easily she could leave this place behind.

The food she had prepared was equally simple—and good. Ben broke open a crusty roll and watched her across the table. She looked cool and lovely and composed, wearing a dress of dark forest green that clung gently to her body, and he found that he had a hard time concentrating on his meal.

Eve, however, proceeded efficiently to do all the tasks of a hostess. She poured Josephine some wine and then listened tolerantly as the old woman discussed at length her dislike of anything alcoholic. When Josephine had exhausted that subject quite thoroughly, Eve initiated a pleasant discussion of the myriad goings-on at Cobb Community: election of the homecoming queen, the soccer game recently won by the school's coed team, the fledgling efforts to start a student newspaper. Ben joined in, determined to keep the conversation upbeat, yet Josephine would not be denied. She seized the opportunity to complain about everything they brought up.

Poor old lady, Ben thought to himself. She'd decked herself out in that hat just so she could come over here and be miserable. Josephine went looking for misery and would not allow herself to be disappointed. Ben shared another meaningful glance with Eve, but just then an eerie yowling noise erupted.

Josephine set down her fork with an air of triumph. "Listen to that, Benjamin! I told you the cat howls something terrible. Who can live with that in the neighborhood?"

Eve retained her composure. "Josie, Oscar is meowing. And he's only doing it because I shut him in a room by himself."

The cat yowled again, making Ben wince. It was a pretty gruesome sound. Josephine pushed back her chair.

"I came over here in good faith, Miss Kearny. I will not be subjected to this."

"For goodness' sake, Josie, stop being fanatical."

"Fanatical," Josephine echoed. "Did you hear what she called me, Benjamin? Fanatical." Josephine seemed to latch onto the word with enthusiasm; she liked being outraged, no doubt about it.

"Josie," said Eve, sounding as if her tolerance had slipped a little, "I made a blackberry pie today from scratch. I hardly ever make a pie from scratch. Doesn't that tell you something about my good intentions?"

"I don't care for blackberries," Josephine said almost with a note of pride. "I don't care for them at all. And my lawyer is a witness here tonight. He's seen. He's heard." Josephine stood and marched toward the front door. "I will not stay and be tormented like this. I will not." It was as if she'd been waiting for an opportunity to make a grand exit. The front door banged shut after her.

Ben and Eve sat across from each other in silence. Finally Eve sighed. "So much for placating Josie. Looks like I blew it."

"On the contrary. You gave Josephine exactly what she wanted. Now she can really be indignant."

"Anything to please her, I suppose," Eve said ruefully. She went to let her cat out of the bedroom. The Siamese bounded into the kitchen, gave Ben a look of disdain and then shot right back into the bedroom. At least Oscar wasn't "meowing" anymore.

"Just so you know, blackberry pie sounds wonderful to me," Ben said. Eve served them both a piece. It was as delicious as everything else she'd prepared tonight.

Blackberries. Blackberries and Eve Kearny. An irresistible combination....

Once again Eve seemed to sense the direction of his thoughts. She finished her own pie quickly and moved into the living room. Ben followed her. She stood in the middle of the floor, as if uncertain of what to do next. An expectant silence had taken over. Ben stepped toward her and, after only the slightest hesitation, she came into his arms. He kissed her, then kissed her again, with a need that could no longer be satisfied merely by a kiss. Moving his hands down her back, he steered her toward the sofa, and they both sank onto it. As he caressed her through the soft fabric of her dress, she moaned a response to him. Her hands tangled in his hair and she pressed him closer.

"Oh, dammit, Ben. Damn you...."

He silenced her with another kiss and now his hand found her breast. She felt good to him, more than good. He fumbled with the buttons of her dress, but it was slow going; they were fastened too firmly. Not like the first day he'd seen her, when that stray button of hers had come undone so enticingly. How vulnerable she had seemed then. How vulnerable she still seemed to him.

"Eve. I want you. I'll stop if—"

"Don't stop." Her voice was shaking. Ben started loosening his tie, only to abandon the effort. At the moment he was far more interested in unbuttoning Eve than anything else. At last, working together, he and Eve managed to slide her dress down over her shoulders, and he bent his head, nudging her silky camisole upward, kissing her skin. He willed himself to take his time, not to rush her, but it was Eve who seemed in a hurry. Grasping his hand, she guided it up to her breast, her fingers trembling on his.

She was so soft and smooth. So tempting. She moaned
again, arching against him, driving him wild with her action, yet he willed himself to take things slowly. "I want
to look at you," he muttered, his voice thick. He pulled
her camisole up farther, revealing her small perfectly
shaped breasts, her skin the pale white he found so alluring, her nipples a deep rose. He kissed each breast in turn,
stroking her with his tongue. Her scent was warm and
feminine, surrounding him.

"Ben...please..."

This time he couldn't tell whether she was begging him
to continue or to stop. But when he lifted his head he saw
the tears on her cheeks. He was far gone by now, but he
couldn't make love to her without knowing what those
tears meant. Groaning, he held her against him, moving
his hands over the bare skin of her back.

"Eve, what is it?"

"Oh, God. I feel ridiculous." She wiped away the tears,
only to have more of them trickle down her cheeks.
"Don't pay any attention to me."

"That's a little difficult right now."

"I want to do this, Ben. I really do. But I just don't
think I can. Dammit, I can't."

Part of him—most of him—wished like hell that he
hadn't gone slowly with her, after all. But another part of
him wanted Eve only if she could come to him completely, willingly, with no doubts about what they were
doing.

No doubts—who was he kidding? He had plenty of
doubts of his own. They didn't stop him from wanting to
make love to her, but they were there, nonetheless.

He went on holding her next to him, not the wisest
thing, considering the state of his arousal. But he figured
she would retreat from him soon enough. So he went on

caressing the soft warm skin of her back, her breasts crushed tantalizingly against the cloth of his shirt. It seemed to Ben that this was about as near to exquisite agony as he could get—cradling a lovely, half-naked Eve next to him while he was fully clothed.

"Damn," Eve said again.

"Want to tell me about it?"

She sighed raggedly. "I'd forgotten what this could be like. And now you've made me start to feel it again. I don't want to feel it, Ben."

"Lust—or something more?"

"I think we both know it's lust—*and* something more."

He couldn't argue with that. He traced his fingers down the delicate bones of her spine, making her shiver with his touch. Now she did draw away, looking flustered as she struggled with her camisole. Ben was sorry when she managed to slip it back into place, but he could tell she was trying for some dignity. It occurred to him that sex was essentially undignified in nature—clothes ending up crumpled and discarded, limbs flung out at awkward angles. The pleasure involved usually compensated for any awkwardness, but tonight he and Eve hadn't gotten far into the pleasure, and maybe that made regaining dignity all the more difficult. Ben glanced away from her, reknotting his tie, giving her time to button herself back into her dress. Then they sat together on the sofa, not touching.

"I wish I could explain," she said, running a hand through her tumbled hair.

"I think I understand. You're still not over your exhusband, no matter what you say."

It really seemed to bother her whenever he brought that up. "I *am* over Ted," she protested. "It's just that— Oh,

I already told you. I don't know how to be casual any-more."

"I wasn't being casual tonight," he said quietly.

She didn't say anything to that for a long moment, but then she shook her head almost sorrowfully. "I wish this hadn't happened tonight. We're both getting in too deep, and you know it, Ben."

"Maybe we're being like Josephine," he said. "Maybe we're looking to be miserable, expecting to have the worst happen if we give in to each other."

She shook her head again, impatiently this time. "You still don't understand, do you? The problem is, I *don't* expect the worst with you. I expect that if we were to get involved, you'd be a very decent and caring man. And an exciting one. I'm quite sure of it, in fact."

"Thanks for the recommendation." He longed to reach out and hold her, but at the moment it seemed the wrong thing to do. She perched rigidly on her corner of the sofa, making it clear she didn't wish to be touched.

"I just don't want any of it," she said, her voice stiff. "I don't want all the caring, the intimacy..."

"Hmm...aren't those the good things in a relation-ship?"

She rose from the sofa, managing to look dignified. "This whole dinner was a mistake. I certainly didn't ap-pease Josie, and I let things go too far between you and me."

"I had a little something to do with the last part," he reminded her gently, moving to stand beside her. He could feel her eluding him once more, retreating further and further away. Could he ever hold onto a woman like Eve? She stopped him every time he tried.

He tried again, anyway. "Eve, I know what you'll tell me. That you're looking for a new job, that you won't be here long. But at least take a chance first. Find out what's between us...."

"No, Ben." She sounded cool and distant, as if she hadn't lain half-naked in his arms only minutes ago. "I don't want to find out anything more. I can't."

He was powerless with her, just as he seemed to be with the rest of his life. There'd been a time when he'd felt in control of things. Not anymore, and certainly not with Eve.

"Good night," he said somberly.

"Good night, Ben."

He left her. The night was cool outside, a touch of winter already in the air. He climbed into his Jeep and started the engine, a heavy sense of disappointment settling inside him. A moment later, he drove away from the warm lights of Eve Kearny's house.

EVE WAS SURPRISED and just a little dismayed at how quickly Kingston University in Denver responded to her job application. Apparently they wished to fill a vacant position as soon as possible, and Eve had been selected as one of three finalists. Only a few weeks after she'd sent in her résumé, she received a phone call from the head of the search committee at Kingston requesting that she fly to Denver for an interview.

She didn't leave her office that afternoon until she'd made all her flight arrangements, and then she drove home slowly. She cruised past Josie's house, wondering if she'd see Ben sitting on the front porch sipping apple cider. He wasn't there, of course. He hadn't been there for two entire weeks. She hadn't talked to him since the night he'd come to dinner, the night they'd almost made love.

Eve swung into her driveway, knowing she ought to be grateful. It was better this way, not seeing Ben. She'd al-

ready learned how easy it would be to get physically involved with him. Getting involved, and everything that
went along with it—no, she wasn't ready for that. Not yet.
Maybe not ever.

She climbed out of her old sedan and went into the
house, Oscar darting ahead of her. She glanced over at her
neighbor's one more time. Even Josie had been subdued
these past few weeks, merely scowling when she happened to meet Eve. If Ben was still Josie's lawyer, there
was no sign of it, nor had the lawsuit been mentioned.

Eve plunked down her carryall and confronted the
closet in her bedroom. What should she wear for the job
interview? Something businesslike yet scholarly, something to show she was ready to move forward in this exciting new position. So why didn't she *feel* excited? This
was a great opportunity.

Eve spread out her navy jacket on the bed, tossing one
of her vests beside it. That would do, she supposed.
Lacking inspiration, she sank onto the bed and fingered
the jacket sleeve. Maybe she hadn't talked to Ben these
past few weeks, but she had talked to his daughter often
enough. Kate would hover at the door to Eve's office at
the most unexpected times, and she always had to be
coaxed inside. But then she would sit and talk intently to
Eve about her favorite authors and about the new stories
she was writing. And more often than not she'd end up
arguing with Eve about what constituted good fiction.
Eve enjoyed the arguments, and she was always a little
sorry when she had to interrupt Kate to go teach a late
class or to attend a meeting.

Now Eve tossed her jacket aside, deciding it was too
businesslike for this interview. She wasn't going to try to
impress anyone; she wasn't going to appear overeager for
the damn job.

Oscar jumped onto the bed and settled on top of Eve's jacket to lick his paws. Eve gazed at her cat for a long while. Then she went into the living room and picked up the phone book. She flipped through the pages until she found a listing for the Cactus Inn. She dialed the number before she could tell herself how foolish she was being.

The desk clerk connected her to Ben's room, and a second later his voice came over the line, deep, confident, energetic.

"Ben Lawrence here."

"Hello. It's Eve." Now she did feel like a fool, but it was too late to hang up.

"Eve...hello." He sounded surprised. "How have you been?"

"Fine. But this isn't a social call."

"Why not? I don't mind social calls. And I'm fine, too, by the way." Now he sounded easy, relaxed, and she wondered if he'd missed her at all. She'd missed *him*, and she couldn't deny that any longer.

"Listen, Ben, I'm glad you're fine. Really. But I have a favor to ask, and that's why I'm calling."

"A favor... hmm. This is something new."

She wished his voice didn't sound so good to her. "I just got the word today," she said briskly. "I'm flying out for a job interview in Denver tomorrow."

"I see." His voice tensed. He paused for a moment, then went on. "I'm happy for you, Eve. I hope the interview goes well."

She found she didn't like his being so polite with her. "The favor I have to ask is something . . . a little unusual. I'll be gone for a few days, and I need someone to, well, someone to look after my cat. Josie certainly isn't a candidate, and Angela at school is already covering my classes for me. I can't ask her to do anything more, and—"

"You want me to baby-sit your cat." He sounded very dubious. Meanwhile, Oscar had prowled into the living room and was staring at Eve accusingly, as if he knew what she was up to.

"I wouldn't call it baby-sitting," she said. "You'll have to feed him, and he does need to be let in and out of the house a few times a day. I guess it's fairly obvious by now that he can't be left locked up all the time."

"Fairly obvious," Ben agreed.

She gripped the phone receiver. "Okay, I was a real idiot to call you," she admitted. "I can't imagine why I did."

"Maybe you just wanted to know how I'm doing." He sounded relaxed again, almost cheerful.

"Goodbye, Ben."

"I'll look after the cat for you," he stated decisively. "How are you getting to the airport?"

"I'll drive in to Albuquerque, leave my car there, and then catch my flight—"

"I'll drive you to Albuquerque, instead. What time should I pick you up tomorrow?"

"I don't want you to do that. It's too much trouble."

"Look at it this way. You'll be doing me a favor. I'd welcome an excuse to get out of Cobb for a few hours, and it's not like my schedule is packed. What time, Eve?"

She gave in all too readily. "This is really nice of you, Ben. Let me think. If you're here by ten in the morning, that should allow plenty of time."

"Nine-thirty," he amended. "See you then." He hung up before she could say anything in response.

Eve replaced the receiver, disgusted with herself. She'd wanted to hear Ben's voice, and she'd used the first excuse that came to mind. If she'd thought a little harder, she could've made other arrangements for her cat. Now she'd be driving all the way into Albuquerque with Ben.

Oscar stalked toward the kitchen, tail held high. Eve followed, opening a can of gourmet chicken-and-liver for him. Maybe chicken wasn't the best delicacy with which to tempt her cat, she realized.

"Stay away from Josie's hens while I'm gone," she warned him.

He blinked innocently and began to nibble his food. Eve propped her elbows on the counter as she watched him.

"Don't concern yourself, Oscar," she murmured. "If I manage to land this job, you won't have to worry about Josie anymore—and I won't have to worry about Ben Lawrence."

It was a dismal thought.

CHAPTER EIGHT

BEN SHOWED UP promptly at nine-thirty the next morning. Eve was ready with one small overnight bag, and she walked out to his Jeep. She'd gone weeks without seeing him, and all she wanted to do now was memorize his strong stubborn features all over again. She let her gaze linger on him, liking the way his hair stirred in the breeze, liking the way he conveyed that hint of elegance even with the sleeves of his shirt rolled up.

He seemed to be taking his time conducting his own perusal, too. "You look different today," he said thoughtfully. "I can't quite figure out why."

She'd pinned up her hair and decided to wear her navy jacket, after all, tempering its severity with a paisley skirt and bright silk blouse.

"I'm the same as always," she told Ben as he tucked her bag into the back seat. He still seemed thoughtful, however, continuing to gaze at her.

She glanced away. "Oscar's fine for now, out making his usual rounds of the neighborhood. The cat food's in the cupboard—you can't miss it. And here's my key, before I forget." It seemed an intimate gesture, handing him her key, but it was one that couldn't be avoided. He closed his fingers over it.

"I'll make sure Josephine doesn't do anything nefarious to the cat while you're away."

"That's reassuring—but I haven't seen you over at Josie's lately."

"These days she likes to come down to my office to discuss legal matters."

"Well, at least she's getting out and about." Eve climbed into the Jeep, suspecting it was Ben's idea that Josie meet him at his office.

As they pulled away from the curb, Eve spoke again. "You know, I didn't get a chance to tell Kate that I'd be gone for the next few days. I'd hate for her to show up at the school and not find me."

Ben remained silent a few moments before answering. "Kate doesn't tell me about her visits with you, but I surmised she'd been to see you again. I suppose I can tell her you'll be gone."

"It'd be a good idea, I think."

"She'll be bothered, of course," Ben said ruefully. "She'll realize that *I* knew about your trip, and *she* didn't. She's possessive of her friendship with you, Eve."

"I'm flattered she considers it a friendship. The two of us never agree on anything."

"It's good for her to talk to you."

Eve gazed out the windshield. She didn't want to admit that she was growing attached to Kate. "Your daughter will be fine, you know. Maybe she hasn't adjusted to the divorce or to moving here, but give her time. She'll come around."

"Do you really think that's all it takes—a little time?"

"Look at me. I'm a walking example of adjustment," she said lightly. "I went through a divorce, moved here...and I'm doing just fine." She glanced at Ben. "Don't argue with me," she warned. "I know you think that deep down I haven't adjusted. But you're wrong. I really have."

"I guess that's why you're planning to leave Cobb," he remarked. "You've adjusted too well to this place."

They were driving down Central Avenue, and Eve glanced at the storefronts: the faded sign in Marta's Dress Shop that had been advertising a half-price sale for two years now, the awning that flapped over the door of the bakery, the battered chairs and lamps and cabinets dragged out each day and displayed in front of the Antique Gallery. "Time seems to have a different meaning in Cobb somehow," she said. "It slows down. You don't have to be in such a hurry anymore."

"But you're leaving," Ben reminded her.

"It's a good idea to slow down for a little while—not forever."

"I'll try to keep that in mind during the next decade or so," Ben said.

"Living here isn't a jail sentence," she protested. "Besides, it's not the same for you. Your kids are here—people you love. That makes all the difference in the world." Even as she said the words, she wondered how it would feel to be anchored to one place because of the people you love. That wasn't part of her experience. Her parents, both retired, were remarkably self-sufficient people and spent a great deal of time traveling from their home in Colorado Springs. They loved Eve, but wouldn't know what to do with her if she visited them for very long. They didn't anchor her, and neither did a husband—neither did children. She told herself she was lucky to be so free of ties, but suddenly she didn't feel lucky. She spoke her thoughts out loud.

"I need to find a place where I can establish myself," she said. "A place where I can create my own ties. Get involved in the community, that sort of thing."

"You seem pretty involved here, being a teacher."

"Oh, outwardly I seem involved. But I never intended to make a commitment to this town, not even in the beginning. I've already told you—I've been hiding, and that's not good."

"First you say you're well adjusted, next you say you've been hiding. You can't have it both ways."

Fortunately she had an answer ready for that. "The important thing is to *realize* I've been hiding and to do something about it. If I get this job in Denver... Well, I do have friends there, and it is where I grew up. It would be a very good place for me to settle down permanently." She was starting to feel better, wanting to imagine herself creating a solid substantial life, something she wouldn't want to leave behind—the way she planned to leave Cobb.

A moment or two later she realized that Ben had failed to turn off for the highway. Instead, he'd turned in the opposite direction, down a narrow road.

"Where are we going?"

"You'll see. I picked you up early this morning because I have something I want to show you."

She sensed a repressed anticipation in him, and she was intrigued. This road took them to the very outskirts of town, where alfalfa fields spread out along the mesa. Ben turned again, this time onto a dirt lane winding beneath ancient cottonwood trees. He came to a halt in front of a large, rambling, two-story adobe house, tucked away behind the trees. Weeds clotted the yard, and several of the windows had been boarded up. It was a solitary place, and looked as if it had been abandoned for years.

"Tell me what you think," Ben said, the undertone of anticipation still in his voice.

Eve wasn't sure quite how to answer, but she tried to be objective. "I imagine the house was beautiful once. It'd qualify as a mansion in this town. A shame it hasn't been kept up.''

Apparently she'd said the right thing; Ben nodded in agreement. "It's suffered some damage, all right, but nothing that can't be repaired. The realtor tells me it hasn't been occupied in about five years because no one in Cobb can afford a place this big.''

Eve glanced at him. "You're going to buy it?"

"Let's just say I'm thinking about the possibility.'' He climbed out of the Jeep, and Eve followed suit. Together they went up an uneven flagstone path toward the front door.

"I'd have to put in new stones,'' Ben murmured. "That wouldn't be so much trouble. I'd redo the stucco for the entire outside of the house, but the basic landscaping's pretty good." He pushed open the heavily carved door, and Eve found it easy to fall in with his mood, helping to list all the possibilities of the house.

"This is a wonderful door," she said. "All you'll have to do is strip it down and varnish it again. You don't see carving like that too often."

"Look at this floor, Eve. Solid oak. I'd have to sand it down, of course.''

"The walls are built thick," she said. "You'd be glad of that. Adobe keeps the heat in during the winter and keeps you cool in the summer. On that sill right there, you could have a window seat . . ." She wandered through the spacious living room with him, seeing beyond the cobwebs draped here and there, the broken glass littered around the fireplace, the soot and grime that had built up in the corners. She could envision the possibilities here, all right. Now she gazed up in appreciation at the aged vigas—the graceful ceiling beams.

"You'll definitely have to leave the beams exposed," she said. "You want the construction of this place to come through. Don't muck it up with anything fussy." It took her a moment to realize that Ben was watching her with an amused expression.

"I wondered how you'd react to this house," he said. "I haven't told anyone else I'm thinking about buying it. Your reaction was the first I wanted to see."

Eve felt uncomfortable. "I guess I'm getting a little carried away, but the place *is* impressive, Ben. Most of the damage appears to be superficial."

"It'd take a lot of work to get the place into shape, but I haven't seen anything else in town that inspires me."

She went to one of the windows where the boards had been torn down and gazed out at the yard. "If anyone tells you to thin the trees—don't listen. They protect the house, and you'll enjoy the shade in the summer." Summertime was long past now, golden leaves swirling to the ground in the breeze. Eve could picture Ben's kids gathering them into great piles and then jumping in, scattering them all over again.

Ben came to stand beside her. "You're only confirming my own feelings about the house. Hell, I just might buy it, after all."

"I don't think you'd be sorry. I wish I could see what it'd look like with all the dirt scraped away, new window-panes put in..."

"If I buy it, maybe you'll still be in Cobb when I finish the remodeling."

"Maybe I won't."

They gazed at each other. Morning sunlight filtered in through the slats of the boarded-up windows, but the room was cold. It needed a fire crackling on the hearth, and Eve imagined this room transformed into a warm inviting place. She was curious to know what Ben's tastes would be; she suspected he'd surround himself with a comfortable sort of elegance.

It was useless to speculate about that, however. Standing here beside him, she was too conscious of his nearness, remembering the feel of his body against hers. Damn. Now she was speculating about something else entirely. She lifted her gaze slowly to Ben's.

"I wish I could take you in my arms right now," he murmured. "The only thing stopping me is that plane you have to catch."

Eve somehow made herself move toward the door. "I can't miss that flight."

"I know. I'll get you there on time."

Once they were outside, Eve breathed in the cool morning air with a sense of relief. She glanced back at the rambling house.

"Buy it," she urged him. "Just go ahead and buy it. This place is meant for you, Ben. I can feel it."

"Anything would be an improvement over the Cactus Inn."

"It's more than that. The house is so solid—built to endure. It's survived all this neglect, and now someone needs to give it a chance. Someone like you." She didn't know why she was telling him all this; the decision was his to make and had nothing to do with her. Yet, deep down, she was glad to be the first one he'd brought here.

He gazed at the house with an air of contemplation, a smile hovering on his face. "Maybe it is meant for me. Until I get some more clients in this town, I'll have plenty of leisure time for repairs."

They both studied the house a moment longer. Then they climbed into the Jeep and made their way back down the lane, heading out toward the highway.

They filled the hour-and-a-half drive to Albuquerque with conversation. Ben told Eve about his days in law school, where he'd been obliged to study so hard he'd begun to think sleep deprivation was a requirement for passing the bar exam. Eve, in turn, told Ben about her time in graduate school, when she'd spent late nights of her own studying Dickens and Shakespeare and Chaucer. It seemed a safe topic, their days as college students, yet Eve sensed a new bond forming between them. Both she and Ben had been driven to do well in the careers they'd chosen, studying hard, making ambitious plans for the future. Ben had clearly gone on to succeed—at least until he'd come to this town—and now she meant to resume her own ambitions. For both of them, Cobb was a barrier to their careers. It seemed like she and Ben had something in common....

They went on talking, few silences between them, as if they had to share as much as possible while they still had the chance. But then they reached the outskirts of Albuquerque, the wide mesas on either side of the highway giving way to the bustle of the city.

"It always looks like such a metropolis to me, coming from Cobb," she said. "I guess my perspective has changed these past few years. I don't know what I'll think of Denver anymore. It'll probably seem huge."

"I hope your interview goes the way you'd like, Eve. You'll impress the hell out of them up there."

She had to smile at that. "You don't know the academic world very well, then. Everyone will frown on me for spending two years at humble Cobb Community. I'll be asked, in a very delicate way, why I haven't had anything published. That's going to be the hardest question to answer, because I really do love to write. Being around your daughter lately has made me realize how much I miss writing.''

Perhaps the conversation between them had grown too easy; she hadn't meant to tell him about her writing. She'd hardly realized she missed it herself until now, but she knew it was true. Kate's intensity about putting words down on paper reminded Eve that she had once felt that same need to capture her thoughts on paper. She'd given up so much after her divorce. Too much. . . .

"With this new job, I'd have more time to write," she told Ben. "I certainly wouldn't have any excuses left."

"Like I said, I hope it goes well for you."

After that, somehow, a constraint formed between them. They arrived at the airport, and Eve experienced an almost forgotten sensation, half nerves, half anticipation.

"Ben, you can just drop me off. You've already gone to far too much trouble."

He parked the Jeep. "You won't get rid of me that easily. I'll stay until your flight leaves."

She didn't want to get rid of him, that was the problem. She was glad he'd be here to see her off.

The airport was busy, and it took a while to get checked in. Afterward, however, there was nothing for her to do but sit and wait with Ben. The constraint still lingered between them, and now they didn't seem to have much to talk about. When Eve's flight was called, they walked together toward the gate.

They reached the point where Ben would have to stay behind. "Thank you again," she said, disliking her own formality.

"I enjoyed bringing you here. I think you know that."

"Still, it was kind of you."

He gave a slight smile. "What time will your return flight get in? I'll pick you up."

"No, that's really too much," she said.

"You don't have a car here—how will you get back to Cobb? Just tell me when you'll return, Eve."

"It doesn't seem right, your doing all this for me," she protested.

"If you don't tell me what time your flight gets in, I'll just camp out here and wait for you."

Eve conceded defeat. "It'll be the 9 p.m. flight, day after tomorrow. Same airline."

"I'll be here. Good luck in Denver."

"Thanks, Ben." There was nothing more to say, but Eve stood where she was, unable to leave his side. She had a crazy vision of herself throwing her arms around him and kissing him, right there on the concourse. Instead, she held out her hand to shake his. She needed to touch him any way she could just now.

He clasped her hand in both of his, and she managed a smile. "I've always hated job interviews," she said, "and the way they make you feel as if you're on trial."

"There's a remedy for that. Just make the employers feel like they're the ones on trial."

"Spoken like a true lawyer." Unexpectedly, they were easy with one another again, and Eve knew the real reason she was reluctant to board the plane: she didn't want to leave Ben, not even for a few days. She'd already gone weeks without seeing him, and she felt almost as if she had to make up for lost time.

It was Ben who nudged her gently toward the gate. "You don't want to miss your flight."

At last a measure of sanity returned to her, and she walked away from him. This was the way it had to be, if she wanted a new life for herself....

CHAPTER NINE

TWO DAYS LATER, Eve had been through a whirlwind of interviews. Kingston University was exceedingly thorough and had required her to meet with practically everyone on campus: the chairperson of the English Department, the vice president of academic affairs, the vice president of student affairs, the dean of the library, the dean of graduate studies. Eve had also been required to attend a tea at the English Department where the faculty could look her over. That had been the most grueling session of all; no group was quite as critical as a bunch of other teachers. But Eve's two years of teaching experience had served her well, and she actually retained her sense of humor while being quizzed by any number of professors. Now the final moments in the whole process had arrived. The chairperson of the English Department was treating Eve to an early dinner before her flight back to New Mexico.

The chairperson, Dr. Margaret Davis, was a tall dignified woman with frosted blond perfectly styled hair. She seemed a difficult person to get to know. She sat in the restaurant with Eve and veered between two personas: busy mother of a teenage girl and ponderous author of several well-regarded books.

"Don't ever have daughters," she advised Eve over the baked shrimp. "I tell you, I can't keep my daughter's boyfriends straight anymore. It's a monumental headache.''

Eve murmured something vaguely sympathetic and felt a headache of her own threaten. Perhaps the last couple of days had worn her down more than she'd realized because Dr. Margaret Davis was starting to get on her nerves. Whenever the woman spoke about her daughter, she used a long-suffering tone that did nothing to disguise a certain smugness. Look at me, she seemed to be saying. I'm the mother of a girl so gorgeous I can't keep the names of her boyfriends straight.

Eve had noticed that many parents did that. They complained at great length about their children, but you could always discern their happiness and pride underneath. It was as if parents felt compelled to display their membership in some exclusive club where both suffering and joy were the required dues. It annoyed Eve. It annoyed her especially now as she poked at the shrimp on her plate. And then she thought about Ben and realized he was one parent who didn't boast about his trials and tribulations as a father. He simply seemed perplexed and a bit overwhelmed by parenthood, struggling to do his best with the job. And somehow that really got to Eve. Other parents might annoy her, but Ben, he made her ache inside for the children she'd lost. Damn him.

''My editor was in town last week,'' Dr. Davis said now, switching to her author persona. ''Too bad you couldn't have met him, Eve. You really do need to start establishing some contacts in the publishing world. All your letters of recommendation praise your dissertation. I'm really quite impressed.''

Dr. Davis didn't sound impressed. She sounded disapproving of Eve for allowing her dissertation to molder in a desk drawer for two years. It was exactly as Eve had predicted to Ben. Her lack of publishing credentials had been delicately but persistently questioned ever since she'd arrived in Denver. No one seemed to care that she successfully carried a teaching load of five courses each semester in Cobb.

"Dr. Davis, Cobb Community College has been an excellent place for me to learn teaching skills. It's been time well spent, and I don't regret it at all."

Dr. Davis looked pained, as if the mere mention of Cobb Community was enough to cause her indigestion. "Our school affords teaching opportunities of the top caliber. We believe all our professors are very fortunate."

The implication was clear: lofty Kingston University was doing Eve a great favor by lowering itself even to consider her application. In return, she was expected to be grateful—and penitent for her years spent at a third-rate community college.

Eve remembered how different her interview had been at Cobb Community two years ago. Everyone had seemed so eager to have her join the faculty, and dear old Professor Halford had made a heroic effort to discuss all of Eve's favorite authors with her. Suddenly she wanted nothing more than to push aside her plate, get on a plane and fly back to New Mexico.

She *did* push aside her plate, glancing around the restaurant where Dr. Davis had brought her. It was a subtly pretentious place, with autographed pictures of poets hanging on the walls. A great many things could be said about Cobb, New Mexico, but pretentious wasn't one of them. Cobb was struggling to survive amid the desert sagebrush, struggling not to be forgotten by the rest of the world.

At last the meal was over, and the parting messages exchanged between Eve and Dr. Davis. The department would let her know about its decision as soon as possible, et cetera, et cetera. A car arrived to drive Eve to the airport, and at last she was on the plane, flying back to Albuquerque—and Ben. He would be waiting for her. She couldn't ignore the lift of her spirits at the thought of Ben's being there. She tried to calm herself, to bring her bouyant mood back down to earth, but it was useless. She wanted to see Ben. Needed to see him.

When the plane landed, she hurried off, and once inside the airport she searched the crowd anxiously. There Ben was, standing off to one side, looking even better than she'd expected. In his jeans and faded khaki shirt, he still managed to look more sophisticated than anyone she'd met in Denver. This time when she went to him, she didn't shake his hand in a stiff formal way. She didn't shake his hand at all. Instead, she found herself caught up in his embrace, his body strong and solid against hers.

"I missed you," he said in a low voice, close to her ear.

"I missed you, too," she said softly. They prolonged the embrace more than necessary, but at last began walking together.

"Are you hungry?" he asked.

"Ravenous," she said. "I had dinner before I left, but it wasn't satisfying."

They ended up at a small coffee shop tucked into a corner of the airport, where they both ordered bowls of spicy southwestern chili. The steam from the chili rose, warming Eve. And she was warmed also by sitting across from Ben, just looking at him.

"How'd it go in Denver?" he asked finally, as if reluctant to bring up the subject.

"Pretty much as I suspected it would. I felt like I was on probation the entire time, but I got through it all right. Whether or not I'll be offered the job . . . ? Right now I'm fairly certain they *won't* offer it to me. I think they'd prefer someone with more stellar credentials."

"You're probably underestimating yourself. But I can't help it, Eve—a big part of me hopes you don't get the job. A big part of me hopes you'll stay in New Mexico. I didn't like it when you were gone. At least before, I always knew you were in town, close by, even when I couldn't see you."

"I've sent my résumé out to a few other places," she said quickly. "My job search has only started."

His expression grew carefully guarded. She didn't understand herself. First she'd felt such an uncomplicated rush of happiness, knowing she'd see him again. But now that she was actually here with him, she seemed compelled to remind him that it was only temporary, this sharing between them. It was as if she'd taken a step toward Ben and then, frightened by what she'd done, needed to take a step back.

"I hope my cat didn't give you too much trouble," she said, and now his expression became disgruntled.

"Oscar and I have been involved in a battle of wills. The cat's been winning, that's what really bothers me. Yesterday the damn animal wouldn't eat a thing I set before him. I went down to the grocery store and bought every kind of cat food I could find—Liver Delight, Tuna Entrée, Country Stew."

"Oh, dear," Eve said, picturing Ben surrounded by tins and tins of cat food. "Did anything work?"

"Beef kabobs," he muttered. "Eleven o'clock last night, the cat finally ate some beef kabobs I brought over from the diner."

Eve smiled. "Imagine that—Oscar condescending to eat something from the Rio Diner. But you went beyond the call of duty."

"In between catering to your Siamese, I found time to buy myself a house."

"Ben, that's wonderful! You actually did it."

He looked pleased with himself. "That's right, I just went ahead and did it. I'm going to have a place for my kids—a place for myself, too, once I get all the work done."

"I'm delighted for you," she said sincerely.

They talked about the plans he already had for the house, and Eve allowed herself to enjoy these moments with him. Long after they'd finished their chili, they sat together, their voices an agreeable murmur in the almost-deserted coffee shop. At last, however, there seemed no choice but to leave. They went out to Ben's Jeep and began the drive back to Cobb.

When they'd finally left the lights of Albuquerque far behind, the mesa on either side of the highway seemed dark, limitless. Eve leaned her head against the seat, lulled by the steady throb of the Jeep's engine.

"You can close your eyes and try to get some sleep," Ben suggested.

"No. I don't want to miss any of this." She hesitated, but the solitude surrounding her and Ben seemed to encourage frankness. "I like being with you. The only problem is that it scares the hell out of me."

"What would you say if I told you it scares me, too? But that doesn't stop me from wanting to be around you. Eve, I told myself I wasn't going to ask you this, but I'll go ahead, anyway." His voice was taut. "Because of my kids, I can't leave New Mexico. If we're going to find out what's happening here . . . you'll have to stay."

"So you're asking me to stay."

"I don't have the right. I know that. And you'd be crazy to spend any time in a place like Cobb out of choice. But still . . . I guess I *am* asking."

Eve stared out at the darkness. She could think of several reasons to stay: her unexpected sense of loyalty to Cobb Community, her impatience with the snobbishness of schools like Kingston University. But to stay for Ben . . . how could she do that, when it was because of him she'd decided to leave Cobb in the first place?

She could lecture herself all she liked about finding new opportunities, new horizons. But that wasn't the real reason she wanted to leave New Mexico. The real reason was tied up with how she felt about Ben Lawrence.

"Dammit, Ben, you make me remember too many things that hurt. Things I thought I'd forgotten."

"What things?" he asked gently.

"You remind me of what I've lost."

"Your husband."

"No, not Ted. It's what Ted and I almost created together. A family . . . Oh, don't you see? I'd almost stopped thinking about the miscarriages. I'd almost decided it could be a good thing, not having kids. I'd resolved feelings, and now you've come along, and I'm starting to get angry again, and hating myself for what happened to my babies. I'm remembering all of it when I just want to forget!"

"What happened wasn't your fault," Ben said. "It was just the worst kind of luck there is. How can you blame yourself?"

He sounded so reasonable. Of course it was just bad luck. Of course she shouldn't blame herself—but she did, anyway. She blamed her body for betraying her. And somehow Ben Lawrence had been the one to reawaken the pain in her, after she'd stifled it all this time.

"I don't know what it is about you," she said. "I don't know why being around you makes me remember again so vividly. Why do you stir up memories that you weren't even a part of?"

He didn't say anything for a long moment, gazing straight ahead, his hands steady on the wheel. When at last he did speak, his voice was still gentle. "A lot of things between you and me don't make sense, Eve. I keep wanting to see you, I've even asked you to stay, but I don't have a damn thing to offer you if you *do* stay. That sure doesn't make any sense."

Ben was putting up his own barrier between them, she realized, making it clear he would give her no promises. But she didn't have any promises of her own to give, either.

"I don't know what I'm going to do," she admitted. "I thought I'd made up my mind to leave, yet now . . . I just need time to think about it."

"Time when I'm not around," he said wryly.

"You do have a tendency to confuse things for me."

They drove the rest of the way in silence. It seemed much too soon when they arrived in Cobb, the town merely a glimmer of light on the dark mesa. Ben pulled over in front of Eve's house, and she didn't know how to say good-night.

"Listen, thanks for looking after Oscar. And thanks for picking me up at the airport. I know it was a lot of trouble."

"I didn't mind."

She sat for a moment, wanting to touch him, as if that would give some closure to their time together this evening.

"Thanks again," she said inadequately. She climbed out of the Jeep, Ben coming along with her overnight bag.

She unlocked the door to the house. When she switched on the light, she saw her cat crouched under a chair, gazing at her with a reproachful expression. No doubt it would take Oscar days to forgive her for going off on a trip without him.

Ben set down her bag, looking serious and preoccupied. "Goodbye, Eve," he murmured, and then he was gone.

It seemed he knew how to say good-night, even if she didn't.

BEN ANCHORED his crowbar, pulled hard and ripped down another big chunk of plaster. He'd been busy in this upstairs room for more than an hour, and plaster dust filled the air. Grit had worked its way under his fingernails and under his collar. But it was good satisfying work, and he was ready for more of it.

He'd moved into his house a week ago, as soon as he'd closed the sale, and then he'd set up camp with a sleeping bag in the living room. He'd be roughing it for a while, but that was a lot better than living at the Cactus Inn. For the first time since his divorce, he felt as if he had a real home. No more efficiency apartments, no more hotel rooms, that was for damn sure.

Ben worked well into the afternoon, tossing his shirt aside, sweat trickling down his arms and chest. He was expending the energy he'd once used for those twelve-hour days at the office, and it was a relief to have something physical to do. His current law practice just wasn't keeping him occupied enough.

He had a total of two clients now. One of them was a man who'd been laid off from the Discount Mart a few months ago and was now trying to get his job back. Ben wasn't optimistic about the case; Discount Mart could barely afford to meet its current payroll. Ben had advised the man to move someplace where the job market was more promising.

His other client was still the cantankerous Josephine Scott. Josephine came to his office on Central Avenue once or twice a week, all dressed up so she could complain about life. The old woman didn't seem to care how quickly the legal process moved along. In fact, in Ben's estimation, she didn't really want it to move along at all. Apparently she just wanted to feel she was in the middle of things, complaining about people like Eveline Kearny who let their cats run amok.

Ben tore down another chunk of plaster. Maybe physical activity was also a way to keep his mind off Eve. He hadn't seen her these past few weeks, not since the night he'd brought her home from the airport. A dozen times he'd almost called her, almost gone to see her. A dozen times he'd stopped himself. It hadn't been easy. He was like someone trying to break a habit—denying himself what he craved, but still craving it. He wanted to be near Eve. He wanted to hold her and make love to her, then make love to her again.

Physical labor wasn't doing the trick, after all. His mind was still on Eve. He couldn't stop wondering how she was doing, what she was thinking. He pictured her pale skin and bright hair, her coolness disguising a warmth and passion underneath....

Ben tossed down his crowbar and went to wash away his coating of plaster dust. To shower he had to stand in an old claw-footed bathtub, but he liked the tub. He was going to keep it. After his shower, he grabbed a beer from the ice chest, then sat on his sleeping bag and leaned against the wall. Mellow evening light streamed in through the dirt-streaked windows as he pondered all the work still ahead of him: plumbing to be revamped, a new water heater to be installed, caulking to be stripped and replaced. He enjoyed adding to his already sizable list. He didn't plan to run out of projects anytime soon.

The phone rang, startling him. It had only been installed for a few days. So far he'd received phone calls from Jenny and Matthew. His two youngest kids, at least, were interested in the fact that he finally had a house in Cobb. No one else had contacted him, however.

He picked up the receiver. "Ben Lawrence here."

"Hello." It was Eve's voice, low and cool and with just a hint of wariness.

Ben smiled. "Hello, Eve. How's it going?"

"Fine. Very fine, to tell the truth."

"Glad to hear it." He was glad to hear *her*. "I hope this is a social call," he said.

"In a way it is." She sounded brisk now. "I wanted to tell you something. Today I was contacted by Margaret Davis, head of the English Department at Kingston University. She offered me the job, Ben."

For a moment he couldn't say anything. The disappointment he felt was like a punch to his stomach.

"Congratulations," he said at last. "I knew you'd underestimated your chances."

"It was a big surprise to me. I didn't expect it at all."

"Congratulations," he said again, knowing he lacked the required enthusiasm. "When do you start?" He was already thinking ahead, deciding how to convince her he needed to see her before she left. Why the hell had he stayed away these past few weeks? He should have been seeing her while he still had the chance. He'd hoped all along she wouldn't get the job. So much for that.

She hadn't answered his question. "When do you leave for Denver?" he asked again.

The silence stretched out between them, then, "I turned the job down."

"What?" Had he heard her correctly?

"I turned it down," she repeated. "There I was, on the phone to Dr. Davis, and she just kept rattling on as if I'd already accepted the position. The way she just assumed I'd take it annoyed me no end. So I interrupted her, and told her very politely that I was turning down the offer. She sounded horrified, as if I'd personally insulted her. It was very satisfying, all around."

Another silence stretched out between them. It was Ben who finally spoke.

"I don't buy it, Eve," he said.

"Don't buy what?"

"This rationale of yours. What's the real reason you said no? You went in knowing they'd disapprove of your...hiatus in Cobb. You knew they'd look down on your lack of writing credentials, yet you still wanted the job. You wanted it badly. So why'd you turn it down?" He was testing her in a way, probing the limits of her decision.

"Dammit, Ben, does this have to be so difficult? Maybe I don't even know why I turned the job down. All I do know is that my life is a muddle, and the only thing I can think about is seeing you."

She sounded angry, but that was okay by him. She could be as angry as she liked, as long as she wanted to see him. That was all that mattered right now.

"Eve, I'm coming over. Just don't go anywhere. I'm coming over."

CHAPTER TEN

IT WASN'T EASY finding a way to celebrate in Cobb. Ben insisted, however, that he and Eve had cause to celebrate, though privately, Eve wasn't sure she agreed with him. She was still in shock over turning down Kingston University. She hadn't planned on doing it. For days she'd stewed about her feelings for Ben, arriving at no answers except that she missed him dreadfully. Then Dr. Margaret Davis had called her from Denver, offering her a position in the most condescending manner possible, and Eve, without thought, without plan, had simply turned the job down flat.

And then Ben had rushed over and swept her into his arms. But Eve was wary, needing more time. She'd finally persuaded Ben to take her *out* to celebrate—to the new drive-in movie theater on the highway. The drive-in was almost halfway to the next town, not really an innovation that Cobb could claim as its own, but at least it was something new and different to do.

So here they were now, sitting in Ben's Jeep at the drive-in theater, some silly romantic comedy playing on the screen. Ben had swept her into his arms again, and she reveled in his nearness, running her hands over the strong muscles of his chest. Her misgivings about intimacy were rapidly melting away, her primary concern at the moment how to get closer to him in spite of the Jeep's bucket seats. The gearshift knob presented a decided inconvenience.

Eve raised her face to Ben's, her lips already tender and swollen from his kisses, and twined her fingers through his hair. Apparently she was still operating on the principle of spontaneity and didn't know how to stop herself. She didn't want to stop.

Ben gave a low groan, crushing her against him. "You know, we'd be a whole lot more comfortable in the back seat," he said, his voice husky.

Eve's laugh was shaky. "My mother warned me never to climb into the back seat with a man."

"Did you ever think that maybe your mother was wrong?"

She didn't answer. She simply cupped Ben's face with her hands and kissed him. When they broke apart a long moment later, they were both breathing raggedly, and Eve nodded her acquiescence.

"Back seat," she murmured.

They climbed awkwardly to the rear of the Jeep, Ben catching Eve as she tumbled on top of him. Still breathing unevenly, they lay together, ignoring the tinny voices coming through the speaker. Once again Eve reached out and ran her hands over Ben's chest, her body suffused with a heat that seemed to spark directly from him. Fingers trembling, she pulled his shirt free of his jeans. She was being swirled away on a tide of emotion and sensation, but she made a final effort to resist—like a marathon swimmer glancing back one last time to the safe familiar shoreline.

"Ben . . . we really can't, not in full view of everyone. . . ."

"It's dark. We're parked in the back row. And besides, I have tinted windows. No one can see in." He was pulling up her blouse now, his hands warm on her skin. Everything was happening so fast, and Eve made yet another attempt to hold on to rationality.

"All the same, we can't do this."

"I know." They both kept doing it. Ben kissed Eve's throat, trailing his tongue downward, and instinctively she arched against him. Now he caressed her breasts, and she was the one who moaned. She was on fire with the touch of him, on fire with her need for him.

The confined space proved a disadvantage, but not an insurmountable one. Eve tugged at the zipper of Ben's jeans, and he tugged at her jeans in turn. Soon her bare skin brushed against his. She caught her breath as Ben moved his hands provocatively over the curve of her hips, and her fingers shook as she explored the hard muscles of his stomach. Her touch drifted lower, and now it was Ben who gasped.

"Eve, you don't know what you're doing to me," he said hoarsely. His hands tightening possessively on her hips, they strained against each other, but even this wasn't close enough. Eve moaned again, opening her legs and straddling him unashamedly.

"Oh, Ben."

"Honey..." His voice was thick, and she could tell that he was holding himself back for her. With deliberate caresses, she asked for more.

He entered her slowly, carefully, his innate gentleness requiring him to do so. But it wasn't gentleness she wanted. She rocked against him, urgently, and now there was no holding back at all. As Ben thrust into her, she arched against him, over and over, tightening around him even as he swept her away.

She came in a frenzied burst, almost sobbing as intensity radiated through her. And Ben gave a deep heavy groan a moment later.

Lying tangled together in the back seat of the Jeep, Ben smoothed the damp hair away from her forehead.

"That was nice," he said, his voice still husky. "Very nice."

"I didn't know I could be like that," she whispered, half embarrassed, half delighted at his words. "Really, I didn't. Sex for me has always been more ... sensible."

He chuckled, smoothing her hair again. "How do you have sensible sex?"

"I don't know. You just do. You plan it out, I suppose. You don't jump in without looking, the way we did ... You were pretty nice yourself, Ben."

He kissed her. "Here's to jumping in without looking."

They kissed for a long time, languorous now, instead of frantic. But gradually Eve surfaced to reality. No longer oblivious, she heard the tinny sounds of the movie issuing from the speaker. Suddenly she had the horrible conviction that if she raised her head, she'd find an entire crowd of people peering in at her. When she finally did raise her head, she was almost surprised. There was only the darkness outside. Thankful for tinted windows, she collapsed against Ben.

"What *were* we thinking?" she asked in dismay.

"We weren't thinking at all. Forget thinking. I could hold you like this all night," he murmured.

She pressed her cheek against his, running her fingers through the swirl of hair on his chest. She couldn't see him well in the darkness, and she was learning his body through touch.

"What are we going to do now? Oh, Ben, nothing's clear to me. In fact, it's all more confusing than ever."

His arms tightened around her. "We take it one step at a time. Neither one of us can turn back now. You know that, Eve."

Her arms tightened in response, and then she slid away from him. She fumbled with her jeans, pulling them on.

"We're crazy, the two of us," she said in a low voice.

Ben zipped up his own jeans and held her again. "This isn't something that's easy for me to talk about, but until tonight, I hadn't made love to anyone since my divorce. I made a few attempts at dating, but they never led anywhere. For a while, I even seemed to have lost the urge—bothered the hell out of me."

"I don't think you've lost the urge," she murmured against his shoulder.

"No. We've cleared that much up, at least."

"I haven't made love to anyone since *my* divorce," she confessed softly.

"I gathered as much."

"It's that obvious?"

"To me it is. But then, I've been paying a lot of attention to you, Eve. I notice these things."

His shirt was still loose, and Eve couldn't resist running her fingers over the bare skin of his chest. It seemed she needed to touch him more now than ever.

He drew a sharp breath as she caressed him. "Lord, Eve. Do you want to get me started again?"

Reluctantly she withdrew her hand. "I want to talk," she said. "I want to figure this whole thing out."

"That's a pretty tall order." He went on holding her, cradling her head against his shoulder. "I don't think we're going to figure it all out tonight, Eve. I just want you to know you can trust me."

"I do trust you," she said. "That's not the problem...." But Eve didn't continue. Ben was right. All her confusion, her uncertainty, couldn't be straightened out in one night. And she knew he was right about something else, too.

In spite of all her doubts, all her fears, there could be no turning back now.

FOR THE FIRST TIME all day, Eve managed to put Ben out of her mind. She sat in her office at Cobb Community, gingerly turning the pages of a diary. The pages were yellowed with age and could bear only the lightest touch. The old-fashioned script was difficult to read, but Eve took her time with it, pulled far back into another era, another life.

A rustling at her office door broke her concentration, and she glanced up. Kate Lawrence hesitated by the door. No matter how many times Kate visited here, she always behaved as if she couldn't make up her mind whether to stay or run.

"Hello, Kate," Eve said, her tone encouraging. "It's good to see you."

Kate slipped into the room, hair swinging against her cheeks. She seemed even more skittish than usual, and she didn't sit down. She glanced at Eve's desk.

"What are you doing?"

"Studying a journal—a fascinating journal, in fact. It was written by Silas T. Cobb, the man who founded this town back in the 1880s." Eve doubted that Kate was interested in Silas Cobb, but she went on speaking, anyway, trying to put the girl at ease. "Silas started this town because he thought to make a sort of paradise for himself and his family."

"He must've been crazy," Kate muttered, wandering restlessly around the office. "I hate this town."

"Kate, your father has a house here now. A place that's going to be beautiful. Maybe that'll make a difference."

"It's so run-down. I can't believe he bought it." Kate twirled a strand of hair around her finger, glancing sharply at Eve. "How come you know so much about my dad? And he knows so much about you? I thought you weren't friends or anything."

Eve closed the diary and set it to one side. "Kate, your father and I—" She stopped, knowing she didn't have the slightest idea what to say. She wanted to be aboveboard with Ben's kids, but you couldn't very well explain to a teenage girl that only last week you'd gone to a drive-in movie with her father and had sex with him in the back seat. And you couldn't very well explain that you'd been seeing him every night since, that you couldn't wait to see him and be in his arms each night.

Eve felt her face heat up just at the thought of Ben. "Your father and I are becoming friends," she improvised. "We've discovered that we like to spend time together, and—"

Kate looked appalled. "You mean you go out on dates with him?"

"I suppose you could say that your father and I are dating." Eve winced. She felt as if she was in high school again, talking about the boy who'd invited her to the prom. Except that she and Ben had gone way beyond anything she'd ever learned in high school.

Kate paced the office, her hair dropping in front of her face. "I thought you were *my* friend," she muttered.

"I am. That's not going to change."

"Everything changed when we moved to this stupid town. Everything." Kate whirled and headed for the door, clearly ready to bolt for real this time.

"Wait," Eve said. "We haven't talked about your writing yet. I'd like to talk, Kate."

The girl stood with her head bowed for a moment, then she stared at Eve defiantly. "I can't hang around here anymore." She strode out of the office.

Eve almost called Kate back, but thought better of it. Everything she'd said today had only made matters worse. She'd tried explaining her relationship with Ben, speaking to Kate like one adult to another. Maybe that hadn't been such a wonderful idea.

Propping her elbows on her desk, Eve rubbed her temples. She'd gained a lover and in the process antagonized her lover's daughter. What would the future bring?

Ben. Her lover. Eve shivered with the newness of it, the unfamiliarity. The uncertainty. She glanced down at the diary of Silas T. Cobb, a man who had sought paradise in the New Mexico desert.

"You were a dreamer, Silas," she murmured. The diary belonged in the school archives—the archives consisting of one cluttered file-cabinet drawer next to the secretary's desk down the hall. Eve had requested the diary on an impulse, and now she wanted to keep it awhile longer. She tucked it into her own file cabinet, and gathering up her usual compositions for grading, she stuffed them into her carryall and went outside.

She started home in her car. Silvery gray clouds were building, threatening a storm, and tumbleweeds skittered across the road. It would be Halloween in a few days, and the weather was appropriate. Turning onto her street, Eve drove past Josie's house. She could've sworn she saw a curtain twitch in Josie's front window, the old woman no doubt peering out disapprovingly. Poor Josie.

Eve parked and let Oscar into the house. The cat turned up his nose at Tuna Entrée and Liver Delight, but finally settled for Country Stew. The fussy eater taken care of, Eve prepared herself a simple grilled cheese sandwich, then sat down at the table with a book open in front of her.

She kept glancing at the clock, unable to lose herself in what she was reading. Ben had wanted to take her out to dinner tonight, suggesting they drive all the way into Belen, a town that actually boasted an Italian restaurant. After all, tonight would be exactly a week since their first time together at the drive-in, and they had both jokingly referred to it as an anniversary. At first Eve had turned down Ben's invitation, telling him they both needed a breathing space. But then she'd wavered. The thought of an entire day without seeing him no longer seemed bearable. They'd ended up with the agreement that Ben would come to her house tonight at eight-thirty. That was more than two hours away, and already she was tensing with anticipation.

Eve finished her simple meal, then spread out her papers on the table and began grading. She couldn't concentrate on the task, however, and eventually gave up. She drew herself a hot bath and soaked for a long while, well away from the clock. As she poured some more bath oil into the water, it occurred to her what she was doing: preparing herself for Ben. Softening herself for him. The thought was so unexpectedly intimate she pulled the plug and watched the water swirl down the drain. Although she dried herself off matter-of-factly, she couldn't seem to halt her preparations. She slipped into one of her more feminine dresses, a flowered print, and opened a bottle of perfume that had been getting a lot of use these past few days.

"Idiot," she told herself, but that didn't stop her from dabbing perfume between her breasts. She frowned at the bottle of perfume, thumping it down on the bureau. This whole situation was getting out of hand. Couldn't she think about anything but hopping into bed with Ben Lawrence?

She sighed. Apparently neither one of them could think of anything else. The way they were going after each other, Ben would have to make yet another visit to the drugstore in search of condoms. Obtaining birth control in a small town was *not* an anonymous undertaking; no doubt Ray the druggist was having a fine time with his latest tidbit of gossip.

Eve frowned at the perfume bottle again, then went back out to her composition papers. She graded a few more, then finally allowed herself to glance at the clock. It was eight twenty-five.... A knock sounded at her front door.

CHAPTER ELEVEN

BEN STOOD on Eve's porch. He didn't touch her or kiss her. He just looked at her, his eyes saying everything that needed to be said. Eve noted that he, too, seemed to have dressed for the occasion. He was wearing tan slacks and a jacket in a soft brown weave; he also wore a tie. Eve smiled. It was such a formal thing to do, wear a tie. And the two of them *were* formal with each other at first, sitting down on Eve's couch at a respectable distance from each other. They talked about their day.

"I'm still gutting walls," Ben said. "I keep telling myself it'll give me an excuse to check the wiring, redo the plumbing, that sort of thing. The truth is, those walls could get by without replastering. I just like the work. I need the work."

"It's going to be a wonderful house when you're finished."

"If I finish." He leaned back on the sofa, and Eve could tell he was starting to relax.

"Today I started doing some research on our town founder," she told him. "For years Professor Halford has been asking someone to write a biography of Silas T. Cobb, but no one ever seems interested—not even Angela, our history teacher. So I thought I'd start looking into it."

"You've been saying you'd like to get back to writing."

"Maybe this is the way to do it. There's a certain perverse satisfaction in choosing a subject that most people scorn. Everyone thinks Silas Cobb was just a crackpot, too insignificant to waste any time on." She grinned wryly. "Writing about Silas won't help my academic career much, that's for sure."

"Eve, are you regretting what you did? Turning down that job in Denver?"

She studied him. His expression was serious, intent, his eyes so dark she felt as if she could melt into them if she gazed at him long enough. She wanted him, but what she felt was more than physical desire. Far more, and that was what scared her.

"No, I'm not sorry," she murmured. "I'm just terrified. Does that make any sense?"

"It does to me." He gazed back at her, still serious, still intent, and she knew that any second now he would reach out for her and she would forget about everything but being in his arms. She couldn't let that happen just yet; there was something else she had to tell him.

"Ben, Kate dropped by to see me again today. And, well, I wanted to be straight with her. She knows that we're dating."

He sat up, no longer relaxed. "How'd she take it?"

"Not very well."

Ben stood and began pacing the living room. It struck Eve how much he and his daughter were alike. This afternoon, Kate had paced Eve's office in the same restless and perturbed manner.

"She's drawing farther away from me all the time," Ben muttered. "Sometimes it seems that way with all three of my kids. It's as if I'm chasing them, trying to catch up, but they always run faster than I do."

"Maybe you should stop chasing," Eve said. "Maybe that's the problem right there."

Ben frowned. "I've changed my whole life around for my kids. I left my job, traveled all the way across the country. After that, I can't just stop trying."

"I didn't mean that. But maybe there's such a thing as trying too hard."

Ben seemed weary as he glanced at her. "You're sure as hell not talking like a parent."

"No, I'm not," she said quietly. "How could I?"

Ben crossed to sit beside her and took both her hands in his. "I'm sorry," he said. "I didn't mean to imply that you don't understand."

"Well, I don't understand parenting, dammit. I haven't had a chance." Then, before she could stop herself, the rest of it came out. "Ben, both my babies were little girls. Both of them."

He pulled her close. "I'm sorry," he murmured again.

Eve buried her face against him, trying to contain the ache inside her. "All I want to do is forget, to go on with my life. I was doing such a good job of that until you came along. You and your daughter and..."

He just went on holding her, as if he knew there was nothing to be said, nothing that could make it right. And that alone helped her. After a moment she straightened, actually able to smile at him.

"I'm fine. Momentary setback, that's all."

He didn't look convinced, but he rose and drew her up beside him. She knew what he was thinking. She was thinking the same thing. Without a word, she led the way into her bedroom.

She had left only her bedside lamp switched on, hoping to soften the spartan aspect of the room. Her plain cotton bedspread, the walls bare except for a few more bookshelves, the secondhand bureau she'd purchased at a garage sale but hadn't bothered to refinish, the old-fashioned wicker cat basket her cat disdained. Ben had seen it all before, but she still felt awkward bringing him in here.

She and Ben stood facing each other beside her narrow bed—the bed she had never intended to share with anyone. But now Ben was with her, part of her life, becoming more of her life with each passing day. Here, in this room, they shared something that needed no words.

And so, with not another word, Eve went into Ben's arms.

THE DAY DIDN'T LOOK very promising. Ben spent the morning replacing a pipe in his upstairs bathroom, only to have water gush all over the damn place. So he wasn't a plumber. He could accept that. But still, he was determined to do the work himself, to get it right, on his own. He fiddled with the pipe for another hour, and the water went from a gush to a trickle. Maybe that was progress.

After lunch Ben picked Jenny up from kindergarten and brought her to his office to spend some "quality time" with him. The way he understood it, five-year-old girls liked spending time at their fathers' offices. It was supposed to be something special.

Maybe Jenny hadn't heard that particular theory, however. She was cranky and kept asking when she could go home to watch TV. Ben finally got her settled in front of his computer, where she tapped away desultorily at the keyboard. Obviously he needed to install some computer games for his kids. They sure didn't seem entertained by *him* these days.

Ben sighed as he watched his youngest daughter. It was harder and harder to believe he'd once felt in control of his life, negotiating all manner of corporate maneuvers with success. Now he couldn't seem to maneuver his way through anything with his children. The more he tried, the more all three of them managed to elude him.

"Pop, are you gonna come over tomorrow and eat Thanksgiving dinner with us?"

"I wish I could, sweetheart. But I'll have a separate Thanksgiving later in the afternoon with you and Matthew and Kate."

"Mom says she won't fix turkey. She says it's a vegetable Thanksgiving."

"Vegetarian. Right. Doesn't matter, though. Eve will have a turkey. That's where we'll eat our Thanksgiving dinner—at Eve's house." Ben tried to sound nonchalant. He'd been wondering how he'd tell the kids about dinner at Eve's place. Make an announcement? Be casual about it?

He and Eve had been together for a month now, and she was the one who'd suggested he bring the kids over. Ben wasn't sure he was ready to invade Eve's life with all three of his progeny. One was enough.

Apparently Kate still dropped by quite often to talk to Eve, and he was pleased the two were building their own friendship. It gave him a sense that he hadn't completely lost his daughter. But Thanksgiving dinner was something else again. His whole family squeezed around Eve's small dinette table—how would she handle it? How would *he* handle it?

He became aware that Jenny was watching him closely. She looked much too astute for her five years.

"Is Eve your girlfriend, Pop?"

"Yes. I think you could say she's my girlfriend."

"Does Mommy know you have a girlfriend?"

"Mommy has a husband. She's glad I have a girl-friend." That wasn't entirely the truth. Rachael seemed suspicious of his relationship with Eve, as if it was some-thing he'd embarked upon just to annoy her. His youn-gest daughter obviously had picked up on some of those undercurrents. Ben definitely needed to get a couple of computer games to occupy his kids. He was relieved when Jenny started tapping at the keyboard again.

Leaning back in his chair, he thought about Eve. That wasn't difficult, because he thought about her most of the time. She possessed him with her coolness, her fire. But always it seemed as if she kept an important part of her-self aloof from him. He felt that way even while they made love. But if he was honest, he'd have to admit that he, too, kept some essential part of himself away from Eve. For one thing, neither one of them ever discussed the future. They were both very careful about that, behaving as if the future didn't exist, as if only the moments they spent in each other's arms counted for anything.

The outer door of his office pushed open, and Jose-phine Scott appeared, wearing her usual scowl.

"You should get yourself a secretary, Benjamin. It doesn't give a good impression, your clients having to announce themselves."

"Hello, Josephine. What can I do for you today?"

"I'm very disturbed about something. Very dis-turbed."

Ben glanced at his daughter. "Jenny, why don't you go out in the waiting room and play with your trucks there."

"I don't want to play. I'll be your secretary."

"Better yet, why don't you be my associate? I need an-other lawyer around here." He handed her a blank sheet of paper and a pen. "Go write a brief for me, and we'll discuss it when you're done."

Jenny nodded happily and disappeared into the outer office. What do you know—he'd finally done something right as a parent.

"Josephine, have a seat," he said genially. "What's the latest scandal in the neighborhood?"

"You needn't be flippant with *me*." Josephine arranged herself with an important air in the seat across from his desk. She was wearing her hat again today, a sure sign she was on the warpath. Ben wondered what imagined crime Eve's Siamese had committed now. He settled back and waited for Josephine's harangue.

She surprised him, however. She didn't talk about Eve's cat. "I know all about you, Benjamin. I know all about what you've been doing."

"Hmm. What's that?"

Josephine gripped the large black vinyl purse she'd set in her lap. Her expression was shrewd. "I know about you and Miss Kearny, that's what. I see you go over to her house every night. Don't think I don't see."

Ben glanced at his daughter. She sat on the floor in the waiting room, blond head bent in concentration over her sheet of paper while she scribbled away.

"Josephine, this isn't the best time to talk about—"

"You're my lawyer, but you're consorting with Miss High-and-Mighty herself. It's not right." Josephine sounded offended, and it struck Ben that a lot of people had been offended lately by his relationship with Eve. His ex-wife, for one. And his oldest daughter, for another. Kate still couldn't seem to accept that she had to share Eve with her father. Why the hell was it so complicated? Ben wanted what he had with Eve to be private, their own oasis in this Southwestern desert. But apparently nothing in Cobb was private.

"Josephine, look," he said. "You and I both know it's about time you dropped this suit against Eve. Why not just let it go?"

The old woman gripped her purse all the tighter, as if he'd threatened to rip it away from her. "I know my rights, Benjamin. You're supposed to be suing Miss Kearny, not carrying on with her. I've a mind to hire another lawyer and sue *you*." Looking satisfied, Josephine got up and made another of her grand exits. Ben glanced at his daughter again and saw that she was watching him.

"How's the brief coming?" he asked.

"I'm not done yet." She bent over her paper once more.

The phone rang and he picked up the receiver. "Ben Lawrence."

"Dad." It was Matthew.

"Hi, kiddo. Need any legal advice?"

"No, Dad," Matthew said with the resignation he reserved for all Ben's jokes. "I need you to pick me up tonight. At five o'clock."

"Sure. Just name the place."

"I'll be at the diner. Five o'clock." Now Matthew sounded odd. Nervous, almost.

"The Rio Diner?" Ben said. "How come you'll be there?"

"'Cause that's where I'm going after school with some of the guys. Just be there, all right?"

"I will. You know, Matt, I'll be putting up that basketball hoop any day now. Just as soon as I fix the plumbing, that is."

"You keep saying stuff like that. But you never do it."

"It'll be soon. I promise. See you at five." Ben set down the receiver thoughtfully. It was true he kept delaying, kept saying he had more work to do before the house he'd bought would be a real home for him and his kids. Now he pondered why he needed to keep putting things off. He glanced around his office and realized he'd been doing some delaying here, too. His law books were still stacked on the floor. He hadn't hung the required diplomas on the walls; they were still in a box, wrapped in newspaper. The file cabinets he'd purchased were still covered in plastic sheeting, for that matter. From the look of the place, you couldn't tell if someone was moving in or moving out. For the first time Ben realized that his surroundings bore a marked similarity to Eve's. It was as if neither one of them could truly decide to settle down in Cobb.

Dissatisfaction stirred in him. But hell, how did you settle into an office when your only client was a belligerent old lady up in arms over your love life? Ben had finished with his other client, the man who'd been fired from Discount Mart. The man had taken Ben's advice and looked for a job elsewhere. He'd relocated to Albuquerque and was now working for a large department-store chain. Ben supposed that could be counted as a success. His client had moved on from Cobb....

Jenny came over to his desk to discuss the legal brief she'd prepared. That went well for a little while, then suddenly she turned cranky again, crumpling up the sheet of paper she'd scribbled on. "When can I go home, Pop?"

So much for quality time. Ben gave up trying to entertain Jenny. He closed up the office and drove her to Phil's house. No one was home but Kate, who barely mumbled a greeting at Ben before planting herself and her little sister in front of the TV. Ben made a few unsuccessful attempts at conversation. Then he returned to his office and stared at his blank computer screen. He was damn glad when the time came to go pick up Matthew.

Ben arrived at the Rio Diner, only to find that his son wasn't there yet. That didn't make any sense; Matthew had implied he'd be hanging around here with some of the other kids from school. Ordering a cup of coffee, Ben sat in one of the booths to wait.

"Ben. What are you doing here?"

He glanced up and saw his ex-wife standing in front of him. It was turning into a hell of a day all around.

"Hello, Rachael. I guess I could ask you the same thing. But I'm here to pick up Matthew."

"That can't be right," she muttered. "He asked *me* to pick him up. He said I needed to be here right at five o'clock...."

Ben and Rachael stared at each other, the truth dawning, but it was Ben who spoke the words out loud.

"Looks like our son has set us up," he remarked. "Matthew Lawrence, matchmaker. I guess I shouldn't be surprised. Lately he's been asking whether or not you and I will ever get back together." To be more precise, Matthew had been asking that question ever since he'd realized that his father had a "girlfriend."

Rachael looked flustered. "Ben, if you think I had anything to do with this, well, I didn't."

"I believe you."

She hesitated a moment, then she slid into the seat across from him. When the waitress came over, Ben automatically ordered coffee for Rachael, extra cream. She interrupted him and spoke to the waitress herself.

"No cream. And make that decaf." Then she turned to Ben. "A lot of things have changed about me. You shouldn't make assumptions."

"You've given up cream, along with everything else?"

Rachael's face tightened. "I'm just trying to live a healthy life-style. There's nothing wrong with that."

Some things never changed, Ben thought, realizing how easily he and Rachael could still fall into an argument. But he didn't want to argue. He wanted to figure out how to get close to his kids. He needed Rachael's help with that, whether or not he liked to admit it.

The waitress who brought Rachael's coffee was the same one who took his order whenever he and Eve came in here for dinner. Now she stared at him disapprovingly, as if he was somehow being unfaithful to Eve. Lord, he was having a cup of coffee with his ex-wife. Did this town have to be in on everything?

As the waitress stalked away to serve another customer, Rachael stirred her coffee, making a clinking noise with her spoon. Ben noticed lines on her forehead that hadn't been there before. Worry lines. Somehow Rachael's new healthy life-style didn't seem to be giving her peace of mind. Back in Boston, when she'd thrown Ben out of the house, she'd thrown out a lot of other things, too—meat, eggs, cigarettes. She'd gotten rid of everything she considered bad for herself, Ben included. He couldn't help wishing the act had made her happier.

"Maybe it's a good thing we're here, away from the kids," she muttered now, still clinking her spoon in her cup. "The truth is, I'm worried about Kate. She has some new friends."

"Isn't it a good thing she's finally making friends?"

"Not these ones. They're girls a few years older than Kate—she's admitted that at least one of them is a senior. From what I've been able to see, they're not exactly the cheerleader type, either. They're . . . scruffy."

Ben shook his head. "There must be something more specific that concerns you about these kids."

"Stop being a lawyer for once. You're always looking for evidence, Ben, and straightforward logic. Well, stop it! Kate is moodier than ever, she disappears at odd hours without telling me where she's going, and her grades are slipping."

He rubbed his neck. "Damn."

He and Rachael sat for a moment, silently sharing their worry over Kate. Concern for their children—that was the only thing they shared anymore. Ben gazed at the window, where someone had taped a few Thanksgiving decorations: a cardboard turkey, ears of harvest corn adorned with tassels of yarn, two plastic Pilgrims with bland smiles on their faces.

"Maybe Eve knows something about Kate," he said at last. "Something that could help."

"Eve Kearny? I don't see why on earth you always bring up *her* name. What does she have to do with this?" Rachael's voice had sharpened.

"I've tried explaining to you before. Kate seems to trust Eve. They have a special rapport."

"I'm Kate's mother, dammit. I'm the one she can trust. I'm the one who has a rapport with my own daughter."

Ben rubbed his neck again. "I'm not saying you don't. All I'm saying is that we should be grateful for any help we can get with Kate."

"For God's sake, how would you feel if I told you that Kate was starting to confide in Phil? Would you be happy and grateful?"

"You know the answer to that."

"Well, you can relax. I was just trying to make a point. Kate *isn't* confiding in Phil. She seems to despise him. And he doesn't make any effort to change that." The bitterness in Rachael's voice was unmistakable.

"Rachael, maybe I don't want Phil to take my place as a father, but I still want the kids to be happy. If there are problems we should talk about—"

"I told you the problem. It's Kate. Nothing else." Rachael acted as if Ben had set a trap for her and she'd avoided it just in time. She slid out of the booth, leaving her coffee untouched. "We have to figure out what to do about Kate. Once we've accomplished that, everything will be fine. Just fine."

She hurried out of the diner, moving in that quick nervous way she had. Cobb didn't have any horse stables or tennis courts, nowhere that Rachael could work off her energy in the ways she'd known in Boston. Did she feel as out of place here as Ben did?

He reminded himself that Rachael had moved to Cobb out of choice. She'd called it returning to her roots, and she'd brought with her the only roots Ben himself had— his kids.

But now there was Eve. Ben sat in the booth, drinking coffee and thinking he would see her soon. It would be a relief after his ex-wife. Rachael was like stormy ocean waves, Eve like still waters of a forest lake. He knew that when he took her into his arms tonight, she would soothe him even as she stirred his need for her.

He paid his check. Then he left the diner, climbed into his Jeep and drove to Eve's. He couldn't wait any longer.

CHAPTER TWELVE

THE FIVE OF THEM barely fit around Eve's table at Thanksgiving dinner. Ben sat next to Eve on one side, and Kate, Matthew and Jenny were all squeezed together on the other side. The kids jostled each other as they ate. But at least they were eating, Ben told himself. Well, at least Matthew and Jenny were eating. His two youngest kids seemed ravenous, despite the vegetarian meal their mother had prepared earlier in the day. Now they dug into Eve's turkey and stuffing and cranberry sauce, eyes wide when they saw the creamy stick of butter that Eve brought to the table.

"Mom says we shouldn't eat butter," Matthew announced, even as he stared longingly at it. "She says it's not good for us."

"Too much butter isn't good for you," Eve acknowledged diplomatically. "But it's Thanksgiving. It's the one day of the year I feel it's okay to indulge myself."

Matthew and Jenny stared at the butter awhile longer, obviously in turmoil. Ben exchanged a glance with Eve and knew she understood. The children wanted to be loyal to Rachael. It wasn't easy for any of them, splitting Thanksgiving between their mother and father. And it couldn't be easy for Eve, having her small house inundated by his kids. Once again, she'd been obliged to lock her skittish cat in the bedroom. Now and then Oscar's mournful meow could be heard. Ben was just glad to have the bedroom door closed. He didn't need his kids seeing where he and Eve made love every night.

Underneath the table, he reached for Eve's hand and gave it a squeeze. She squeezed back. Kate glared at the two of them.

"I don't know why we have to do this," she muttered. "It's stupid. We just ate at Mom's three hours ago." Kate didn't seem to have any appetite, and she merely picked at her food.

"Eve went to a lot of effort here," Ben said. "Please try to show her some courtesy."

"Eve thinks maybe this is a bad idea, too," Kate answered defiantly. "We were talking about it the other day, and she told me she was starting to wonder about getting herself into—"

"Kate, I'd like you to come help me in the kitchen," Eve said, pushing back her chair.

"How traditional," Kate scoffed. "The women in the kitchen, while the *men* sit down to eat."

"Kate," Eve repeated in a quiet voice.

Kate looked mutinous, but at last she pushed back her own chair and followed Eve into the kitchen. Ben could hear the low intense murmur of their voices. He sat at the table with his other two kids and tried to inject a little holiday spirit into the proceedings.

"There's nothing like turkey and stuffing, is there?" he asked Jenny. Too late he remembered this wasn't a neutral topic. Jenny set down her fork and stared at her plate.

"Mom says it's cruel to eat turkeys. She says they have feelings, too." Jenny's expression grew miserable. "I don't want to hurt any turkeys."

"Sweetheart, this turkey is already dead." Hell, that wasn't the right approach, either. Jenny's eyes welled with tears. Fortunately Kate and Eve appeared just then with the pumpkin pie, and nobody could refuse generous portions of that.

Ben was glad when the meal came to an end. He got all three kids situated in front of Eve's television set to watch the last of the football game. This seemed to suit Matthew, but Kate took a book from one of the shelves and hunched over it, as if to shut out everyone else. Jenny sat on the floor with her model trucks, spinning their wheels with a melancholy air. Ben looked at his kids. Maybe the image they provided wasn't one of perfect domestic tranquillity, but it would have to do for now. He escaped to the kitchen to help Eve clean up.

She turned to him. "Listen, about what Kate said. About me regretting this dinner..."

"You don't have to explain. You'd be crazy if you didn't regret it."

Eve scraped mashed potatoes from a pan. "Kate and I were just talking the other day," she said in a low voice. "Like friends. But I'm really starting to think that might be a mistake. It's as if she remembers everything I say, no matter how casual it is, so that later she can use it against you. Against me, too, I suppose."

"She's a mixed-up kid right now." Ben kept his own voice low. It seemed that Eve's kitchen was the place for private whispered conversations today.

"It's not that I hold it against Kate. She's struggling to find out where she fits with us, Ben, and I know that. I just have to be more careful. I can't allow her to play the two of against each other— Damn." Eve held her hand against her stomach.

"What's the matter?" he asked, instantly concerned.

"Just a little queasiness, that's all. An expected part of every Thanksgiving."

"You didn't eat much. It must be the stress of my kids."

"They're good kids, Ben."

"Yeah, but stressful."

She smiled. "Maybe you're right."

He made her sit down. Then he proceeded to wash the pans at the sink. It was a good feeling, taking over Eve's kitchen while she watched him, her legs stretched out in front of her. But even so, the presence of his kids in the other room intruded. The house was too small for them— or perhaps he just didn't want to share this place with his children. This was where he and Eve spent their private moments.

Raised voices in the living room indicated that Matthew and Jenny had started to squabble over television programs. Ben did his best to ignore them.

"I'm sorry about this," he said. "I wish it could be different."

"They're trying to adjust, that's all. Adjusting takes time."

"That's what you keep telling me," he said with a slight smile. "When will they stop adjusting and just start living?"

"Maybe when you do, Ben."

He dried his hands and drew a chair over to sit beside Eve. "I'll admit I haven't accepted this town yet. But you haven't, either. Sometimes, Eve...I get the feeling you're still thinking about applying for another job." He brushed his fingers over her palm. There. He'd said it. This was the closest he'd ever come to discussing their future. It didn't escape him that he was putting the burden of that future on her—questioning what she would do. But for now, it was as far as he was willing to go.

She didn't answer right away, her brow furrowing. Then she stirred, as if she felt confined by his touch. "I haven't sent out any more applications, if that's what you're asking."

"You still have the option to leave, though."

"You almost sound as if you envy me. What are you really getting at?"

He smoothed her hand in his, trying to make her fingers unclench. "Maybe I wish we could both leave," he murmured. "Just take off together, the two of us. And that makes me feel guilty as hell. I came to this town to be with my kids, and now I fantasize about leaving them behind."

Eve leaned toward him, a smile playing over her features. "I've heard that parents often entertain the fantasy of leaving their offspring behind. You shouldn't feel guilty. You're just being normal."

How neatly both of them had sidestepped the real issue: their own relationship and where it would lead them. But for the moment, Ben no longer felt inclined to press the point. It struck him once again how alluring Eve was. Wisps of her fiery hair curled next to her face, and the savory warmth of the kitchen seemed to have wrapped itself around her. He wanted to wrap himself around her, too.

"I'm entertaining quite a few fantasies right now," he said, still keeping his voice low.

"It's not the most convenient time...." Eve's eyes had darkened to a smoky blue, revealing her own desire. They sat with their hands entwined, gazing at each other. No, it wasn't the most convenient time. It was probably the most inconvenient time, but he couldn't help wanting her, more than ever before—

"Pop, it's a Christmas movie and Matthew won't let me watch!"

Ben drew back from Eve. His youngest daughter stood in the doorway to the kitchen, cradling a model truck as if it were a doll and staring at Eve and Ben accusingly. He tried to remember that he was a father before anything else. Around Eve, he was finding that more and more difficult to keep in mind.

"Uh, sweetheart," he said to Jenny. "Why don't we all watch the movie together?"

"I want to go home."

"I think your father's idea is better," Eve said. "I'd love to watch a Christmas movie with you." Wisely, Eve didn't give Jenny a chance to think twice about it. Ben looked on in admiration as Eve shepherded his five-year-old into the living room, appropriated the remote control from Matthew and soon had everyone settled in front of the television—even Kate.

An old movie was just beginning, Cary Grant playing the part of a witty, debonair Christmas angel.

"I've seen this one before," Eve remarked. "It's wonderful, and I'm sure we'll all enjoy it." She sounded determined.

Kate grimaced and bent her head, hair swinging forward. Matthew looked glum. Jenny climbed into Ben's lap and stared distrustfully at Eve. Oscar meowed from the bedroom. Only Cary Grant seemed to be having a good time.

Under other circumstances, Ben knew he might have enjoyed himself. He'd seen the movie before, too, and he agreed with Eve that it was a good one. He would have liked sharing it with her, just the two of them—alone. He felt guilty again. Here he was, spending Thanksgiving with his kids, and all he could think about was getting rid of them.

His life was a jumble of different pieces, worse than any jigsaw puzzle, none of the pieces meant to fit together.

Maybe he didn't even want the pieces to fit, and that was the real problem.

IT TOOK SOME DOING, but Ben finally convinced Eve to spend the night at his house. She'd resisted the idea for quite some time, arguing that all his remodeling had turned the place into a construction zone. She'd even joked that she'd have to wear a hard hat in bed—except that Ben didn't have a bed yet. Ben suspected that her real objections went deeper. Whatever the problems, all he knew was that he needed to spend time with Eve on his territory, as well as on hers.

And so, at last, two weeks before Christmas, he persuaded Eve to pack her toothbrush and spend the night with him on the floor of his living room. She'd left her cat behind, which was fine with Ben. Let the animal yowl all night and really give cantankerous old Josephine something to complain about.

Now morning light filtered in through the sheets that Ben had tacked over the windows. He and Eve hadn't gotten a whole lot of sleep during the night, what with one thing and another. It was a snug fit for the two of them in his sleeping bag. And how could a man be expected to sleep with a beautiful naked redhead next to him?

Ben smiled and pulled a drowsy Eve into his arms. "Good morning," he murmured.

"Good morning," she whispered back.

He gave her a lingering kiss, trailing a path from her mouth to her throat and molding her limbs against his. "Mmm. You're soft . . . and warm . . . and tempting."

She laughed. "You make me sound like a pastry fresh from the oven. Was that a compliment? Or are you just hungry?"

"I can wait for breakfast...." They kissed for a long while, then simply lay there content merely to nestle in each other's arms.

"I wonder if you'll ever get a bed," she teased him. "I'm beginning to think that at heart you like roughing it, that you'd just as soon be out in the mountains living in a tent."

"You could be right. When I was a kid, my dad used to take me camping a lot."

"Where are your parents now?" Eve asked, resting her head on his shoulder, her hair fanned out against his chest.

"My mother lives in New Jersey, where she can be near my older brother. Steven's the favored son, so she has an apartment about half an hour from his house. She's the perfect grandmother to his kids—the works." Ben kept his tone good-natured. Long ago he'd learned to accept his mother's preference for Steven. It was simply part of family lore by now.

"And your father?" Eve asked after a pause.

That was a more difficult subject. "My dad died a few years ago. A heart attack, very sudden. I'm only glad that I made it to the hospital before he was gone."

"I'm sorry, Ben."

He buried his fingers in her hair. "I've never been close to my mother, but my dad was something else. We liked the same things. We looked at life the same way. The dynamics in my family were a little bizarre. It almost seemed as if my parents couldn't relate to each other, so they each picked one of the kids to be an ally. My mother got Steven, and my dad got me. Definitely not the perfect family you tell me we all dream about, but I was friends with my dad. Good friends, and that counted for a lot.''

Eve sighed, and he felt her breath against his skin. ''Maybe no one has the perfect family. Maybe it's impossible, but we all keep trying.''

He kissed her again, and then he pulled down the sleeping bag so he could look at her. As if to thwart him, she turned onto her stomach. He traced a hand along the curve of her spine.

''Eve, is anything wrong?''

She rested her head on her arms and smiled at him, but her mood seemed cautious. ''Why do you ask?''

''Nothing in particular. Just an intuition I have. Maybe it's nothing. But I spent a lot of my married life sensing that something was bothering my wife, trying to figure out what it was and then trying to fix it. Maybe I just can't get out of the habit.'' Instantly he was sorry he'd brought up Rachael. He felt Eve stiffen.

''I'm not like your ex-wife, Ben.''

''Believe me, I've noticed. But I'm still good at picking up on what's left unspoken. Lately you've been…even more distant than usual.''

She frowned, propping herself up on her elbows. ''Even *more* distant? I thought we'd been getting fairly close. Too close, for that matter. And now you tell me I've been distant.''

Ben propped his own elbow on the pillow, realizing that he was bungling this discussion. He knew he ought to stop before he really made a mess of it, but somehow he couldn't.

''I never know what you're thinking, Eve. I'm not sure I even know how you feel about me.''

"You haven't been all that forthcoming yourself," she returned. "Let's face it—that's the way we've both wanted it. No promises on either side."

He had to admit she was right. So why the hell was he needling her? Maybe . . . maybe it was just that he'd never known that coolness of hers to thaw entirely. Now he ran his fingers once more down her back to the curve of her hips. Her skin was like silk. He smoothed her hair aside and leaned over her to press his lips against the back of her neck.

"Ben, if you think making love will solve anything between us . . ."

"It never solves anything," he murmured, shifting position so that his legs tangled with hers. "It just makes things more complicated."

"So why are you doing—" Eve caught her breath as he brushed a finger along her lower lip. Her mouth possessed its own silkiness, a softness that required kissing. But he held off the kiss until Eve slowly raised her eyes to his, and he saw what he needed to see. Her own desire, her own wanting. Only then did he bend his head over hers.

Across the room, at the front door, came the sound of someone turning a key in the lock. The door swung open and Ben's oldest daughter burst inside, long hair flying. "Dad," she called urgently. "Dad, we have to talk—" Kate's voice broke off with a gasp when she saw Ben and Eve in the sleeping bag. She stood frozen for a moment, her expression one of horror. Then, with another gasp, she whirled and dashed out of the house, banging the door shut behind her.

"What the devil . . . ?" Ben muttered.

"We've done it now," Eve said with a groan. "We've really done it now!"

CHAPTER THIRTEEN

BEN STRUGGLED to his feet and grabbed for his jeans. Eve sat up, clutching the sleeping bag to her chest, looking embarrassed but also concerned.

"Maybe I should be the one to go after Kate," she said. "Maybe I should be the one to talk to her."

He zipped his jeans and pulled on a shirt. "No, Eve." He sounded grimmer than he'd intended. "Given the circumstances, I think I'd better handle this." Still barefoot, he opened the front door and stepped out onto the porch. He'd expected Kate to be halfway down the lane by now. Instead, he found her sitting hunched on the porch steps, shivering in the frosty morning.

He sat down beside her. "Kate, I think I'd better explain—"

"You don't have to explain anything," she said fiercely. "I know what you were doing. I'm not stupid. You were having *sex*."

The bluntness of her words made him pause for a moment before continuing. "Okay, I know you're upset by what you just saw, but surely you'd guessed by now that Eve and I—"

"Can we *please* talk about something else? Except you were the one who gave me a key! You were the one who said I could come by anytime I needed to." Kate's voice sounded brittle in the cold dry air.

"I meant exactly what I said. This is your house, too."

"So how could you *do* it? With Eve! Right there on the floor."

Ben pushed a hand through his hair. He'd never been at a loss for words with a client, but at the moment he had no idea what to say to his fifteen-year-old daughter.

"Look," he tried at last, "I know your friendship with Eve is special. It'll go on being special."

"This is so humiliating," Kate muttered, hugging her knees tightly. "Just don't talk about it. Just stop." She sounded like Rachael all of a sudden, and Ben stifled an oath of frustration. Why couldn't he have a straightforward conversation with anyone these days?

"How did you get here?" he asked.

"My friends dropped me off."

Ah, the mysterious "scruffy" friends that worried Rachael. "I'd like to meet them sometime."

"Right. Like I can really bring people here after today. Every time I open the front door, I'll be wondering if it's safe."

"That's enough," he said quietly. "You know I'm working on the house and that's why everything's ...unsettled. Something like this won't happen again."

"I have to go now." Kate stood, rubbing her arms. The denim jacket she wore looked inadequate for this chill morning, but Ben knew better than to comment on the fact.

"Kate," he said, standing beside her, "obviously you came here this morning because you had something important to tell me. What is it?"

She rubbed her arms some more, staring up at the bare branches of the cottonwoods. He didn't actually expect to get anything out of her, and he was surprised when she turned back to him, speaking in a monotone.

"Mom and Phil had a big fight this morning. She told him he never tries to be part of the family, and he told her that he's sick of having three bratty-ass kids around. They yelled at each other, right in front of Matthew and Jenny." Kate was trying hard to sound like an adult, and almost succeeding. "I thought you should know what's going on. It's not good for Matt and Jen."

It wasn't good for Kate, either. But he couldn't say that. He couldn't treat her like a kid, even though she still was one.

"I'm grateful you told me this," he said. "It means we can take care of the problem before it gets out of hand."

As usual, he'd managed to say the wrong thing. Kate stared at him.

"You can't make it better!" she exclaimed. "You don't live there with us. You can't change Mom, or Phil, or anything. So don't act like you can." She hurried down the steps and along the flagstone path.

"Hold on," he called. "I'll drive you wherever it is you're going."

"Don't bother," she yelled back. "My friends are waiting for me down the road. Goodbye, Dad."

He wanted to chase after her, but he knew that would only alienate Kate all the more. He could only stand there on the porch, watching her go. She moved with a stiff proud stride, her hands stuffed deep into the pockets of her jacket. She didn't turn to look back at him, not even once, although he suspected she wanted to. She'd come here today because she needed him, and he'd let her down.

By the time she was out of sight, his feet were numb with cold. He went back into the house. Eve was fully dressed and zipping up the sleeping bag, as if that would obliterate this morning's embarrassment.

"Maybe you overheard some of that," he said.

"No, I didn't. I stayed in the kitchen until just a moment ago. I didn't want to intrude on your privacy."

That was how it was between him and Eve, he realized. They were always very careful not to intrude on each other's privacy. But maybe a little intruding wouldn't be such a bad idea. He sat down and pulled on some socks.

"You didn't need to hear Kate to imagine how she took it—seeing the two of us together. But that's not all. She came here because she's upset about the way Rachael and Phil are fighting."

Eve smoothed her bulky sweater over her jeans. "I don't think you should tell me anything more, Ben. Kate already tells me too much."

He glanced up as he laced on a running shoe. "She talks about Phil and Rachael?"

"Not exactly. But she wrote a story about them."

"I'd be interested in reading that story."

"Kate shows me her writing in confidence."

"Just tell me one thing, Eve. Does her story show Phil being abusive in any way?"

"No, nothing like that. She just writes about the way Phil and Rachael interact. The misunderstandings between the two of them." Eve looked uncomfortable. "Reading Kate's stories is like eavesdropping on a private conversation."

Ben put on his other shoe, yanking at the laces. He was always prepared to believe the worst about Phil Marcus. Okay, maybe the guy wasn't physically abusive, but he yelled in front of Ben's children. He called them "bratty-ass kids." That was bad enough.

Eve began moving around the room, tossing items into her night bag: her brush, a bright scarf, the sexy nightgown he'd slipped from her body the instant she'd crawled into his sleeping bag last night. Now she wore that heavy thick sweater almost like a barricade. Making love was the one way he knew to reach her. How did he reach her now?

"Eve, about what happened this morning. Kate's angry and upset, but I guarantee she'll show up at your office again sometime soon. She needs both of us."

Eve swung her bag over her shoulder. "Sometimes I feel like I'm coming between you and your kids. All three of them are unhappy with our relationship."

"Sometimes I feel like it's the other way around," he said. "I feel like my kids are coming between me and you. I don't have answers for any of it."

She came over to him, holding her hand against his cheek for a brief moment. "Take me home, Ben," she said softly. "Then maybe you can try to work out some solutions."

They went outside and climbed into the Jeep. It didn't take long to reach Eve's neighborhood. As they passed Josephine's house, the old woman pulled a curtain aside and glared out the window at them.

"Do you think she's just been sitting there waiting for us?" Ben asked.

"Probably. We're the only excitement in her life, I'm afraid."

Ben pulled into Eve's driveway. She leaned toward him and gave him a quick kiss. Then she slipped out of the Jeep and disappeared into her house. Once again she'd eluded him. Having her spend the night at his house hadn't narrowed the distance between them. Perhaps it had only widened it.

Ben backed out of the drive and waved at a scowling Josephine as he accelerated down the street. He returned to his own place, but instead of going inside, he began jogging along the row of cottonwoods, taking the cold air into his lungs. He had no particular destination in mind.

Maybe he couldn't play racquetball in this town, but at least he could run. At least he could do that much.

"CONGRATULATIONS, EVE," the doctor said in a somber voice. "You're pregnant."

The words came as no surprise, yet shock rippled through her, anyway. She sat across from Dr. Cole, gripping her hands together as if to quell the deep trembling inside. She wished her emotions were as tidy and sterile as this office, but they were threatening to spill out all over the place.

"Ben and I, we've been so careful," she said automatically. "How could this have happened?" But she already knew the answer. *The first time*. When she and Ben had made love so recklessly in the back seat of his Jeep, they hadn't been careful at all. Afterward Eve had been terrified by their foolishness, and from then on they'd always—*always*—used condoms. Yes, they'd been careful—when it was already too late.

For weeks now, Eve had been battling the knowledge of this pregnancy. She'd denied all the signs: the tenderness in her breasts, the sudden bouts of nausea, her period being late—and later still. She'd argued with herself, told herself it was just stress. After all, when she'd been married, it had taken months of trying for her to become pregnant. How could those few moments of unthinking desire with Ben have resulted in this?

Yet, all along, underneath her denial, she'd known the truth. She was expecting Ben's child. She hadn't been able to force herself to take a home pregnancy test, but at last she'd accepted that she could no longer delay a visit to Albuquerque to see her doctor—Jonathan Cole, the man who'd tried to help her through her first two pregnancies. Her first two losses.

Dr. Cole was still a young man, although he'd been prematurely gray for several years. The combination always disconcerted Eve: the doctor's fresh unlined face and his full head of silvery hair. It gave him a look of both innocence and wisdom at the same time. But Eve knew he was a good physician—good enough to be honest with her now.

He sat forward in his chair, studying her gravely. "I'll do everything I can to save this baby for you, Eve. But I think you know what kind of fight we're up against."

"Yes. I know."

"I'm willing to fight. Are you?"

Suddenly she was angry. It wasn't Dr. Cole's world that was coming apart, yet there he was launching into a pep talk. She knew all the answers he wanted to hear. Yes, of course she'd fight. She was a trooper. She never gave up.

But even if she told him all that, her heart wouldn't stop breaking. She'd fought twice before, with everything she had, and still she'd lost. How could she possibly go through this again?

Eve stood up and reached across to shake the doctor's hand. "Thanks for seeing me on such short notice, Jonathan. Don't worry, I'll be back for my next appointment."

"I never lose hope about these things, you know."

"I appreciate that. Really, I do." She simply couldn't talk to him anymore, or listen to his optimistic words. All she wanted to do was escape.

Outside the doctor's office, the day was bright and sunny, warm for December. In a week it would be Christmas, and as usual there didn't seem much chance of snow. Eve wondered if Ben's kids felt disappointed. They were used to snow.

She climbed into her car and bent her head over the steering wheel, refusing to let the tears come. How long she sat there she didn't know, but at last the prickling behind her eyelids subsided, leaving only a dull pain.

She knew that she should start back for Cobb, that Ben would be waiting for her. But somehow right now she couldn't bear the thought of seeing him. Needing to delay the moment any way she could, she started the engine and drove to one of the city's largest shopping malls.

Eve wanted to be surrounded by people—people she didn't know. The mall satisfied both requirements. Holiday shoppers rushed from store to store, and Eve fell in aimlessly with the crowd, allowing it to carry her along. Festivity confronted her everywhere: tinsel and ribbon adorning the shop windows, children lining up to sit on Santa's knee, a choir giving energetic renditions of all the old carols.

Eve stopped for a moment to listen, which turned out to be a mistake. Christmas carols had always made her feel vaguely melancholy, but today the music seemed to pierce her with its improbable sweetness. She turned and hurried on, knowing only that she needed to keep moving.

She saw women pushing strollers, women cradling weary toddlers . . . pregnant women, their immense bellies jutting out in front of them. Eve tried to concentrate on other figures— elderly couples, teenagers jostling each other. But always her attention returned to the young mothers. Why did there have to be so damn many of them?

Eve hadn't yet bought a Christmas present for Ben, and she had no idea what to get him. She went into one of the department stores and walked distractedly up and down the aisles. Then she came to the section where Christmas decorations were sold and realized that Ben hadn't even put up a tree. He kept saying his place was too much of a mess, what with all his remodeling projects. Eve didn't know what he had planned with his kids. After the apathetic response the children had shown to Thanksgiving at Eve's house, it seemed best to refrain from inviting them over for Christmas. But where did that leave Ben? How would he engineer a family celebration?

It seemed that even the smallest details became complicated when you had an ex-wife and three children to juggle in your life. Eve wondered how Ben would react when he learned there was another child on the way. A child who had so little chance of surviving...

She placed a hand over her stomach as if that would somehow protect her baby. Blinking angrily against those wretched tears, she examined a wreath made of pinecones and embellished with a plaid bow. It was something that would look nice against the carved front door of Ben's house, and it would add a touch of Christmas, at least.

Eve paid for the wreath, then wandered through the mall again. This time she ended up in a bookstore. She supposed that was inevitable.

Books had always soothed her before; perhaps being among them now would blunt the edges of her pain just a little. She gazed at all the rows and rows of hard covers. With their jackets of shiny embossed paper, they looked like so many gaily wrapped gifts. She ended up buying one for Ben's present—a time-travel mystery set in the eighteenth century.

Then Eve thought about Kate. Ben's daughter hadn't come by to see her lately. Cobb Community College was closed for the holiday season, which might partially explain Kate's absence. Yet Eve had told Kate she was welcome to drop by the house. Kate hadn't taken her up on it. Eve wondered if she ever would—especially after the other morning when she'd stumbled in on her and Ben.

Nonetheless, Eve selected a gift for Kate, too, an elegantly bound volume of *Wuthering Heights*. The stormy dramatic tale reminded her of Ben's daughter. And for the first time, Eve allowed herself to wonder if the child she was carrying was a boy or a girl.

That was a mistake. Now, her baby seemed all the more real, all the more fragile. She pressed a hand to her stomach again, knowing that all the books in the world couldn't soothe her despair. She had to get out of here. She had to keep moving, even if it meant returning to Cobb.

Clutching her packages, Eve made her way from the mall. Outside on the sidewalk, a Salvation Army volunteer rang his bell. As Eve donated a few dollar bills, she almost started crying again. It seemed that anything could set her off today. She strode to her car and headed for Cobb as early dusk painted the sky.

An hour and a half later, she drove down Central Avenue. Christmas lights sparkled along the line of old-fashioned lampposts that marked the street, and Eve felt a rush of affection for this little town. It celebrated every special occasion with enthusiasm. If only she felt like celebrating, too.

Eve's phone was ringing as she let herself in the door of her house. She knew it was Ben, but she didn't know how on earth she would talk to him. She was tempted to let the phone keep ringing, but that wouldn't be fair. At last she picked up the receiver.

"Hello." She tried to sound as normal as possible.

"I was starting to get concerned about you." Ben's voice was deep and warm. "You said you'd be home earlier than this. I wish you'd let me take you into Albuquerque, instead of driving yourself." Lately he'd been more protective of her, as if sensing somehow that she needed more of his care.

"I had some Christmas shopping to do," she said with forced cheerfulness. "I couldn't very well bring you along for that."

"I'm leaving right now to come over."

"No! Ben, don't. I need some time to myself tonight."

He didn't say anything for a long while, but then he spoke again. "I know something's been bothering you. I wish you could tell me about it."

"Not just yet."

"Then there *is* something. It's not my imagination."

"No...no, it's not. But I need some time to deal with it on my own."

There was another long pause. "I'm sorry," he said at last. "It makes me a little crazy, I guess, trying to prod you into telling me your thoughts and feelings and not getting any response. So then I just prod all the more."

"It reminds you of the way things were with Rachael," she said, finishing it for him, her voice tight. "But I'm not Rachael. I don't make a habit of hiding from you."

"Yes, Eve, you do. Can't you trust me?"

"You just have to give me some time. Please, Ben—at least tonight. Just give me some time."

She hung up quickly, no longer able to hold back the tears.

CHAPTER FOURTEEN

BEN FOUND a stray paintbrush and stacked it in the corner with the rest of his gear—rollers, pans, cans of paint. Soon he'd be done remodeling his living room at least. For now, all he could do was straighten up the place a little in preparation for Rachael's visit this afternoon.

He didn't know why it seemed important, what his ex-wife thought of his house. Rachael wasn't an expert at interior decoration. She'd furnished their house in Boston with a fussy blend of different styles, as if needing to move on to French Provincial or English Gothic before she'd quite finished with American Rustic. As for himself, he'd been too engrossed in his career to concern himself with home decor. Now, for the first time, furnishing a house was his responsibility alone—but, hell, he wasn't on trial here. So why did he feel as if he was?

The hour for their appointment came and went. Ben had begun to think she'd changed her mind when a rather abrupt knock came at the front door. That had to be Rachael. No one else could make a simple knock sound so combative.

When Ben swung open the door, Rachael stayed on the threshold, peering inside his place with a suspicious air.

"Is it really necessary for us to meet here, Ben? Surely we could have arranged something else."

"We never seem able to get anything sorted out at Phil's house."

"It's my house, too," she said, her voice sharp. "I really wish you'd stop talking as if I were merely a guest in my own home."

"Rachael, I didn't ask you here to fight with you. We really need to talk."

She remained where she was for another moment, then finally stepped inside. As Ben started to close the door, he glanced at the pinecone wreath he'd tacked up on it, the wreath Eve had given him yesterday. When he'd arrived at her house last evening, she'd presented him with the wreath and sternly advised him to get going on some Christmas spirit for his kids.

Yet Eve herself hadn't seemed imbued with the Christmas spirit. She'd seemed edgy—distraught almost, once again stubbornly refusing to talk about what was bothering her. When Ben had started to make love to her, she'd asked him only to hold her. And so they'd lain together all through the night, Eve sleeping fitfully and Ben sleeping hardly at all. He sensed that something was very wrong with Eve, but he didn't know what to do about it. Never had he felt so powerless.

"Ben, you *did* say you wanted to speak with me," Rachael reminded him. "I have a lot to do today, so can we just get on with it?"

Making an effort, he pulled himself away from thoughts of Eve. He shut the front door and motioned Rachael into a chair, then sat in the chair across from her. These were his only pieces of furniture at the moment: folding lawn chairs that he'd purchased on sale down at Discount Mart.

"I'm worried about the kids," he began, only to have Rachael jump in with an interruption.

"I've tried talking to Kate," she said. "Over and over, I've tried to draw her out. I've suggested she invite her friends to dinner. I've even told her she can have a party at Phil's house—at *my* house. But she seems outraged that I'd even make the suggestion. Ben, whatever you do, don't tell me anything right now about Eve Kearny, and how *she* can talk to Kate."

"This isn't about Eve, or about Kate's friends. It's about the situation between you and Phil, and how it's upsetting our kids."

Rachael stared at him angrily. "What situation?" she demanded. "I can't believe you'd even bring this up. Whatever happens between me and Phil is private, do you understand?"

Ben hated doing this, but he saw no other choice. "I wish it *was* private, Rachael. But it's not. It's affecting the kids. They say you and Phil are fighting more and more. Don't you realize why Matthew called me the other day and asked me to pick him and Jenny up? You'd just had a big argument with Phil, and the kids couldn't bear to be around the two of you. They actually preferred being with me for once. That should tell you something right there."

Rachael stood up so quickly she almost sent the flimsy lawn chair flying. "I can see what you're doing, Ben. You're trying to play the children against me."

"You're not listening to me," he said. "And you know me better than that. You're their mother, Rachael. I want them to be happy with you. And right now they're *not* happy."

Rachael turned away and remained with her back to him, as if to shut him out of her life. But they'd had three children together, and that meant their lives would constantly be bumping up against each other. Didn't she realize that yet?

Ben raked both hands through his hair, considering the irony of it all. Lately he seemed to be spending most of his time trying to get the people he cared about to talk to him. His son, his daughters, his ex-wife. Eve. Eleven-year-old Matthew was the only one willing to talk with him. Tradition had it that men were reticent, and women were ready to share their feelings. It didn't always work that way.

At last Rachael swiveled toward him, the anguish he saw on her face surprising him.

"You think it's so easy," she said. "I'm supposed to tell you all my problems, you'll come up with a logical solution, the kids will be happy, and that's the end of it." She took a deep breath. "Well, it's not so easy, Ben. Do you want to know the real reason I married Phil Marcus? Because he seemed so damn *different* from you. He seemed like a person who had both a job and a personal life—not a career that took up every spare minute of his time. And he wanted to be a husband and a father more than anything else. That was how he made it sound, anyway."

Ben was hearing more than he'd bargained for, but finally Rachael was coming to the point. He couldn't stop her now. He went on sitting where he was, waiting to hear the rest.

Rachael took another deep breath. "The joke's on me," she said bitterly. "It turns out that maybe Phil likes the *idea* of being a husband and father, but the reality is something else again. He doesn't like having kids mess up his routine. And he doesn't like a wife messing it up, either. So what's your solution to that, Ben? Just tell me."

He moved to stand beside her. "Look, there has to be an answer. Maybe not an easy one, but still, there's an answer. The kids can't go on like this."

"It's amazing how concerned you are about the children's welfare these days. It used to be that you left all that to me. You didn't care about any of us."

He felt awkward, wishing this episode were over—wishing he could, indeed, find a quick easy solution to the problem. "Listen, Rachael," he said gruffly. "Maybe I was a lousy husband and a lousy father. But I still cared. Now I just want to know that my kids are okay. I wouldn't mind seeing you happy, too."

She gazed at him, her eyes large in her taut face. When they'd first met years ago, her big eyes and angular features had given her a charming gaminelike quality. These days, however, she only looked strained.

"Dammit, Ben," she said, her voice harsh. "Why couldn't you have been like this when we were married?" She stepped toward him and for a second he thought she meant to push him out of her way. Instead, she leaned her head against his chest, and he ended up patting her on the back consolingly.

Rachael seemed to be all sharp angles next to him. There'd been a time when this angularity of hers had attracted him. At the moment, however, he longed only for Eve's softness. And he longed to be comforting Eve, not his ex-wife.

It took Rachael a few seconds to recover herself. Then she stepped back from him, looking resentful. "I said too much today. I want you to forget it."

"We finally have something out in the open, and that's good."

"What are you going to do—become a marriage counselor for me and Phil? I hardly think so. Just forget it!"

After she'd gone, Ben wondered what he'd accomplished by asking her here today. Probably nothing. The last thing he really wanted to know about was Rachael's marital problems. But what else could he do when all three of his kids seemed to be getting more and more miserable?

Ben didn't have any answers. And so he did the same thing he'd been doing every day for the past week. He shrugged into a sweatshirt, left his house and went running. He ran and tried unsuccessfully to forget all the chaos in his life.

TWO DAYS BEFORE CHRISTMAS Kate finally showed up to visit Eve. She came to the house and hovered on the front porch, much the way she'd hovered outside Eve's office. But eventually Kate made it inside and wandered restlessly around the living room. Surprisingly, the cat didn't retreat from this unexpected visitor. He simply remained where he was, draped regally across the top of the sofa, watching Kate with his shrewd turquoise eyes.

Eve herself sat down on the sofa, placing Silas T. Cobb's journal on the coffee table. Kate glanced at it.

"Are you still reading that old diary?" she asked.

"As a matter of fact, I am. It's more and more interesting all the time. I've just reached the part where Silas is getting married again. He wore out his first wife, poor woman. I wonder how the second one will fare." Eve didn't mention that researching Silas T. Cobb was the only task she seemed able to concentrate on these days. The complications of Silas's personal life were much easier to reflect on than her own.

Almost without volition, her hand moved to her stomach. Lately she'd been feeling queasy almost all the time. Her first two pregnancies hadn't been like this; she'd hardly been sick at all.

Kate went on wandering about the living room, pausing only now and then to frown at a shelf of books, or at Eve's small potted Christmas tree. She poked one of the ornaments.

"This is more like a bush than a tree," she muttered.

"I'm going to plant it outside after New Year's," Eve said. "I've always hated the thought of all those trees being tossed into the trash when they've served their purpose. I like knowing my Christmas trees get to keep on living."

"You sound like my mom," Kate said disdainfully. "She doesn't like picking flowers because that means killing them. She won't even step on spiders. Instead, she chases them all over the house so she can put them outside."

Eve could admire someone who refrained from stepping on spiders, but she didn't particularly enjoy being compared to Rachael. She hadn't even met the woman, but she still didn't like being compared to her.

"Kate, I think what you really want to talk about is what happened last week—the morning you came to your father's house."

"*Please*. That's the last thing I want to talk about." Kate scowled at Eve's potted evergreen again. "Yesterday my dad dragged all of us over to decorate his house. It was pathetic. We had to buy a Christmas tree, then make strings of popcorn for it. Where'd he get an idea like that, anyway?"

"From me, actually." Eve gave a faint smile. "When I was growing up, I used to like to string popcorn for the tree. I suggested to your father that you and Jenny and Matthew might enjoy doing that, too. I even supplied the popcorn."

Kate stared at her. "That kind of thing's okay for Matt and Jen, but not me. I don't need any family rituals invented by you and my dad. Don't you realize how *phony* that is?"

Eve leaned back, Oscar's tail tickling her cheek. Kate was clearly looking for an argument, but Eve refused to give her one.

"I know family traditions take time," she said mildly. "The best thing, of course, is for you and your brother and sister to develop some of your own. I suppose I was just trying to help the process along."

"Are you going to marry my dad?" Kate demanded brusquely.

This question was enough to make Eve sit up straight. She moved too suddenly, however, and had to fight the queasiness that washed over her. Marriage to Ben—that was the last thing she'd consider right now. Surely this difficult pregnancy would only threaten their relationship. She couldn't tell any of that to his daughter, however.

"I don't know what's going to happen between me and your father," she said carefully. "But I don't think it's something you should worry about, Kate."

"In other words, it's none of my business."

"That isn't exactly what I meant."

Kate gave her a skeptical glance, looking more like Ben than ever. Then she headed for the door. "This has been a real thrill," she muttered, "but I have to go."

"You haven't shown me any work lately. I miss reading your stories."

"I haven't had time to write," Kate said loftily. "I've been too busy."

"With your new friends? I'd like to meet them." Eve tried to sound casual, but Kate instantly took a wary stance.

"Did my dad tell you to say that? Did he tell you to get a look at my friends so you could report back to him?"

"I'm not a spy, Kate. But if your father's concerned about you, that's only natural."

"How much do you talk about me?" Kate sounded truculent. She also sounded as if she'd like knowing that Ben and Eve discussed her.

"Your father loves you very much," Eve said gently. "Why don't you just give him a chance to prove that to you? Talk to him yourself."

Kate whirled around and yanked open the door. "I have to get out of here." She stood looking back at Eve, her expression unreadable, cold air pouring into the room. Josie Scott wasn't the only person who knew how to orchestrate a grand exit. Kate always seemed to prefer banging out the door in the middle of a conversation, as if to punctuate it with a misplaced exclamation mark. But this time Eve ruined her effect.

"Before you leave, I have a Christmas present for you," she said. "It's under the tree. Go ahead. Take it."

Kate hesitated, then stalked over to the tree and stared at the two presents underneath: one for her, one for her father. She read the tags, then grabbed her own gift.

"Thanks," she mumbled.

When she left, she surprised Eve. Instead of banging the door shut after her, she closed it slowly, almost cautiously, the lock making a subdued click as it fell into place. Eve was sorry to see her go. In spite of all Kate's prickliness, for a few moments, at least, she'd kept Eve's mind off her own problems.

Oscar twitched his tail and stretched out comfortably along the back of the sofa. Closing his eyes, he napped with a lazy purr.

Eve suddenly felt tired, too. It was another symptom of pregnancy, this overwhelming weariness that could hit her at any time. Or perhaps her weariness was a symptom more of sadness than anything else. Because that was how she'd felt these past few days: sad and guilty.

She still hadn't told Ben about the baby. She knew she would *have* to tell him, and soon. But for now she guarded the knowledge to herself, convinced that telling Ben would only make her pregnancy all the more difficult and painful to cope with.

Sighing she curled up on the sofa, resting her head on one of her ruffled throw pillows. She remembered the time she'd told her ex-husband she was expecting their second child. After all they'd been through with the first, Ted's reaction had been one of mingled hope and despair. She and Ted had tried to cling together, but in the end, they had only turned away from each other. How could she stop the same thing from happening to her and Ben?

Eve closed her eyes, but in spite of her exhaustion she couldn't sleep. She thought about Ben, and sadness swept over her again. It seemed to her their relationship was almost as fragile as the tiny life she harbored inside.

EVE AND BEN LAY in each other's arms in front of her fireplace, and Ben was making another one of his silly endearing jokes.

"I'm spending Christmas Eve with my own Christmas Eve," he murmured, crowning her with a sprig of holly. "What do you think of that?"

She answered him with a kiss. "I think it's fine. Just fine."

She was proud of herself. So far this evening, she'd managed to set a cheerful mood. She'd spread a quilt invitingly before the fire, supplied glasses of eggnog and turned the lights down low. She'd almost managed to convince herself the cheerful mood was real.

Now she and Ben sat up to exchange gifts. He smiled over the book she'd chosen for him, stating that he would read it right away. Then he presented his gift to her. She tore off the wrapping paper and found an elegant jewelry case. Inside was a silver pendant with one small exquisitely cut diamond that sparkled in the firelight.

"It's much too extravagant," she protested. "A diamond, Ben..." Her tears, always too close to the surface these days, threatened to spill over.

In her mind, a diamond meant promises, a commitment between two people. Did it mean the same to Ben? She didn't pose the question out loud, because she didn't dare offer him a commitment of her own.

Eventually her tears did spill over, and she turned her face just in time. As she lowered her head, he smoothed her hair aside so that he could fasten the pendant around her neck. His touch lingered against her skin.

"Eve, what is it?" he asked quietly. "You're pulling away from me more and more. You won't talk to me... and I know you don't want to make love with me."

"Oh, Ben, it's not that! I want you so much...."

He gathered her into his arms, crushing her against him. "What is it, then? Tell me."

She dreaded saying the actual words, and searched for a way to begin. "Ben... I need to ask you... do you ever consider having more children?" She said the last bit in a rush, cursing herself for her awkwardness.

"If I'm going to be honest with you, no, I haven't. Three kids are already more than I can handle. I don't need any more. Is that what you're worried about? That I'll ask you to have children?"

He'd misunderstood. Before she could say anything else, however, he lifted her chin and gazed at her with a serious expression. "Eve, this is one concern you can set to rest. I know what a bad time you went through before, trying to have kids. I won't ask you to go through that again. What we have...it's separate from everything that's happened in the past, for either one of us. Can't you believe that?''

He made it sound as if they were two shipwrecked survivors, cast adrift together, getting ready to sail off to a completely new life. She wanted it to be that simple. But she was carrying his child—and he'd just stated categorically that he didn't want any more children. Even though her baby had only a small chance of surviving, it deserved two parents who would fight for its existence!

Her mind flashed back to her husband. She'd tried so hard to believe in that second baby of theirs, yet Ted had given up. He'd stopped believing, and after the miscarriage she'd almost hated him, as if it had been all his fault.

But in the end it had been *her* fault, her body that had failed. And her body would most likely fail this new baby. It wouldn't matter if she and Ben believed in this child with all their hearts. Her damn body was defective, and there was no way to get around that.

Eve felt a fury like nothing she'd ever known before. It shook her with its strength, burning inside her. She was furious at her ex-husband, Ben, herself—even her unborn child. Only Ben's arms, still folded tightly around her, kept the anger from consuming her.

''Eve, talk to me,'' he said. ''Please talk.''

It was past time for that. Now Eve was seized with recklessness, a hot defiance born of her anger. Fingers trembling, she pulled at Ben's shirt, at the zipper of his jeans. He needed no further encouragement. Unbuttoning her shift, he pulled her camisole up over her shoulders, kissing the spot where the pendant dangled between her breasts. And then he lowered himself over her, his strong muscles outlined in the flickering firelight.

They made love with a desperation both of them seemed to share. And for a few moments—a few moments only—Eve forgot everything but the touch of Ben's skin against her own. She forgot everything but the wild sweet passion between them.

CHAPTER FIFTEEN

EVE STOOD at her office window, gazing out at Cobb Community's shriveled cactus garden. She was almost three months pregnant. Physically she felt amazingly well. The bouts of nausea had subsided entirely, and an energy coursed through her she couldn't seem to contain. She always had to be walking, moving about. Emotionally, however, she was a wreck, and she knew it. Her mood swings arced from wild optimism to sudden despair. She still hadn't told Ben about the pregnancy. She didn't want to tell him until there was simply no other choice. Right now the problem was hers alone, and she guarded it almost jealously. The pregnancy was hers to worry over, and to hope for against all the odds.

The guilt was hers, too. Everyone said that motherhood brought with it a heavy dose of guilt, and they were right. It started from the day you learned you were expecting a child. After Eve had made love so frantically to Ben at Christmastime, she'd been terrified that she'd harmed the baby somehow, and she'd phoned Dr. Cole to broach the subject.

"Hmm...sex for the next few weeks is acceptable," the doctor had said matter-of-factly, as if speaking about a laboratory experiment rather than Eve's personal life. "You can also exercise and go about any normal activities, except for heavy lifting. It's not time to concern ourselves with the real restrictions yet." The doctor's unspoken message was clear. Enjoy your freedom while you have it, Eve. We're in for a rough ride ahead.

Yet Eve hadn't made love to Ben since then. She hadn't wanted him to see the new fullness in her body and guess her secret. She had to be the one in control of this situation at least for a little while longer. All too soon, Ben would learn the truth, and the disintegration of their relationship would begin in earnest. Could it really be any different this time than it had been with Ted?

Eve pressed her cheek against the cool glass of the window, fingering the diamond pendant she wore like a talisman. Of course, her relationship with Ben was already suffering. Their best form of communication had always been making love, or simply touching each other, holding each other. These days, Ben no longer even attempted to touch her, as if he knew she would turn away from him.

Oh, she was in control of the situation, all right. She controlled it so completely that both she and Ben were inventing more and more excuses not to be together. She hadn't even seen him in two days.

Eve left the window and went to her desk. She was finding it difficult to sit still lately, but Kate had finally brought her another story to read. That was worth some concentration. Oddly enough, she and Kate had shared a new ease with each other these past few weeks, as if they'd reached some sort of truce. The truce consisted of never mentioning the most important tie between them: Ben.

Eve sighed and began reading Kate's story. Her perusal was automatic at first, but after a page or so she paid growing attention to the words in front of her. This was one of the best things Kate had written. It was also one of the most disturbing.

Half an hour later, Eve turned the last page. The story had her concerned—very concerned, indeed. She read through it once more, quickly, and her apprehension only deepened.

"Oh, dear," she murmured. "Poor Kate. What sort of predicament have you gotten yourself into?" Kate, of course, wasn't there to answer. She had arranged to come back tomorrow to discuss the story. Until then, Eve would have to speculate about it on her own.

There was another solution. She could call Ben up right now and discuss the matter with him. She imagined what she would say: Hello, Ben. I know I haven't let you come near me in a while, but never mind that now. Your daughter's written a story that really troubles me. You see, I think she's writing about herself, and what she's describing isn't at all reassuring. You have more to worry about as a father than you ever imagined....

No, she wouldn't make that call just yet. She needed to speak to Kate first and hear her explanation. After that was soon enough for Ben to worry—to hit the roof, more likely.

When Eve drove home a short time later, she glanced across and saw Josie in her front yard, poking among her iris beds. The iris stalks were brittle and faded by winter, rather like Josie herself.

Eve stepped out of her car and went to the edge of Josie's yard. "Hello," she called.

Josie scowled at her. "Your cat's been mauling my flowers," she announced. "Sure as anything, that beast has been over here, tearing everything up!"

"Josie, there aren't any flowers right now."

"My bulbs are tucked into the ground, waiting for spring. That foul animal of yours is trying to dig them up." Josie poked a stick among the irises, making a dry rustling sound as she searched for evidence.

"Oscar would never dig up your bulbs. They're quite safe." There was something pathetic about Josie and her bulbs, as if Josie herself was buried away from life, waiting for a spring that never seemed to come.

"Damned cat," Josie muttered, brandishing her stick. She glared at Eve. "Don't think you'll get away with this, *Miss* Kearny. I know all about what you've been trying to do. That plate of cookies you left on my porch at Christmas—thought you could butter me up, didn't you?"

Eve pretended innocence. "I can't imagine what cookies you're talking about."

"Hah. I also know exactly what you've been up to with my lawyer. You've buttered *him* up fine, haven't you?"

Eve had accomplished exactly the opposite with Ben. Lately she'd done everything in her power to push him away, and she'd succeeded.

"Josie . . . were you ever married?"

The old woman looked affronted. "Certainly not. I knew better than that."

"But maybe you loved someone."

Josie pursed her lips, her wrinkled cheeks seeming to draw inward. Then she found her voice. "Don't you mind about me, Miss Kearny. I'm proud to say that I've never made a mess of *my* life."

Eve walked back to her own side of the property line, calling to her cat as she went. Once again, Oscar was skulking under the hydrangea bush, and he came bounding out only when Eve opened the door to the house. He streaked past her.

"Stay away from Josie's chickens—and her bulbs," Eve admonished him. Then she sank onto the sofa and stared at the Christmas tree she still hadn't planted outside. She hadn't even put away the ornaments yet. Nothing was more forlorn than a Christmas tree left standing past its time.

Pulling her feet up on the couch, Eve groaned. Unlike Josie, she was managing to make quite a mess of her life.

THE NEXT AFTERNOON, Kate showed up at Eve's office ahead of schedule. She wore a denim jacket that was too big for her, a plaid shirt that was also too big and jeans with strategically placed tears at the knees.

"I can't stay long," she said, from the start. "A friend of mine is picking me up in a few minutes." She perched on the edge of a chair. The sense of ease she and Eve had recently shared had vanished; clearly Kate was nervous about the effect of her story.

Eve searched for a way to start, arranging Kate's typewritten sheets in front of her. "This is excellent writing," she said at last. "It's very...powerful. A little rough here and there, but—"

"It's supposed to be rough. That's the tone I want. The *style*. I mean, if you've going to be bugged by that..."

"As I told you, Kate, it's very powerful. You've given me the story of a girl—Emily—who feels lost in a new town. Then she meets people who make her feel as if she belongs. One boy in particular makes her feel that way. But what you've portrayed most effectively is Emily's fear, deep underneath, that she's going too far."

Kate sprang up from her chair and paced the office with her usual restlessness, hands jammed into the pockets of her jacket. "You don't get it at all. Emily isn't afraid of anything. She's in love, and that's the only thing that matters to her. That's the only thing that *should* matter."

"On the contrary. I think Emily is very afraid. She can't help wishing she was still a child. The scene where she locks herself in her bedroom, bringing out all her old toys and remembering what it was like to play with them— that's a very good scene, Kate. Very perceptive."

"This is stupid!" Kate burst out. "I can't stand how you're always looking for symbolism. I have to go."

Before Kate could escape, Eve went to the office door and closed it. She gazed at Ben's daughter. "There's a reason you wanted me to read that story. It wasn't just so I could comment on your tone or your style. You wanted me to know that you're Emily, and that you're scared and don't know what to do next."

Kate stood rigidly, hands still stuffed in her pockets. "Do you think I actually came here for advice?" she asked scathingly.

"Maybe you did."

"Well, I'm not Emily. It's just a story." She began inching toward the door, and Eve could tell it was time to be straightforward.

"Kate, you're having sex, aren't you? With a boy who's older than you, just as Jack is older than Emily in the story."

Kate tossed back her hair, looking all the more defiant. "So what if I am? Everybody else has sex. You have sex."

"That's different," Eve said firmly. "I'm thirty-seven. You're only fifteen. You're not ready yet."

"What's the magic age?" Kate taunted. "When will I suddenly be ready? When did it happen for *you?*" Underneath Kate's sarcasm, Eve heard uncertainty. She longed to reach out and take Ben's daughter into her arms, the way she would comfort a frightened little girl. But she refrained, knowing that Kate was balanced too precariously between childhood and womanhood.

"Don't look to me as an example," Eve said wryly. "I've made plenty of mistakes. But maybe that's why I can help you avoid some mistakes of your own."

Kate stared out the window. Her hair had fallen in front of her face, and Eve could no longer read her expression. "When was the first time you did it?" Kate persisted. Her voice was anxious, as if Eve's answer would offer some important clue to her own predicament.

Eve didn't have any experience with this type of conversation. Perhaps when adults were around teenagers, they were supposed to behave as if sex didn't exist. Then again, perhaps they were supposed to be honest.

"I was eighteen," she said. "It was my first year at college, and I made love with a boy who said he wanted to marry me. At the time I thought I wanted to marry him, too. It didn't work out for one reason and another. But the point is, I was too young then for either sex or marriage. In a lot of ways, that first love affair of mine was devastating. If I had it to do over again, I'd have waited."

"What happened next? After you broke up with him." Kate spoke in a mumble, and Eve sensed she needed to cling to someone else's story right now—anyone's story but her own.

"Well, eventually I met the man I did marry," Eve said. "By then, I was finally ready for a permanent relationship."

"But you're divorced now. And you're...you're *doing* it with my dad!"

Not lately, Eve wanted to amend, but she stopped herself. "Listen," she said, "I've just been trying to explain that I've made my share of mistakes, and—"

"Being with my dad—is that a mistake?" Kate almost sounded hopeful.

Eve didn't know how to answer. She thought about Ben all the time, and thinking about him made her ache with longing. She'd allowed him to become part of her in a way she'd permitted no other man, not even her ex-husband. That seemed like a mistake, all right. A very big mistake.

"Kate, you're only trying to avoid the real issue here," Eve said. "We should talk about what's going on with you, not me."

Kate hunched her shoulders inside that too-big jacket. "Nothing's happening with me. Nothing you need to know about."

"Do you really believe you're in love with this boy? Can you honestly say he loves you in return?"

"His name is David," Kate said haughtily. "And I know he loves me. Just because he hasn't said the exact words yet doesn't matter. He wants to be with me all the time."

This didn't sound good at all. An older boy and fifteen-year-old Kate. Oh, poor Ben when he learned about this. And he did have to learn about it.

"Kate, you need to tell your father. He can help you through this a whole lot better than I can."

"I don't want anybody's help. I just wrote a story, okay? Can we just talk about the story?"

"Very well. Let's talk about Emily. She's frightened. Things are moving too fast for her. David is pressuring her, and she's giving in to him, but she doesn't know what she wants—"

"You won't tell my dad, will you?" Kate looked straight at Eve for once. "You can't tell him!"

"Think about it. When you left this story with me, you knew I'd guess the truth. And you knew the next logical step would be my telling your father about it. That's what you really want."

"You don't understand anything." Kate's voice was shaking. "You can't tell him. You just can't! He'll...he'll hate me if he finds out." Kate visibly clenched her face muscles. Eve recognized that expression; it was the expression of someone trying very hard not to cry. Eve had seen it in her own mirror often enough these past weeks.

She went to Kate and this time she did gather the girl in her arms. Kate was trembling, but her tears didn't come. It would have been easier on them both if she'd actually wept. As it was, Eve could only hold her, wishing with all her heart she could protect Ben's daughter from harm.

"Everything's going to be fine," she murmured. "Don't worry. Your father loves you so much. Nothing could make him hate you. Nothing."

Kate didn't seem to register a word Eve was saying. "Don't tell him—you can't tell him!" she pleaded, over and over. She went on shivering uncontrollably. And Eve continued to hold her, the way she could imagine holding a daughter of her own.

"Kate, if you can't talk to your father, what about your mother? Won't you confide in her?"

"No." Kate stiffened and drew away. "That's even worse than talking to my dad. I can't do it." She hugged her arms against her body, the too-long sleeves of her jacket falling over her wrists. "Don't tell him," she said again, as if she could defend herself only with these familiar words. "Promise me you won't tell him."

"I can't do that."

"You have to promise!" Kate sounded desperate.

Eve realized she was the only adult Kate seemed willing to confide in. It was a heavy responsibility. "Answer one question," she said. "Are you and this boy—are you and David using any type of birth control?"

"He's not *stupid*. Neither am I."

"That didn't answer my question."

Kate was getting a stubborn look on her face, but after a pause she nodded reluctantly. "David takes care of everything," she muttered. "He uses *condoms*." She was obviously trying to sound sophisticated, yet she sounded like a child.

"All right, here's the deal," Eve said decisively. "I'm giving you one week, Kate. One week exactly to tell either of your parents what's going on with you and David. After that, it's up to me."

Kate backed away from her. "I thought I could trust you."

"You can. I know that what you really want is for your parents to help you through this. One week, Kate."

Kate whirled, flung open the door and made her usual abrupt disappearance. Maybe her friends were waiting for her outside. Or maybe it was only David this time.

Eve sank onto the chair behind her desk and buried her face in her hands. She could think of a dozen different ways she might have handled this encounter with Kate. What would have been best? Did any parent really know?

Eve reminded herself that she didn't qualify as Kate's parent. She was simply a thirty-seven-year-old pregnant single woman—the last person who should be counseling a teenager on birth control and other such matters.

Eve made a sound that was somewhere between a groan and a laugh, although she quite failed to see any humor in the situation.

CHAPTER SIXTEEN

IT WAS ONLY the first day of February, but Ben noted that the plate-glass windows of Cobb's Rio Diner were already adorned with decorations to celebrate Valentine Day: old-fashioned paper hearts trimmed with lace, a cardboard Cupid aiming an arrow.

Ben had never felt less like celebrating Valentine Day. He sat in a booth at the diner, staring at a piece of cherry pie and wondering how much longer he could go without making love to Eve. It was very clear she wanted a strict hands-off policy, yet she hadn't actually broken off her relationship with Ben. That was the puzzler. Only yesterday she'd called him up to say she'd missed seeing him these past few days. Hell, it didn't make any sense. She missed him, but she didn't want him around. The problem was, he missed *her* so much that the sensation was like an actual physical pain in his gut.

"Sorry I'm late." Rachael slid into the seat across from him. They'd developed something of a ritual these days: meeting at the diner once a week or so to discuss their kids. These were never jocular occasions, but they were an improvement over open combat.

Now Rachael frowned at the piece of pie in front of her. "You shouldn't have ordered any for me. They probably bake with lard in this place." She said "lard" as if it were an illegal substance.

Ben shrugged. "I'll have both pieces, then. But the coffee I ordered for you is safe. Decaf. No cream, no sugar."

"Don't start again. I know you think the children would be a little more cooperative with me if I fed them junk food now and then."

"Hey, I'm glad you insist on a healthy diet. Let me be the one who gives them junk food."

"Very funny." Rachael gazed into her coffee cup as if suspecting Ben of slipping her a little sugar, after all. "You'll be happy to know that Phil and I aren't fighting anymore," she said. "In fact, we hardly talk to each other now, which makes for a very peaceful atmosphere." She paused.

After fifteen years of marriage to her, Ben knew all the cues: the potent silences, the glances of apparent disinterest, the tidbits of information thrown out to tempt his curiosity. Even when Rachael wanted to share her thoughts, she was coy about it. Today she obviously wanted to tell Ben more about Phil, but she expected him to wheedle it out of her. He was supposed to take responsibility for whatever she ended up saying.

It wasn't like that with Eve. There was nothing coy about her. He knew something was troubling her deeply, but as far as he could see, she simply didn't want to tell him about it. She was determined to handle it on her own, whatever it was.

Rachael cleared her throat, a signal he wasn't paying enough attention. Lord, she was behaving as if they were still married. He refused to fall into the old patterns.

"Listen, I realize your problems with Phil are none of my business," he said. "I just wanted to point out that the kids weren't happy, so that you could take some kind of action."

"Well, they're much happier now. Like I told you, Phil and I don't even *talk* anymore. He goes about his business, I go about mine. You'd almost think we were two strangers living in the same house."

Again the pause, the silent request that Ben grill her for more information. He changed the subject as adroitly as possible.

"You say the kids are doing better. Is Kate still giving you a hard time about her friends?"

Rachael was successfully diverted—for the moment, at least. "I finally got a chance to meet some of these so-called friends. Nowadays when they come for Kate, they've taken to parking around the corner from the house. They act like they're hiding from me. But the other afternoon I got the better of them. I marched around the corner, went straight up to the window of that disreputable truck and introduced myself. 'Hello,' I said. 'I'm Kate's mother. How do you do.' I gave them the whole polite routine, even though I *really* wanted to tell them to get the heck out of there and never come back."

"Where was Kate during all this?" Ben asked.

"She was still in the house. I had to sneak out ahead of her. When she showed up and found me talking to those delinquents, well, what could she do? I'm her mother, after all."

Ben could well imagine his oldest daughter's reaction. "Just because they drive an old truck doesn't mean Kate's friends are delinquents. You don't know anything about them."

"You know, you *could* trust my judgment for once. If I tell you they're delinquents, believe me, that's what they are."

"Just give me details, Rachael."

"Oh, for goodness' sake. We're talking two girls who look like escapees from reform school, and a much too good-looking boy with a goatee."

"You never mentioned anything about a boy before. I thought this was about Kate and a few girlfriends."

"That's what I thought, too," Rachael said. "I've caught glimpses of the two girls before, but the young man appears to be a new addition."

"You allowed Kate to get in a truck with this guy?"

"What else was I supposed to do, Ben? I'd already alienated her just by introducing myself to her lovely associates. I couldn't very well make a scene and try to physically restrain her. Besides, her girlfriends were there, too. It's not like I let her go somewhere on her own with a boy."

Ben rotated his shoulders, trying to loosen the tension in his neck muscles. Sooner or later, he and Rachael would have to let Kate start dating. For now, though, he didn't like to think of boys anywhere near his daughter.

"I think I preferred it when she didn't have any friends in town," he said.

"I preferred that, too."

He and Rachael shared a woeful glance. It was almost a look of camaraderie. They were finally starting to cooperate a little when it came to their kids.

"I don't know what we're going to do about Kate," Rachael said now. "If we forbid her to see her friends, you know she'll manage to disobey us. Even though I've been insisting she do her homework, her grades are still slipping, and she's moodier than ever."

"Instead of picking up all three kids tomorrow, why don't I just spend the day with Kate? Maybe if the two of us are off on our own, she'll finally open up a little with me. I'll take her into Albuquerque, make a real occasion of it.''

Rachael nodded. ''That sounds like an excellent idea. Matthew and Jenny will be envious, of course, but you can promise to give each of them a special day, too.'' She stared thoughtfully at Ben. ''Maybe you really have changed,'' she said. ''I didn't want to believe it at first, but maybe you relly have.''

Ben didn't particularly like the speculative way his ex-wife was looking at him. ''Listen, Rachael, I hope you work things out with Phil.''

Rachael frowned at the mention of her husband's name. But then she glanced at her watch and announced in virtuous tones that she had to be off to pick up Matthew and Jenny from the neighbor's. This sounded more like the Rachael he knew. She liked to remind him of all the motherly things she did for the kids: picking them up, ferrying them about, caring for them when they were sick. More than anything, she liked to remind him that he still hadn't put in his fair share of parenting.

As usual she left the diner before Ben, allowing him to pay the check for both of them. He sat in the booth awhile longer, considering his options for the afternoon. He could go to his office and pretend he had work to do. Or he could go home and lay the new tile in the kitchen. Then again, he could go to Eve and demand to know why she'd withdrawn from him.

He ended up leaving his Jeep in front of the diner and taking off for a run. He fell into a steady pace, not pushing too hard, letting his breathing find its own rhythm. Already his daily runs were starting to take effect; he could go for longer and longer distances. This afternoon he chose his favorite route. He cut across Central, following a maze of quiet residential streets until he came to the edge of the river.

The Rio Grande stretched wide and shallow before him, so shallow that in many places the muddy river bottom was visible. Ben ran along the bank, the moist earth spongy under his shoes, cattails and marsh grasses swaying as he passed through them. On either side of the river rose dense clusters of trees: always the cottonwoods, spreading their leafless branches above him.

He jogged on for another mile or so. He knew right when to slow his pace, right when he had to stop making any noise at all. He stood very still on the bank, shading his eyes as he gazed farther up the river. He'd already learned from experience that one false move, and the entire flock of sandhill cranes would rise up in majestic flight.

Even today, with all his caution, the cranes sensed his presence. They became restless, curving their long necks to glance all around. But gradually they settled down again, tucking their wings back into place.

The cranes were large birds, by turns graceful, by turns comic. They took mincing steps through the water, bending their long legs and speaking to each other in soft deep guttural sounds that carried surprisingly far.

Now the subdued gray of their feathers took on a pearly sheen in the waning sunlight. As Ben watched, more cranes circled above and came wheeling in for a landing. They always looked agile to him when they took off, but when they landed, their movements became almost clumsy, awkward.

No matter what they did, the cranes provided entertainment, and Ben wondered why he hadn't shared this with his kids yet. The answer came quickly: he wanted to share it with Eve first. He wanted to show her that he'd found something truly pleasing in Cobb, New Mexico. She alone would understand how important it was for him to find *anything* redeeming.

So why wasn't she here, enjoying the cranes with him? Why had she pulled away? They needed each other, he knew that much. How could he reach her again?

There were so many cranes on the river now that they jostled each other. They didn't seem to mind the contact, though. They were sociable creatures. Ben knew they migrated from the north in enormous flocks to winter in the area. He doubted there was any such thing as a lonely crane.

Watching them, Ben felt his own pervasive loneliness, like a chill that had worked its way under his skin. It was a sensation he'd never known before Eve. When he and Rachael had started to grow apart, he'd known anger, confusion, even depression. But he hadn't experienced the elemental sense of loss cutting through him that he felt now.

The sky had mellowed to a rich dusky blue when Ben, moving as quietly as possible, turned and headed back the way he had come. He didn't break into a run again until he sighted the residential streets of Cobb.

This time he didn't choose a leisurely pace. He pushed himself to the limits of his endurance, sprinting hard. Yet, no matter how fast he ran, he couldn't get Eve out of his mind.

It was late that night when he finally gave in to his need and drove to Eve's. In spite of the late hour, he could've sworn he saw a curtain twitch at Josephine's window as he went past. Didn't the old lady ever relax her vigilance? Maybe she was afraid she'd miss some vicarious thrill if she started paying attention to her own life, instead of everyone else's.

Ben parked in Eve's driveway and climbed the steps of her porch. Her house was dark. She was probably already asleep, and Ben knew he should leave her. But he couldn't help himself. He knocked at the front door. When there was no answer after several moments, he knocked again, louder this time.

The porch light came on and a few seconds later a tousled, sleepy-eyed Eve peered out at him.

"Ben! Is anything wrong? Are you all right?"

He didn't answer. He just looked at her. She was more lovely than he could ever remember, her hair tumbled luxuriously about her shoulders, her face slightly flushed. She wore a loose flannel nightshirt that stopped at midthigh. Ben hadn't known that Eve wore a nightshirt to bed. He'd seen her in sexy nightgowns, and he'd seen her in nothing at all. It made him realize that when he wasn't around, Eve indulged in habits of which he knew nothing. How much of her real self did she keep private from him? No matter what, she looked damn good now.

"I think you'd better come in," she murmured. "It's cold out there."

Once he was inside, he leaned her against the door and kissed her. A hundred times he'd remembered the taste of her lips, but it was still new to him. Light spilled out from the bedroom, barely reaching them. Enveloped in shadows, Ben went on kissing her.

She was pliant, then eager, her hands moving up over his shoulders as she pressed against him. Unexpectedly she pulled away.

"Ben . . . there's so much that's wrong between us. You can't even know . . ." Her voice seemed to catch on the words, and he didn't wait to hear any more. He bent his head and captured her mouth again, burying his hands in her hair.

When Eve broke away again, it was only to lead him into the bedroom. Moving quickly, she turned off the lamp on her nightstand. In the darkness, she lowered herself onto the bed, drawing Ben down beside her.

The mattress was narrow, but by now both Eve and Ben had learned to be inventive in confined spaces. He traced his hand up her thigh, her skin soft to his touch. Tonight Eve seemed especially round and womanly. And she wasn't wearing anything under the nightshirt.

He made love gently, quietly to her, only a few sounds disturbing the stillness of night: the rustle of sheets and blankets being cast aside, the creak of the box spring, the quickening of Eve's breath and then his own.

Afterward they clung together for a long while. As the heat of their passion subsided in the cool air, Ben smoothed a blanket over both of them, neither of them speaking. He was grateful that she seemed to realize the same thing he did. Talking right now would only create more distance between them. Coming together tonight had been a gift, one that shouldn't be questioned.

Ben held Eve until she fell asleep. Then, very carefully, he slid his arm out from under her shoulders. She stirred, only to turn and nestle deeper against the pillow. Still carefully, Ben slipped from the bed. He'd done the same thing this afternoon, moved stealthily so he wouldn't disturb the cranes. Now he didn't want to disturb Eve, or the memory of making love to her tonight.

Picking up his shoes, he walked barefoot to the door. He hadn't counted on Eve's cat, however, and in the darkness he almost tripped over the Siamese. Oscar gave a yowl of protest. Ben stopped, afraid that Eve would wake. But no sound came from the bedroom, and after a moment Ben slipped out the door. Tossing his shoes onto the front seat, he started the engine and eased his way out of the drive. This time, as he swung down the street past Josephine's house, he was positive he saw a curtain twitch.

IT HAD BEEN THREE DAYS since Ben had come to her house late at night, and he hadn't called once. To be fair, she hadn't called him, either. She didn't really have a right to blame him for his silence—for staying away. After all, she was the one who refused to tell him the truth.

She was carrying his child, but she still wanted control over that monumental fact. And maybe she was being superstitious, too. An illogical part of her believed that as long as she didn't tell Ben, she could pretend that her pregnancy would proceed exactly as she wished: no problems, no fears. It was as if she were living in a small precious pocket of time where the rules were hers to make. She could dream of a baby growing strong and healthy inside her, a baby she would carry to term and finally cradle in her arms. Once she told Ben, however, she'd have to deal with the real pregnancy, the very real problems involved. Yes, it was all completely illogical, but at the moment Eve needed to grasp any illusion she could.

She went to the kitchen, escorted by her cat. Oscar never ate this early in the morning, but Eve poured herself a large glass of milk and popped some whole-wheat bread into the toaster. She always ate a healthy breakfast these days, following to the letter Dr. Cole's instructions. She was like a hopeful kid, crossing her fingers and not stepping on any of the cracks in the sidewalk. When you got down to it, she was trying to make a bargain with her body: I'll do everything right if only you'll allow me to have this baby....

She ate a bowl of oatmeal, as well as the toast. The phone rang while she was still working on the milk, and she took her glass with her into the living room.

She reached the phone on the third ring. "Hello?"

"Eve. it's Ben."

At first all she knew was happiness at hearing his voice. But then she realized that he sounded different—almost brusque. Before she could ask any questions, he barreled ahead.

"Eve, Kate didn't come home last night. We've looked everywhere for her, and then it occurred to us that she might be with you."

Eve set down her glass. Part of her registered the way Ben so naturally said "us." He had to be referring to himself and Rachael, of course. But that was only a fleeting thought, quickly submerged by her concern for Kate.

"No, she's not with me. I haven't seen her in nearly a week." A dread grew inside Eve. She'd given Kate an ultimatum—you've got one week to tell your father you're having sex or I'll do it for you. Had Kate run away to avoid facing that? It was one of many possibilities, all of them frightening.

"Ben, I have something I need to tell you."

"I'm sorry. I just don't have—"

"It's about Kate. Where are you calling from?"

"My house. But—"

"I'll be right there." She hung up before Ben could say anything more. The last thing she wanted to do was talk about this over the phone. She didn't relish doing it in person, either, but she felt obligated to tell Ben about his daughter face-to-face.

Fingers trembling, she dressed hurriedly in a skirt and sweater. With her thickening middle she couldn't quite fasten the top button of the skirt. No matter; her bulky sweater would disguise her waistline. She was due for a faculty meeting at the college in an hour, but she suspected she'd be missing it. Kate was far more important. She strode out to her car and headed for Ben's house.

When she arrived, she found that he wasn't alone. His ex-wife was there with him. Eve cursed herself for not taking the possibility of Rachael's presence into account. Their daughter was missing. They were searching for her together. It was only to be expected.

It was the first time Eve had met Rachael, and Ben introduced the two women distractedly. It bothered Eve that the other woman was so striking. Rachel wasn't beautiful, but her looks were distinctive. Her hair was cropped dramatically short, and her pointed features were the kind you'd expect of some offbeat fashion model. Her body was as willowy as any model's, too. Eve felt pudgy in comparison, and then she reminded herself that right now her only concern should be Kate. She turned to Ben.

"I have something to tell you that might help," she said in a low voice. "Maybe it would be better if I spoke to you in private, though."

"If you know something, just tell us," he said. "We don't have time. Anything could have happened to Kate."

Ben looked as if he'd been up most of the night, his eyes bleary and reddened. He'd never been this abrupt before, but Eve figured he had justification. And so she faced both of them: Ben and his obviously resentful ex-wife. Rachael stood close to him, gazing at Eve with a frown.

"Almost a week ago Kate showed me another of her stories," Eve began. "It was about a girl involved in a sexual relationship with a seventeen-year-old boy. It became very clear to me that Kate was writing about her own experiences, and—"

"What are you saying?" Rachael demanded. "You think Kate is having sex?"

Rachael's agitation somehow helped Eve to be calm. "Kate has a pattern of writing about the things going on in her life. That's why I believed that this latest story was more than her imagination. When I confronted her, she finally admitted the truth to me. She's involved with a boy."

Eve looked at Ben now. He hadn't said anything, but the expression on his face was a mixture of pain and anger. She had no doubt that the anger was directed in at least some measure toward her.

"Ben," she murmured. "I wanted to tell you. I was going to tell you. But Kate was so scared you'd stop loving her once you found out. She begged me not to say a word. I explained to her that she had a week to confide in you herself—and, after that, it was up to me."

Ben still didn't speak. He simply gazed at Eve as if she'd suddenly become a stranger to him—someone he didn't recognize. Someone he didn't care to recognize.

CHAPTER SEVENTEEN

RACHAEL SPOKE NEXT, her strident voice filling the empty spaces in the room.

"I can't believe my own daughter would do such a thing. She's too young! I don't believe it, Ben. I just don't."

"I think we have to start believing it," he said quietly. "It's possible Kate's gone off somewhere with this boy. Eve, do you know anything else about him?"

Before she answered, Eve sank onto a chair. Her legs had gone wobbly on her. She didn't know if this was because of her pregnancy or because Ben was still regarding her with such a cold expression. He was so controlled and logical right now. She'd far rather see him get his anger out into the open.

"I'm fairly certain that the character in Kate's story matches up with a boy in real life. His name is David. He has a beard and he drives a pickup truck—"

"Oh, my God," said Rachael. "That's the young man I met. The one I told you about, Ben."

"Go on," Ben said curtly to Eve. "What else?"

"In the story, David has graduated from high school, and he works at a grocery store. I don't recall any other details." Eve bit her lip, remembering the evocative description of sex between Jack and Emily in Kate's story. She didn't care to describe those particular details to Ben.

"We have enough to go on," he said. "There are only two grocery stores in town. This jerk shouldn't be hard to track down. He'll be damn sorry when I find him, too. I'll beat the hell out of him." Ben's anger was finally starting to boil over.

"Ben," Eve said urgently, "Kate's involvement with this boy is very complex. He makes her feel that she belongs somewhere, and she sincerely believes she's in love with him. But she's scared, too. She's afraid of losing your love, your good opinion of her. Perhaps if I hadn't given her an ultimatum..." Eve's voice trailed off. Was she seeking some sort of reassurance from Ben—a pat on the back for having done the right thing? If so, she was out of luck.

"You should have told me," he said. "As soon as you found out, you damn well should've told me."

"You had no right to keep this from us," Rachael added. "She's our daughter. We love her, and she needs us." The two of them went on standing together, Ben and Rachael. Eve could see what a handsome couple they'd once made: Ben with his dark eyes and golden brown hair, Rachael providing a contrast with her smoky black hair and large gray eyes. They were both lean and elegant.

Clasping her hands tightly in her lap, Eve battled her own anger. She detested the way Ben so naturally allied himself with his ex-wife.

"Somehow Kate feels she can talk to me," Eve said, "I believe that gave me a certain responsibility. I had to respect her wishes as much as I could. Maybe I made the wrong decision, I don't know. But I've always had Kate's best interests in mind."

"You're not her mother," Rachael shot back. "You're trying to take a place that doesn't belong to you."

"I never wanted to be Kate's mother. I just wanted to be her friend."

"Kate doesn't need friendship right now," Ben said. "She needs parenting. But first, dammit, we have to find her." He shrugged into a Windbreaker and escorted Rachael out of the house.

Eve remained where she was, and only gradually did the absurdity of her situation assail her. Here she sat in her lover's house, while her lover went off with his ex-wife. But she couldn't make herself move just yet. She glanced around, noting all the changes in the living room since she'd last been here. Ben had painted the walls ivory. He'd sanded and polished the wooden floor, and scraped clean the stones of the hearth. She saw that he had followed her suggestion, fashioning built-in bookshelves along one wall. Now he needed only to furnish the room. At the moment, Ben's lawn chairs and sleeping bag held pride of place.

Eve stared at the rumpled sleeping bag. Then, slowly, she stood and walked out the door of Ben's house, weariness sweeping over her. She wanted nothing more than to go home, curl up in her own solitary bed and drift into a sleep where she wouldn't have to think or feel.

Instead, she climbed into her car and drove to the college, where she'd be only a little late for her faculty meeting. Somehow, in spite of everything, she had to keep going through the motions of her life.

LATE THAT AFTERNOON, Ben walked into her office. He looked even more tired than she felt, his hair rumpled, a stubble of beard on his jaw. Eve dropped her pen on the desk, too many emotions swirling through her: intense relief at the mere sight of Ben, pain at the memory of his coldness, anxiety for his daughter.

"Did you find Kate?" she asked hopefully.

He didn't sit down, but went to stare out the window at the cactus garden. "No. We haven't found her yet. But we know she's with that damn boy. He didn't show up for work today. One of Kate's girlfriends finally broke down and admitted that Kate and David had been planning to run off together."

A heaviness settled inside Eve. "Do you know where?"

"They're probably in Albuquerque. I have one or two leads to follow. Nothing very promising at this point."

Eve crossed to him and put her hand on his arm. "I'm so sorry," she said softly. "If only I could have done something differently, something that would have convinced her to confide in you."

"It's not your fault. If I blamed you this morning, I was wrong. I'm her father. I'm the one who should've handled things differently. It never even occurred to me that she could be dating, let alone..." He didn't seem capable of actually saying the words. He just went on staring out the window.

Ben had exonerated Eve, but it didn't make her feel any better. She still felt as if they'd become strangers.

At last she found herself wanting to tell him about the pregnancy. Today she'd witnessed how parenthood could bring two people together. In spite of their divorce, Ben and Rachael unmistakably shared a great love for the daughter they had created. Now Eve realized how jealous that made her feel. She wanted that same bond with Ben.

She could also imagine how ludicrous dropping the news on him right now would be: your daughter's run off with some boy, and by the way, I'm carrying your child, Ben. Just thought you'd like to know....

"How's Rachael coping?" she asked, wondering why she had to mention Ben's ex-wife.

"She's doing all right. Sometimes Rachael puts on a front of hysteria, but she actually handles crises well."

Was that admiration she heard in Ben's voice? Eve couldn't be sure, and she was disgusted with herself for bringing up Rachael at all, but now she knew why she'd done it, at least. She'd wanted to find out how close Ben and Rachael had grown during this crisis. It sounded as if it was pretty close.

Eve hadn't realized jealousy could feel like this: miserable and mean and petty. "I wish there was some way I could help," she said.

"You helped this morning. You gave us the information we needed."

Eve wished fervently he wouldn't keep saying "we." It was as if, when it came to the children, he and Rachael no longer existed separately; parenthood had united them in some irrevocable way.

Now Ben stared through her office window up at the sky. Eve followed the direction of his gaze and saw a flock of cranes passing overhead, silhouetted in a long V against the horizon.

"They're already migrating north again," Ben murmured. "Leaving this place behind, just like everybody else."

"They always come back, though. Sometimes I think Cobb isn't such a bad place to return to."

Now Ben looked at Eve, his gaze searching. She almost believed he would take her in his arms and they would bridge the distance between them in the only way they knew how: touching each other. But then an expression of sorrow came over Ben's face.

"I wanted to tell you what we'd discovered about Kate. I knew you'd be worried, too."

"I was very worried. I'm glad you came."

"I'll let you know if anything else develops."

They might have been the most formal of acquaintances, until Ben reached out as if to brush a strand of hair from her cheek. But he arrested his movement, and he didn't touch her. Eve wondered if he would ever touch her again.

BEN FOUND HIS DAUGHTER in a scuzzy motel room in Albuquerque. The carpet was so thin and ratty it looked like nothing more than shreds of dirty terry cloth tacked to the floor. The walls bore the stains of age-old water leaks, and a pervasive scent of mildew filled the air.

Kate sat cross-legged in the middle of a sagging bed, and the infamous David stood leaning against one of the stained walls, affecting an air of nonchalance. The kid wore the usual uniform of a teenager—baggy jeans and oversize T-shirt, but his goatee was meticulously styled. He probably spent half his time combing the damn thing, and the other half seducing Ben's daughter.

Ben felt murderous. All he wanted to do was grab David by his scrawny neck and pound him senseless. It took a great amount of willpower not to do precisely that.

"Out," Ben said to the kid. "Just get out of here."

At the tone of Ben's voice, David seemed to forget about nonchalance. He sidled through the door, leaving father and daughter to confront each other.

"You can't treat him like that," Kate said, her back stiff and unyielding. "I won't let you."

Ben had to hand it to his daughter: she had guts. At first she'd looked terrified when he'd burst in here, but now she acted as if she were holding court in a suite at the Ritz. Only the tears glistening in her eyes betrayed her.

Ben remembered what Eve had told him—Kate was afraid of losing his love. So, instead of yelling at his daughter, he settled himself on a corner of the bed.

"Your mother and I have been very worried about you," he said almost conversationally. "Eve's been worried, too."

"She told you, didn't she? I asked her and asked her not to tell, but she did, anyway!"

For the first time, Ben sympathized a little with Eve's conflicting loyalties. "She kept your secret until you ran away. After that, she had to tell us."

"I'm not coming home. I want to be with David, and you can't stop me."

Ben thought about his daughter and that punk sleeping on any number of sagging beds, and he felt murderous again. Yet today, when he'd surprised them here, he'd found both of them fully clothed, watching TV and sharing a bag of potato chips. They'd looked like children rather than two sex-crazed teenagers.

"I think you do want to come home," Ben said. "It'd probably be a relief for David, too. He has a good job waiting for him, and I'm sure he doesn't want to lose it."

"He hates that crummy store and that crummy town. Just like me. He can get a job anywhere."

"What exactly did you plan to do, Kate? Follow this kid around the country while he works as a bag boy?"

"When I turn sixteen next month, I can get a job, too. I wish you'd just *leave,* Dad."

"I'm not going anywhere."

Kate scooted farther away from him. "I'm not going home!"

"I'm your father," he said, because apparently she needed reminding. After a moment, he added, "I love you." According to Eve, these were the words Kate needed to hear. He meant them, too, even if he didn't understand his daughter.

He said them again, more forcefully this time. "I love you, Katie."

"Don't call me that!"

"You used to like it when I called you Katie."

She kept silent now, picking at a hole in her jeans. Her feet were bare, and he could see that she'd painted her toenails a bright pink. It was an oddly innocent color.

"Let's just go home," he said. "Your mother can't wait to see you."

"I *hate* living with her and Phil."

"She's doing her best. We all are."

"I'm staying here with David. We're going to get an apartment and be happy. I don't need anybody but him." No longer teary-eyed, she stared at Ben with an obstinate expression, as if daring him to contradict her. "I belong with David," she insisted proudly.

That was it. Ben decided he'd given kindness and tolerance enough of a shot. It was time for some good old-fashioned parental authority.

"You're coming home," he said grimly, taking her duffel bag from the corner and setting it in front of her. "Start packing. You're coming home and you're staying there even if we have to place you under house arrest. Get moving, Kate. I'm your father!"

TALKING TO EVE on the telephone that night was exactly what Ben needed. Her low voice was soothing and sexy at the same time, almost making him forget all the problems between them.

"I'm so glad you found her," Eve said. "How did you know where to look?"

"The uncle of one of Kate's girlfriends owns that scumbag motel in Albuquerque. Next time Kate shouldn't involve so many people in her escape—except there won't be a next time. She's on a strict curfew."

"Will you let her see David?"

"We're still discussing that. Rachael believes if we forbid her to see him, it'll only make things worse. She's willing to let him visit Kate as long as one of us is there to chaperon. But the kid had sex with my daughter. Now we're supposed to sit there and watch them play tiddledywinks together?"

Eve sighed. "You're asking the wrong person, Ben. I don't have any answers. And I think my days of counseling your daughter are over."

"You're the only person she'll talk to. I don't want her to lose her friendship with you."

"Are you sure?" Eve's voice was lightly mocking. "I made a mess of things this time around."

"You did what you thought was best. I couldn't see that at first, but after having to drag my daughter out of that motel room, who the hell knows the best way to deal with her? At least she talks to you, Eve."

"How does Rachael feel about that?"

"You already know how Rachael feels," he said. "She's envious of your closeness to Kate."

"I'd say she's envious of my closeness to you. Except that we're not all that close anymore, dammit." She sighed again, a sound that came to him like the mournful whisper of a breeze. After that, she didn't say anything more for such a long while Ben wondered if she'd set down the receiver and quietly walked away from it. She startled him when she did speak.

"Ben, in a few days I'll need someone to look after my cat again. I don't suppose you'd mind doing me the favor. I'm going away for... for just a little while."

"You have another job interview." It was a statement, not a question. All along he'd been afraid Eve would keep on applying for a new job. She had an out he didn't possess. But once more she startled him.

"It's not an interview. I'm going into the hospital, Ben."

He sat up straight, gripping the receiver. "What's wrong? Are you sick? Eve—"

"I'm not sick—not exactly. But I think you'd better come over and let me explain it to you."

"Damn right I'm coming over."

EVE SAT in one of her armchairs rather than on the sofa. Ben saw that as a significant choice. If she'd picked the sofa, he would have been able to sit next to her and hold her hand. Apparently she didn't want that. He tried to settle into the armchair across from her, but he couldn't get comfortable. The cushions might just as well have been stones. He had to face it—he wasn't going to get any comfort until he knew what was wrong.

The house was warm, but Eve wore one of the bulky sweaters that seemed to be her favorite type of clothing lately. She kept pushing up the sleeves, then pulling them down again. She looked outfitted for winter weather at an alpine ski lodge in Colorado, not a mild February evening in New Mexico.

Ben saw that she was also wearing the necklace he'd given her for Christmas, the diamond almost lost among the folds of her sweater. She reached up to clasp it.

"I'm pregnant," she said.

Ben stopped wrestling with the cushions and stared at her. Ever since Eve had mentioned the hospital, he'd been envisioning all manner of dangers and disasters. Pregnancy hadn't been one of them.

His first reaction was intense relief. His second reaction was something he couldn't quite put a name to. But he left the uncooperative chair behind and went to sit on the coffee table, instead. Leaning toward Eve, he took both her hands in his.

"I don't know what to say," he admitted. "I guess I'm a little stunned. I thought we'd been so careful."

"That's what I thought, too." She was very composed, as if she'd rehearsed telling him about this and now she was merely repeating her lines. "But the first time we had sex we weren't careful, Ben. And that's when it happened."

"Lord . . . you mean the drive-in?" He did some quick calculations. "You must be almost four months along. . . ."

Ben was more than a little stunned, and he was having a difficult time absorbing it all. In the forty-eight hours since Kate had run away, he hadn't gotten any sleep, and even though Kate was home now, he still hadn't relaxed. He'd reached the stage of exhaustion where his nerves were stretched so tight they had no slack left. Sleep deprivation—maybe that was why he couldn't think clearly right now.

"Four months," he repeated. "That means . . . How long have you known, Eve?"

"I suspected almost from the beginning, but I didn't want to believe it. It wasn't until I went to the doctor right before Christmas that I knew for sure."

"You've known since Christmas and you didn't tell me?" He chafed her hands between his and for the first time her composure seemed to slip a little.

"Every time I started to tell you...somehow I couldn't make myself go on. Dammit, for such a long time I didn't want the pregnancy to be real. And then you said you couldn't imagine any more children in your life. That wasn't encouraging... Oh, hell. Where's a handkerchief when I need one?"

Ben remembered the first time he'd seen Eve cry. They'd been tangled together on her sofa, and she'd wept because they hadn't made love. Now it occurred to him that she was weeping because they *had* made love.

There was a box of tissues on the coffee table, and he handed it to her.

"Thanks." She blotted her eyes. He noted that her nose turned red when she cried. Somehow that only made her seem lovelier. He put his hands on her shoulders, drawing her toward him.

"You should've told me," he said. "All that time we spent growing apart...you should've told me. How many secrets will you keep from me?"

"You don't want any more children, Ben."

That statement held too much truth, so he skirted it. "Do you want this baby?" he asked.

"Of course I do." She stared at him, as if amazed he'd even venture the question. "I want it more than anything in the world. But that doesn't do me a whole lot of good, does it? I've already lost two babies. Chances are I'll lose this one, too."

He didn't want her to go through that again. He'd do just about anything to keep it from happening. But another kid... He couldn't handle the three he already had. He'd started to wonder more and more lately if he was cut out for fatherhood. It seemed that being a parent required a special talent he just didn't have. After everything that had happened with Kate, how could he feel otherwise?

"We'll get through it," he told Eve, although he knew his voice lacked the proper conviction. Sleep deprivation again; he didn't have what it took to muster up any false enthusiasm. He couldn't be like the men on TV commercials who babbled foolishly and joyfully when they learned they were going to be fathers.

He knew he was letting Eve down. She pulled away from him and blotted her eyes again. Her nose was still red.

"The day after tomorrow I'm going into the hospital. It will only be overnight. There's a . . . a surgical procedure that has to be done."

"No more secrets, Eve," he said. He hadn't intended to sound irritable, but it came out that way. He tried again. "If you don't tell me exactly what's going on, I'll only stew about it and drive both of us nuts."

"It's so humiliating," she said angrily, twisting the soggy tissue in her fingers. "My body . . . it just won't allow me to carry the baby for the nine months. My damn cervix is too weak. The doctor's going to put a suture in it, stitch me up as if I were nothing better than a flimsy sack. There. Is that enough?"

He got the picture. Eve's entire face turned a rosy color as she flushed with shame. Ben knew her well enough by now to understand a few things. Eve wasn't ashamed of speaking frankly about her body. Instead, she hated admitting that her body didn't function perfectly. She seemed to take it as a personal failure.

"This procedure. Will it do the job?" he asked.

"Maybe. Maybe not. It didn't save my last baby."

Ben might be exhausted, but the lawyer in him took over, looking for practical alternatives and solutions. "Have you had a second opinion? Maybe you need another doctor. Don't believe what only one person tells you—"

"Ben. The problem is me, not my doctor."

There it was again, the heavy weight of blame she placed on her own shoulders. What would it take for Eve to absolve herself?

He didn't know how to help her. He suspected that she'd only told him about the pregnancy at this point because she had to go into the hospital. Otherwise, she would have kept it from him even longer, hiding the evidence from him under her big sweaters. He'd never known a more stubborn person. He was starting to comprehend her reluctance to betray Kate's trust. But to harbor this knowledge from him, the knowledge that she was carrying his child... Ben had a lot more difficulty comprehending that. Why did she believe that she had to carry all her burdens alone?

"We'll get married," he said. "That's the first thing we have to do."

She pulled away from him. "No," she said emphatically. "Absolutely not. I can't think about marriage at this stage."

"It's the only option that makes any sense."

"No," she repeated, her expression fiery. "We wouldn't even be discussing marriage if it weren't for the pregnancy. Dammit, I don't want you to do the noble thing. Forget it, Ben. Don't talk about it anymore."

He felt too tired to be noble. He just wanted to be with her, and he wrapped his arms around her again. "We'll table the marriage discussion—for now. But somebody else can look after your cat when you go to the hospital. I'll be there with you. No argument, Eve."

For once she didn't even try to protest.

CHAPTER EIGHTEEN

EVE DETESTED HOSPITALS. She'd hated them ever since she'd been a kid and her parents had taken her to visit her sick grandmother. The hospital had seemed to change plump happy Nana Rosalie into a shrunken stick of a woman who kept calling plaintively for a glass of water. Ever since, Eve had associated hospitals with ominous transformation. You went in one person and came out another. Her two miscarriages had only reinforced that conviction.

However, this particular visit to the hospital introduced a new element—Ben.

His was a forceful presence. He established himself as her protector, her mediator, from the very beginning, creating a flurry of activity. Suddenly the nurse produced an extra blanket without having to be asked twice, a candy striper showed up with doughnuts smuggled in from the hospital cafeteria, and Dr. Cole stopped by to chat more with Ben than Eve.

It was all rather overwhelming, Ben taking charge. He did it so well. Maybe too well. He seemed to believe that if he organized enough details and learned enough facts, this entire procedure would go exactly according to plan.

He was waiting in the recovery room when Eve awoke from the anesthesia.

"Is the baby all right?" she whispered groggily.

"The baby's fine. You're fine," he informed her in a tone of great relief, bending over and peering at her as if to make sure of this for himself. "The doctor says you need to take it easy. No teaching, no work, no exertion. Nothing but relaxation for an entire week."

When Ben drove Eve home from Albuquerque the following day, he insisted on taking care of her while she recuperated. He even made lunch, which turned out to be a pair of no-nonsense sandwiches of his own devising— grilled cheese, bacon and tomato. He wasn't a fancy cook, but he got the job done. Eve sat up against her pillows and gazed at him over the grilled cheese.

"Ben, I appreciate everything you've done for me. But it's not necessary to do any more. You can leave now. I thought you said something about having to put in a new shower head at your house."

"How long are you going to act like this baby is your burden and no one else's?"

"As long as I'm the only one who really wants the baby." She crossed her arms over her stomach and frowned at him. "Dammit, Ben. You're taking charge like this is a court case you're determined to win. But what you're really doing is avoiding the fact you don't want another child! You say I try to hide my emotions, but you're just as bad."

He pulled a chair in from the kitchen and sat down. Those quizzical lines around his eyes were etched in deeper than usual and Eve had a suspicion that Ben's world puzzled him more and more. That couldn't be easy for a man like him.

"Eve, won't you at least eat lunch?"

She obliged, but insisted he eat one of the sandwiches, too. If they were going to argue, at least they could both do it on full stomachs.

"Okay, so I'm not overjoyed at the thought of another kid," Ben said reluctantly. "Can you blame me, Eve? My youngest daughter still acts like 'Pop' is a stranger she hopes will go away soon, and my oldest daughter insists she's in love with the local bag boy. For all I know, *she's* pregnant."

"Don't say that. Don't even think that," Eve said with a shudder.

"You're right." Ben looked pained.

"You seem to be getting along with Matthew," Eve reminded him.

"Matt only wants two things from me—a basketball hoop and a reconciliation with his mother. So far I haven't delivered on either count."

"Maybe Rachael wants a reconciliation, too," Eve said tartly.

Ben gave her a keen glance. "We have enough real problems. Like you say, let's not imagine any more. It's true Rachael and Phil aren't getting along, but they'll have to work it out somehow."

Eve smoothed the quilt over her knees. She'd seen the way Rachael had looked at Ben that day. She'd looked at him as if she wouldn't mind having him back.

"We're off the subject," Eve said, wrenching her thoughts away from Ben's ex-wife. "The point is, you don't want any more children, so I'm damn well going to handle this pregnancy on my own."

"I'm as responsible for this baby as you are."

"You're not responsible for me. Get it?" Eve gripped the quilt in both hands. She knew she wasn't being fair. She wasn't telling Ben how scared she felt right now, wondering if her baby was going to make it. Instead, she was picking a fight with him, focusing all the attention on whether or not he wanted another child. That was safer than confronting her fears head-on.

He reached over and took her empty plate. "You won't get rid of me, Eve," he said with determination. "I'll be here today, tomorrow and the day after that. You'll be tired as hell of seeing me, but there isn't a damn thing you can do about it."

Ben remained true to his word. During the next week, for all intents and purposes, he moved into Eve's house. The first night he started out on her sofa, but after it gave him a backache, he spread his sleeping bag on her living-room floor. Eve grumbled and told him he could share her bed. Just because the doctor had strictly forbidden sex didn't mean Ben had to sleep on the floor.

He continued to choose the sleeping bag, claiming she'd be more comfortable that way. Eve didn't buy his excuse. It was obvious Ben didn't really know how close he wanted to get to her right now. Just as she'd feared, her pregnancy was changing things, widening the gap between them still further.

The worst of it was she wanted him in her bed. Lying alone each night, she worked herself into a state of heated dissatisfaction, dreaming of his touch and fantasizing about the feel of his bare skin next to hers. From the restless noises Ben made in the other room, she suspected that he, too, found it difficult to sleep. Although, dammit, he certainly seemed able to resist her. But she was too proud to beg him to come to her.

It was, therefore, a strange week, Ben pampering her and serving her meals, but hardly ever kissing her. Signs of him confronted Eve everywhere: his plaid robe hanging on the bathroom door, his razor left on the rim of the sink, the out-of-town newspapers he liked to read piled on her coffee table. Anyone would think she and Ben were living and sleeping together—except for that wretched sleeping bag on the floor.

Ben did go to his office at least a few hours every day, putting up the front of a busy lawyer. And one day he brought Kate over to Eve's house for a visit, dropping off his daughter while he ran a few errands.

"I'll be back to pick you up in about an hour," he told his daughter, then discreetly disappeared.

"Oh, wonderful," Kate muttered in Eve's direction as soon as he had gone. "This is just great. He won't let me see any of my friends, but he dumps me *here*."

"Last time I checked, I qualified as your friend, too," Eve remarked mildly.

"I know why my dad brought me here. I'm supposed to confess all my deepest thoughts to you, and then *you're* supposed to tell him everything I said. Why don't you just use a tape recorder? That'll make it easier for you."

"Don't be melodramatic," Eve chided. "Your father doesn't have ulterior motives. He thought it would be nice if you got out of the house for something besides school."

Now that Eve had met Rachael, she could see similarities between mother and daughter. The way Kate had of dramatically emphasizing certain words came straight from Rachael. Both mother and daughter were vivid brunettes, with the same rich dark shade of hair. Rachael had cut hers very short and Kate wore hers very long, as if in rebellion.

But Kate had inherited Ben's dark eyes and his distinctive features. Together, Ben and Rachael had produced a daughter unmistakably their own. A wave of bittersweet longing swept over Eve. Would her baby look like Ben? Like her? If her child survived...

"What's wrong?" Kate asked warily. "Do you have a stomachache?"

Eve became aware that she'd been pressing a hand to her middle. "Not exactly," she hedged.

"My dad said you went to the hospital. Are you sick?" Kate was trying to sound nonchalant, but Eve heard the worry in her voice. Kate would have to learn the truth, sooner or later. Perhaps sooner was better.

Eve took a deep breath. "I'm going to have a baby," she said.

She was prepared for the shock that registered on Kate's face, but not for the accompanying flash of revulsion. "A baby? You and my dad..."

"Yes, we're going to have a baby," Eve said, already regretting her frankness. Here she was, telling a fifteen-year-old girl that a new brother or sister happened to be on the way. Obviously it wasn't something you should just drop on a teenager like this.

It was too late to turn back, however, and Eve tried to remedy the situation. "This will have no effect on how your father feels about you," she said quickly. "He loves you and Matthew and Jenny very much, and—"

"A baby?" Kate repeated in horror. "You and my dad didn't just have *sex*. You made a baby!"

"The two happen to be related," Eve said dryly. "I would hope you'd figured that out by now."

"I'm not dumb. At least David and I used *condoms*."

"A very wise decision, but that doesn't change the fact that you're too young to be involved in a serious relationship."

"Don't turn this around," Kate said scornfully. "I'm not the one who was stupid enough to get pregnant."

Eve struggled to hold on to her patience. "I told you before not to look to me as an example. Yes, perhaps I was foolish. But I want this baby more than anything. I can also support my child and provide a good home.

That's the advantage of being thirty-seven. If you were to become pregnant, Kate, your situation would be very different. Can't you see that?''

Kate stared at Eve. ''You sound like you're not going to marry my father. You sound like you're going to have the kid and raise it on your own.''

Eve watched as her cat strolled across the room and jumped onto the windowsill. Oscar settled down, tucking his paws underneath him and assuming his usual expression of impassive wisdom—as if he knew the answers to all questions, but couldn't be bothered to share them. Eve wished she had some answers of her own. She and Ben hadn't discussed marriage again, but she knew it was something very much on his mind. She tried to avoid the subject. The truth was, she couldn't bear to think that far ahead. All her concern was centered on just keeping this pregnancy a success from one day to the next. She didn't dare hope for anything more. She didn't dare picture herself actually raising her baby—with or without Ben at her side.

''Kate, I know you'd probably be overjoyed if I didn't marry your father. But that isn't the point—''

''I'm not like my little brother,'' Kate interrupted. ''I don't expect my mom and dad to get back together. I'm not *that* naive.''

''Good for you.'' Eve knew she was botching this conversation. She didn't seem any good at being the mature adult who could guide someone younger. Yet she wanted to be a mother! Was she crazy?

She tried again. ''The important thing is for you to realize that no one is going to take your father away from you. Not me, and not this baby. Can you believe that?''

Kate was starting to look belligerent. She stared pointedly at Ben's sleeping bag, still rumpled in the middle of the floor. "I don't care what you and my dad do. All I care about is seeing David again. Everybody thinks they can stop me from seeing him—but they can't."

Too late, Eve realized that Ben's daughter was setting the stage for another grand exit. She'd had her say, and now she stormed out of the room before Eve could stop her.

"Kate! Hold on. You know you're supposed to wait here for your father."

She might as well not have spoken, because Kate just kept moving.

Eve was under strict doctor's orders to move slowly and carefully. By the time she reached the front door and could glance up and down the street, Kate was nowhere to be seen. The girl had made a break, and she'd used Eve to do it. No doubt she was headed straight for her boyfriend.

"This is dreadful," Eve said to her cat. "Just dreadful. I've done it again, Oscar. When it comes to Ben's daughter, I can't seem to do anything right."

She didn't know why she was standing here confiding in her cat. She grabbed her keys and went out to her car, only to meet Ben pulling into the drive. He swung out of his Jeep.

"What are you doing?" he demanded. "You know what the doctor said—"

"No time to talk now," she said urgently. "Kate's gone. I have a feeling she's on her way to the store where David works."

Ben swore under his breath and started to climb back into the Jeep. But then he came over to Eve and took her arm. He guided her toward the house, rather as if he were ferrying a crystal vase.

"Don't be ridiculous," she protested. "The doctor said I could walk by myself as long as I was careful."

He didn't listen, refusing to leave until he had her situated once again on the sofa. Only then did he go off in search of his daughter, a grim expression on his face.

Eve didn't envy Kate, once Ben found her. She didn't envy Kate's boyfriend, either.

BEN TURNED DOWN first one corner, then another, choosing the most direct route to Landmark Foods, the grocery store where David Flanders worked as head bag boy. Ben's hands tightened on the steering wheel. Whenever he thought about the Flanders kid, he still wanted to beat the hell out of him.

He and Rachael had decided that, for the time being, they wouldn't allow Kate to see the boy. They'd give her at least a few weeks to cool off, maybe get some sense into her head. So much for that. Just as Eve had predicted, Kate was headed straight for Landmark Foods. Ben could see his daughter up ahead, cutting across the street toward the grocery store.

He slowed the Jeep as he came up behind her. She walked with a proud no-nonsense stride, swinging her arms at her sides, instead of stuffing them into her jacket pockets as usual. She looked determined.

Ben pulled up alongside her. "Kate, you know the rules," he called through the open window. "You were supposed to stay at Eve's until I picked you up."

She didn't act surprised to see him there. She just kept striding along. "Go away, please," she said. She sounded icily polite.

Ben inched the Jeep forward. "You're not allowed to see David, Kate. So forget about even trying."

"What'll you do—force me into the car?"

"If that's what it takes."

Now Kate whirled and stared at him. Her eyes were huge and dark. "After what *you* did, you don't have any right! You...you got her pregnant, Dad. How could you?"

Ben almost pressed down on the horn. Damn. He and Eve hadn't even discussed how they were going to tell the kids about her pregnancy.

They'd both been avoiding the subject; they hadn't talked about the baby at all these past few days, and it never occurred to him that she'd tell Kate. Maybe he should've known better.

Today he'd hoped that Kate would drop her mutinous attitude and confide in Eve. Instead, it appeared to be the other way around.

"I think you'd better get in so we can talk about this," he told Kate.

She gripped the edge of the door, still staring at him with that betrayed expression. But then she did climb into the Jeep. She huddled there, pressing herself as far away from him as she could get. Gone was the girl with the proud determined stride. This Kate seemed lonely and uncertain.

"How could you do it?" she muttered. "First you took Eve away from me. She was *my* friend. And now..."

Ben pulled over to the curb. A few young kids pedaled their bicycles along the quiet street; one of them had training wheels. Ben could remember Kate's first set of training wheels, although he hadn't been around much to help her learn to ride. He'd missed out on so much with her, and maybe it was just too late to catch up.

"Eve and I didn't plan for this to happen," he said now.

"That's supposed to make it better?"

"Kate, Eve wants this baby very much. Give her a break, okay? She's terrified."

"Eve isn't scared of anything," Kate scoffed.

"Sometimes she gives that impression. But she's terrified, all right. She lost two babies when she was married, and she's scared she'll lose this one."

For a minute he thought he'd reached Kate. She glanced over at him. "Eve's been pregnant before?"

"That's right, but the babies were born too soon. So of course she's worried about this one. She doesn't need any added stress."

If he'd meant to play on Kate's sympathies, he hadn't succeeded. His daughter shivered and huddled down again inside her jacket.

"Gruesome," she declared. "I'm *never* going to get pregnant."

"You should think about that before you get involved with a kid like David Flanders."

"He's not a kid. And it's none of your business, anyway. I love David."

Ben was tempted to floor it over to Landmark Foods and finally give David Flanders the pummeling he deserved. But when he did press down on the accelerator, he ended up at Rachael's. He followed Kate as she hurried into the house.

Everyone was in the living room, a room that still looked more like a bachelor's den than anything else. A big-screen television now took up most of Phil's battered old desk, and Phil and Rachael sat in opposing armchairs, staring at the five-thirty news. Matthew and Jenny were sprawled on the floor, playing Monopoly and squabbling as usual. It wasn't exactly the picture of domestic tranquillity, and Kate didn't improve it any by marching in and making her announcement.

"They're going to have a baby!" she exclaimed, her voice quivering with outrage. "They're going to have a baby and I guess that's okay with everybody, but I'm not even allowed to see David. *I* didn't get pregnant, but I'm the one who gets punished!"

Rachael grabbed the remote control and switched off the television. "What on earth are you talking about, Kate? Who's having a baby?"

"I was watching the news," Phil said. "Does anyone mind if I just watch the news in my own house?"

"*Dad's* having a baby," Kate said. "Dad and Eve."

Now every head swiveled toward Ben. Even Phil brought himself to attention, studying Ben with an expression of interest. Ben felt like some sort of oddity on display. This wasn't how he'd planned to break the news about Eve's pregnancy. For a moment silence filled the room, then Jenny scrambled to her feet, paper money scattering around her.

"Pop's having a baby?" she asked, gazing cautiously at his stomach.

"No, stupid," Matthew said. "Boys don't have babies. Only girls."

"Is Mom gonna have a baby?"

"Not Mom, stupid. Eve." The implications of that statement seemed to register with Matthew for the first time. He scrambled to his feet, too, staring at Ben in a distraught manner.

"I think I'll go down to the Red Carpet for a beer," Phil remarked to no one in particular, and he made his getaway. Ben felt tempted to go with him. He stood his ground, however, confronting his family.

"I'd like everybody to settle down about this," he said. "It's true that Eve's going to have a baby. Eve and I are going to have a baby,'' he amended. ''But that should be a happy thing. You'll have a new brother or sister.''

Jenny looked disconsolate. Matthew simply looked miserable. Kate looked both disconsolate and miserable. Rachael, who hadn't spoken, suddenly went into action.

''All right, children, upstairs. The three of you. Your father and I will discuss this on our own.''

''But, Mom—'' Kate began to protest.

''I said upstairs. All of you. Now, please.'' Rachael sounded preternaturally calm, in itself a bad sign. When Rachael was this quiet, Ben had the eerie feeling he was caught in the eye of a tornado.

The children seemed to sense the advisability of retreat. The three of them trooped past Ben, averting their gazes. He knew they'd probably hide at the top of the stairs and listen to everything he and Rachael had to say. That couldn't be helped.

As soon as the kids were out of sight, Rachael turned to Ben.

''How could you?'' she demanded, echoing Kate, her expression twisted in pain.

''I didn't intend for the kids to find out this way. Everything snowballed. But now they know about it, and we'll go from there.''

''That's not what I mean! How could you even consider another child? With *her*, of all people.''

Rachael almost made it sound as if they were still married, as if he'd personally betrayed her. The irony of that didn't escape him. He'd been faithful to her all the years they'd been together. She'd never questioned his integrity then, only his devotion to his career. But now that he had a right to be with another woman, Rachael was accusing him.

"What Eve and I do is private," he said. "At least, it should be private. Think about it, Rachael. If you and Phil decided to have a child, I wouldn't have any say in the matter."

"Don't be ludicrous," she snapped. "My having a child with Phil is hardly a possibility. Lately we haven't even—" She broke off abruptly. "Anyway, that's not the issue here. The issue is that our children are just starting to adjust to their new lives. You throw something like this at them, and who knows how far it will set them back. Ben, you have a responsibility to your kids! Doesn't that mean anything to you?"

He knew she wasn't talking about the children this time. She was talking about herself, attempting to make her claim on him.

Suddenly Ben felt weighed down by all the claims being made on him—and the only thing he wanted to do was escape.

CHAPTER NINETEEN

JOSEPHINE SAT in Ben's office, wearing another hat. This one had a large floppy brim and a bright blue ribbon tied around the crown. It made her look like an aging ill-tempered Bo Peep.

"Benjamin, I'd be well in my rights if I decided to file a grievance about you with the state bar, or even the district attorney's office. I'd have an ironclad case, too. You were supposed to sue Eveline Kearny, not breed with the woman!"

Eve was five and a half months along now, and she was showing. Or rather, since everyone knew about the pregnancy, anyway, she'd decided to *let* herself show. She'd abandoned the bulky sweaters for soft dresses that draped her body. To Ben, she'd never looked prettier, the gentle roundness of her body an enticement to him.

Unfortunately, it was an enticement he had to resist. The doctor had strictly forbidden sex for the rest of Eve's pregnancy. When Ben shared her bed these days, gentle caresses of her ripening body were all he could allow himself. It was an exquisite sort of denial.

Ben found himself in a peculiar situation. The child Eve was carrying still didn't seem real to him, yet unquestionably it had already caused endless uproar in his life. Kate, Matthew and Jenny objected to the very idea of a potential rival. Rachael took the baby as a personal affront.

And Eve . . . Eve still hadn't forgiven him for not wanting this child.

But even with all the turmoil, the baby simply didn't seem a reality. Ben couldn't picture it as part of his life, no matter how hard he tried. Of course, that was what Eve couldn't forgive.

"Benjamin," said Josephine sternly, "you don't seem to be listening. I have every right to report you to the state bar. You're my attorney, but instead of prosecuting my case to the fullest, you've—"

"I know, I know. I've bred with the defendant. Guilty as charged, Josephine. I'm impressed by your grasp of the law."

She tilted her chin proudly under the hat. "I know what's what. After all, I worked at Duke City Insurance for thirty years. I practically ran that office, Benjamin."

More likely she'd terrorized the office. Josephine had mentioned her career a few times before, and now it gave Ben an idea. Not a very pleasant idea, to be sure, but it might just do the trick. At this point, he was willing to be creative in order to solve his problems with Josephine.

Ben squared his shoulders. "How'd you like a job?" he asked.

"A job," she echoed suspiciously.

Ben nodded. He had to find some way to reconcile the situation with Josephine. Besides, the old lady got to him. She was cantankerous and difficult in the extreme—but she was also lonely and badly in need of something to occupy her mind besides lawsuits against cats.

"That's right, a job. I could take you on part-time. You'd be doing some legal research for me—preparation for taking cases to trial, that sort of thing."

"There's one small detail you seem to be overlooking. You don't have any clients except for me."

"Josephine, it's precisely that type of astute observation I could use in my law practice."

"Don't try to be smart with me, Benjamin. What's the catch? You're not offering me a job out of the kindness of your heart."

Sometimes he almost enjoyed sparring with the old woman. "The catch is that you drop all complaints against me, Eve and Eve's cat. Seems like a fair trade. We'll all get along for once, and you'll embark on an exciting legal career."

"Hah. I don't like any of this. I don't like it one bit." The brim of Josephine's hat bobbed as she shook her head. "You can't get around me this way, Benjamin. You can't buy me off!"

After she'd stalked out of his office, Ben supposed he should be relieved. One thing was certain, though; in another lifetime, Josephine might have made a fine litigator. She was adversarial by nature, and she was also a nitpicker—a winning combination.

Ben faced his blank computer screen. Technically, he did have one other client besides Josephine—yesterday he'd advised a man on estate planning. But Ben knew he couldn't go on like this. It wasn't a matter of money. After all his years as a corporate attorney, his financial situation allowed him plenty of time for a breather. But he didn't want a breather. He was a lawyer at heart, and he needed to practice law. How the hell could he do that in Cobb, New Mexico?

He heard the blast of a trumpet from outside—or rather, he heard the bleat of a trumpet. The Cobb High School marching band was not known for its musical ability. Today was Saint Patrick's, and the way Ben understood it, the marching band formed a significant part of the town's celebratory parade.

Ben went out to catch a glimpse of the festivities. All up and down Central, townspeople gathered for the event. Children sat on the curb, parents pushed baby strollers into line for the best viewing position, and teenagers lingered in small clumps, trying to look bored.

Kate wasn't among the teenagers, Ben noticed, although he and Rachael were gradually allowing their daughter more freedom, hoping she would find new friends. Outings with her "scruffy" associates were forbidden, yet even these friends were allowed to visit Kate at home. And Ben had grudgingly agreed that David Flanders could also visit Kate—under supervision. There was just a slight hitch. David Flanders had not yet availed himself of the opportunity. Neither had he attempted to telephone. Kate, of course, didn't blame David for this oversight. Instead, she blamed her parents for misunderstanding the boy—that is, not allowing him the opportunity to exercise his hormones to the fullest.

Ben clenched his fists. He found the idea of that kid having sex with his daughter intolerable. So, instead, he concentrated his rage on the boy's goatee. What was with the goatee, anyway? A full-fledged beard, Ben could understand. He could also understand clean-shaven. Either way, a definite choice was being made, a stand taken on the issue of facial hair. But a goatee—that was somewhere in between, a sort of no-man's land. Ben was starting to hate goatees.

Ben could feel his blood pressure rising, and he tried to think of something else. The Cobb High School band was marching slowly past him, white uniforms looking just a little smudged and timeworn. Green crepe-paper streamers fluttered in the warm spring air, and then came the rest of the parade: a few vintage cars noisily honking their horns, the passengers tossing candy from their windows;

a small float bearing the princess of St. Patrick's, re-
splendent in a green velvet gown; the town's junior base-
ball team strutting along, caps planted at rakish angles on
their heads. The team pitched candy at spectators with
enthusiasm, and peppermints came hurtling at Ben like so
many fastballs.

Ben grinned reluctantly. These kids were about Matthew's age. As a matter of fact, why hadn't Matthew
joined the team? Okay, he was small, but he was a good
athlete. Ben would have to look into this. In too many
ways, his family was holding back from full involvement
in the town. He was guilty of that himself.

Ben glanced up and down the street. Rachael had said
she'd bring the children out to watch the parade, but so
far Ben hadn't seen any sign of them. Already the event
was petering out, and if they didn't hurry, they were going to miss it.

A few kids pulled by dogs on leashes went scurrying by,
forming part of the parade for no discernible reason. Then
along came the Cobb Police Department, a couple of guys
mounted on stocky horses that seemed better suited to
plowing than galloping after criminals.

And that was it. End of parade. Just when it had started
to build up steam, it was over, leaving Ben with a feeling
of dissatisfaction. He wished Eve was here with him. But
she and her fellow teachers planned to watch as the parade wound its way past the community college for a
grande finale; meanwhile, Ben and Eve had agreed he
would share Saint Patrick's Day with his children.

Yet Ben's kids hadn't made it, after all. It was as if the
two parts of Ben's life canceled each other out—no kids,
no Eve.

He went back into his office where, a short time later, Rachael and the children did arrive, all of them looking breathless and out of sorts.

"Where is it?" Rachael demanded. "Where's the parade?"

"You missed it."

"How could we possibly miss it? We drove up Central. There's only one major street in the whole damn town."

"It's over," Ben informed them.

Kate slouched off to a corner by herself, but everyone else stared at Ben accusingly, as if somehow he had let them down. Matthew, Jonny, even Rachael.

It was a relief when Ben's telephone rang. He hoped it was Eve, but instead, he heard the raspy voice of Samuel Wexter, senior partner of Wexter, Hollis and Greene, calling all the way from Boston. Sam was not only his former associate, but also his mentor.

"Ben, hope I haven't caught you at a bad time," Sam said as if fully confident it wasn't a bad time. "I have a favor to ask. We're finally working on that merger for Carlisle Labs. The thing is, Carlisle keeps insisting you're the only one he can talk to about it. Think you can fly out here for a few days? We really need you." There was no question in Sam's voice. He stated the problem as if to do so were merely a formality, as if he already expected Ben to be on a plane headed for Boston.

Ben, however, could think of a dozen reasons to turn Sam down. He was no longer a partner in Wexter, Hollis and Greene. He'd started a new life for himself. He missed the old life too much; returning, even for a few days, would be a mistake. It would remind him of everything he'd given up. More importantly, he didn't know if he should go that far away from Eve right now. The doctor had allowed her to continue with her teaching duties, but the pregnancy was undeniably a fragile one. Anything could go wrong at any time. He needed to be close by.

Then he glanced up and saw his family still watching him. Rachael had narrowed her eyes, obviously speculating about who might be on the other end of the telephone line. Matthew and Jenny gazed at him as if they were still expecting a parade to materialize from his pockets. Kate refused to look at him at all, but even her rigidly held back seemed to make some obscure demand of him.

Suddenly he knew that he had to get away from all of them—Rachael, Kate, Matthew, Jenny. And, if he was completely honest, he'd acknowledge that he needed to get away from Eve for a little while, too. This last thought bothered him, but it was the truth.

"I'll book a flight as soon as possible," he finally said. "I'll be there, Sam."

To Ben, it always seemed that Boston managed to combine a hectic pace with a reflective outlook on the world. Downtown, businessmen strode along in their dark suits, briefcases slapping against their legs. Businesswomen rushed by wearing socks and athletic shoes with their subdued jackets and skirts. Later, in their offices, the women would exchange their comfortable footwear for shoes with heels, but they'd still keep moving fast.

Yet, in spite of the hurried pace, the city itself afforded a sense of timelessness. Shadowed by modern skyscrapers were the historic bookstores, apothecaries and meetinghouses of weathered stone and wood. In a place where you could stumble upon a graveyard more than three hundred years old, not to get a little philosophical now and then was difficult. It could make you slow down, for a moment, anyway, before you hurried on again toward the skyscrapers.

Ben enjoyed the combination. Hell, he enjoyed everything about being back. He liked walking through the plushly carpeted corridors of Wexter, Hollis and Greene, hearing the greetings that were called out in casual welcome.

"Ben, glad to see you back."

"Mr. Lawrence, what a pleasant surprise."

"Ben, we'll hit the racquetball court tonight."

He liked feeling that he hadn't been gone at all, that his place was here for him, waiting. He liked the endless intense meetings, the coffee consumed by the quart, sandwiches and doughnuts brought in at odd hours. He liked the way high-strung Rob Carlisle looked to him for advice. He'd forgotten the sense of power that being a real lawyer could give. It was like adrenaline pumping through him, and he wondered how he'd existed without it.

Late his first evening in Boston, he pounded up and down a racquetball court, and he wondered how he'd lived without this, too. The sport allowed him a release of aggression that running didn't permit. He lost a game, then won two in a row.

He arrived back at his hotel room, drenched in a healthy sweat. All day long, he'd made an effort not to think about Eve. It hadn't been easy, because he had a tendency to compare her to every woman he saw. He'd note that Eve would never wear a drab business suit; she chose colorful vests and flowing skirts. Her skin was creamier, her hair brighter than any woman's he saw....

Now he didn't even stop to shower or clean up. He sat down and dialed Eve's home number.

"Hello." Her tone was reserved, even though she'd answered on the first ring.

"It's me," he said. "I miss you."

She allowed just the slightest hesitation. "I miss you, too."

"How are you feeling?"

"I'm fine. Really, I am. I told you that you didn't need to worry about taking this trip."

"Yeah, but I still miss you."

"You already told me that." Her tone was lighter now.

"Eve, I needed some time away. From everything. But I wish I was holding you in my arms right now."

"I wish the same thing. But maybe we both needed a time-out."

He paused. He didn't like thinking about Eve needing time away from him, too.

"How are your classes going?" he finally asked.

"As well as can be expected. My students are still afraid to mention my pregnancy. I think they're concerned about embarrassing me. But Professor Halford is just the opposite. He won't stop pampering me. Today he brought in a cushion for my back and told me all about his daughter's three pregnancies." She spoke quickly, as if reluctant to allow any silences to creep into the conversation. "How did your meetings go today?"

"Not bad. Although Carlisle's such a nervous person I can't figure out how he got to be a multimillionaire."

"He relies on good lawyers like you, that's how."

They spoke a little while longer, and it was Eve who neatly ended the conversation.

"It's two hours later there, Ben. Get some sleep. I have a feeling tomorrow's a big day for you."

"Good night, Eve."

"Good night."

After they hung up, Ben pondered the fact that he and Eve were careful not to share endearments. It was always just "good night," never "good night, dear," or "good night, darling." It was one more way of keeping a space between them.

Ben didn't enjoy his next two days in Boston nearly as much as the first. The negotiations for Carlisle Labs proceeded as smoothly as could be expected, and that was satisfying, but somehow Ben was losing that sense of rightness about Boston. He felt as if he'd come back here and slipped into a familiar suit of clothes, only to gradually realize that the suit didn't fit anymore. His satisfaction faded.

Take Rob Carlisle, for instance. At first it was flattering to have the multimillionaire turn to Ben so assiduously for counsel. It was flattering to think that Carlisle had actually required Ben's presence. But what, really, made Rob so different from cantankerous old Josephine Scott? In the end, both were self-centered fussbudgets.

All the years Ben had worked as a corporate lawyer in Boston, he'd been convinced he was doing something important. Even when he'd given it up for his kids' sake, he'd felt what he was relinquishing was special. It was damn unsettling now to wonder about the contribution he'd really made all those years. What was happening to him?

And then it began to bother him like hell that he didn't feel he belonged in Boston anymore. Was he just missing Eve? He tried to imagine a different scenario. What if he could transplant Eve to Boston and stay here with her? How would he feel then?

He couldn't imagine it. There was so much distance between them that had nothing to do with the miles from here to New Mexico. He didn't know where he belonged with Eve.

On his third day in Boston, his last meeting wrapped up earlier than expected. He declined a racquetball game with one of his former partners and walked to the Common.

It was early evening. The park rolled gently before him, new grass already heralding spring. Ben wandered on and glanced across the street toward the public gardens. A memory came back to him of a time when Kate had been small and he'd taken her for a ride on one of the swan boats that plied the lagoon.

It had been one of those unblemished afternoons when everything had been just right: the balmy weather, the relaxed mood, the easy companionship he'd shared with his daughter. After that, however, it had seemed he was always too busy to try repeating the experience. What had stopped him? Perhaps simply his absorption in his career, or the conviction that perfect days didn't come along too often. Whatever the reason, he'd let too many opportunities for closeness slip away.

With Eve, he had another chance. The realization came to him quietly, without fanfare. All this time, he'd essentially blamed her for the distance between them, but wasn't he the one who'd been holding back most of all? He had his excuses, perhaps. He'd failed with one family, and he didn't want to fail with another. But he had to take a risk before it was too late. Perfect times didn't just happen; he had to make them happen. Forget his damn career. Forget everything else. All he wanted right now was Eve.

Ben turned and walked back to his hotel. First he called the airline. Then he called Sam Wexter to say he couldn't stay an extra day in Boston, after all.

He was going home to Eve.

CHAPTER TWENTY

"I LOVE YOU."

It was the second time Ben had said the words, but they didn't seem to be registering with Eve. She and Ben lay together in her narrow bed. Between the two of them and Eve's stomach, there wasn't much room, yet they were managing. Perhaps the doctor had forbidden sex, but that didn't mean they couldn't indulge in a healthy bout of cuddling. Nestling against Ben, Eve had turned her face so that he couldn't see her expression, but he felt the rigidity in her limbs.

He said the words again. "I love you, Eve." The phrase had a certain ring, and he liked repeating it. Too bad it didn't produce the same effect on Eve.

"Dammit, Ben," she mumbled against his chest. "Things are just too complicated for you to talk about love all of a sudden."

"What's so complicated?" His hand rested on the swell of her stomach. She was wearing her flannel nightshirt again, the fabric soft and sexy, heated by her body. Still, he wanted nothing more than to peel the nightshirt from her and caress her skin, but he could tell this wasn't the time. Tonight he needed to lure Eve with words.

"Everything's too complicated," she said now. "The situation with Kate, your ex-wife..."

"They're not in the room with us. No one's here but you and me," he reminded her.

She sighed. "You never said anything before about loving me. What's different now?"

He smiled, filled with an incredible sense of well-being. "Nothing's different. I've loved you since the minute I first saw you with your button undone. I wanted to undo the rest of your buttons."

"That's lust, not love," she protested.

"I'd say it's been a generous amount of each right from the start." He leaned over and kissed the hollow of her throat. As always, her warm feminine scent enveloped him. Never had he felt so certain of anything as this: the rightness of being here with Eve. Maybe she needed a little convincing, but he had time. He wasn't going anywhere.

"Ben . . . there's one thing you can't deny. You don't want this baby."

Slowly he moved his hand over her stomach, claiming the child she carried. "For a long time I didn't want it," he conceded. "I'd been feeling flat-out inadequate about my first three kids, and another one . . . I wasn't looking forward to feeling inadequate all over again. But that's changed."

"People don't just change. It doesn't work that way." Now the light from her bedside lamp spilled over her face, giving her pale skin a golden cast. She looked lovely and solemn, all her efforts concentrated on disproving his love for her.

"I've changed," he murmured. "I still feel inadequate about being a father, but I want our baby, Eve. I want it because it's yours and mine, and because it gives me a chance to start over again. I can make all sorts of new mistakes this time."

"Maybe you won't have the chance. You know how unstable this pregnancy is." Her voice had tightened and she drew her eyebrows together as if in pain. "You know too much about raising children, Ben. I know too much about losing them."

"I thought the doctor said things are going much better than expected."

"Sure, things are going well—for now." She sounded convinced that if she let her guard down for even a second, she'd lose the baby. Ben traced her eyebrows with a finger, trying to massage the tension away. But as soon as he removed his hand, lines etched their way into her forehead again.

"I love you" was all he could tell her.

"Oh, Ben..." She clung to him, her grip surprisingly strong. "Just be here with me, please. Don't say anything more."

He drew her as close to him as he could, their feet tangling in the sheets, while the lamplight cascaded over them. And Ben held Eve with his own fierceness, as if he alone could protect her and the baby from harm.

IT WAS TOO GOOD to be true. She was well into her sixth month now, and still the doctor said that everything was going well.

"The suture's holding," he'd told Eve on her last visit. "I want you walking as little as possible, but you can teach your classes as long as you do so sitting down."

"What's wrong?" she'd insisted. "Something has to be wrong!"

"Everything's holding," Dr. Cole had answered patiently, but even that choice of words filled her with vague dread. Everything's holding. It made her sound like a dam capable of crumbling at any time.

When Ben drove her back and forth from her weekly appointments with the doctor, he always told her that he loved her. For almost a month now, he'd been repeating those words like an incantation to banish her fears: I love you, Eve. I love you.

She loved him in return. Oh, damn, she loved him from the deepest part of her soul, but she just didn't know how to tell him. If she said the words out loud, she feared her emotions would simply break loose, and she'd be lost after that. Truly lost.

Eve gave a weary sigh, forcing herself to concentrate on the work at hand. She sat in her office, her back supported by a cushion in one chair, her legs propped up by a cushion in another, reading the letters Silas T. Cobb had sent to his first wife, Marianna, more than a hundred years ago.

Silas had written from New York City, where he had been busy trying to raise funds for his little utopia—his namesake, the town of Cobb, New Mexico. He'd envisioned the town as a cooperative venture where high-minded individuals would share their goods, and so he'd gone off to New York, seeking high-minded investors. When he wrote to Marianna, he didn't speak of missing her. He spoke only of his own ideas. It made Eve sad, picturing his wife struggling by herself, trying to make a reality of her husband's dreams—trying to feed her four children.

Ben was a very different man than Silas T. Cobb. When Ben had gone off to Boston, he'd called her every night. And he had rushed home to her, sweeping her into his arms, and telling her that he loved her.

She was very lucky and she knew it. Countless times a day she would stop whatever she was doing and examine the amazing knowledge that Ben Lawrence loved her. He loved her, and he wasn't afraid to tell her so. She was the one who was afraid.

The yellowed page in Eve's hand was so fragile it threatened to tear. She placed it back in the box with the other letters. Already she knew how she wanted to fashion her biography of Silas, how she wanted to capture the fact that he'd been a visionary even as a boy. It consoled her, having this project to work on, knowing where she was headed with it. This was something she could foretell, shape to her own will. So unlike her pregnancy.

The shadows of dusk were gathering as Ben appeared in the doorway. Even in the dim light she could sense that he was full of energy, his movements purposeful and sure as he came to kiss her.

"Tonight we're celebrating," he announced.

"What's the occasion?"

"You'll have to come with me and find out." He was smiling.

"Ben, is it about your career? Have you made a decision about what you want to do?" These past few weeks he'd been brimming with new ideas, as if somehow his trip to Boston had released him from mourning his old career.

"I'm looking into a few interesting possibilities, but that's not why we're celebrating."

"Tell me, then," she urged. "I'm no good at surprises."

"You'll see," was all he'd say. He helped her up. She went outside with him, stepping gingerly as he supported her arm. Nowadays, she walked only when absolutely necessary, reclining on cushions most of the time. It made her feel rather like a plump partridge settled down to nest

Ben assisted her into the Jeep and then headed out of town. She didn't realize where they were going until he turned in at the drive-in theater. It was too early in the evening for the movie to be showing yet, and they were the only people here. Ben paid the admission, anyway, and parked in the middle of a row of speakers. He turned to her.

"I figure this is our place," he said, his tone so serious that at first she didn't realize he was teasing her. The memories of that first night were still branded vividly in her mind, and even now she almost expected to see curious faces peering in the windows.

"I hope you're not expecting a repeat performance," she said dryly, clasping her hands over her stomach. "I'm not very agile at the moment."

"I think we can confine ourselves to the front seat for what I have in mind." He reached into his pocket and brought out a small velvet jewelry box. With a self-conscious flourish, he opened the box and held it out to her.

Inside sparkled a ring: a lovely diamond set in white gold. Eve stared at it with a mixture of dismay and wonderment.

"Ben . . . no. Don't do this."

"Marry me, Eve. Don't think about it. Just put on the ring and say you'll marry me."

She refused even to touch the jewelry box. It took a great effort to keep her voice from shaking as she spoke. "I thought we already discussed this. I told you I couldn't even consider marriage, not with everything so up in the air right now."

He moved closer to her, not an easy task with the gearshift knob in the way. The darkness of night had thickened around the Jeep, and she couldn't read his expression. She could, however, hear the intensity in his words.

"Eve, just listen to me. Everything's up in the air for me, too. My ex-wife suddenly thinks I'm the solution to all her problems, Kate talks to me less than ever, I still don't know what I'll do about my career—but none of that changes the fact that I want to marry you. I need to marry you. Nothing else matters."

Eve's hands tightened on her stomach. "The baby matters. Oh, I can't possibly marry you now, Ben! If something goes wrong with...with this pregnancy, marriage is the last thing we should be concerned about."

"If something goes wrong, I want us to be married so we can deal with it together. Like a real couple. I'm not your ex-husband, Eve. I'm not going to abandon you."

"Ted didn't abandon me. Not intentionally. He tried his best—"

"Don't make him out to be a saint," Ben said harshly. "The guy wasn't strong enough. But you and I, Eve, we can be strong, whatever happens next."

Part of her yearned desperately to trust him. But another part of her demanded with equal desperation that she hold back. "If we could just wait until it's all over. Until we...know the outcome. Then we can talk about marriage."

"I see." Ben's tone hardened. "You want to make our relationship conditional. If the baby's fine, you'll marry me. If there's another tragedy, well, what then, Eve? Will you say goodbye to me just because you're convinced I'm as big a coward as your ex-husband?"

"No," she whispered. "It's not like that."

"It's exactly like that. Dammit, I know how it feels to be afraid of taking risks. You were right when you told me I didn't want to start a new family. I didn't like the idea of being a failure again. I don't like to fail. Maybe that's my worst fear. But I'm finally facing it, and that feels damn good. I want you, and I want our child."

She knew her own worst fear. She had two, to be exact: the baby wouldn't make it, and Ben would leave her—in that order. He talked about love and strength, but he didn't know what an ordeal losing a baby could be. There was no way to know what that was like unless you went through it yourself. You were shattered, and your relationship was shattered, no matter how strong the two of you thought you were.

She needed to explain all this to Ben, but she could tell he didn't want to hear any more. He took the ring from its box, smoothed out the clenched fingers of her left hand and slipped it on.

"Does it fit?" he asked.

It was a little snug, yet she didn't want to tell him that. "It's perfect, but that's not the point. I can't wear it."

"Hell, Eve, you won't even consider being engaged to me? Our baby will come into the world, and we won't make even one promise to each other?"

"All I can say is . . . I love you." The words slipped out before she was prepared for them. They made a promise she hadn't been ready to give. But it was too late to take them back. The words didn't destroy her, didn't sweep her out of control, as she had believed they would. Instead, they left her with a deep aching melancholy, a knowledge that Ben had spoken the truth. He was right. No matter how much she cared for him, she needed to put conditions on their relationship. She could take only one small uncertain step at a time with him.

"I've loved you for such a long time," she said, her voice dropping back to a whisper. "Maybe since the day I first saw you and my blouse came unbuttoned. I always come unbuttoned around you, one way or another. But I can't marry you, Ben. Not now. Not yet."

He didn't say anything. He didn't need to speak. His disappointment and bewilderment were almost palpable. By now darkness had completely fallen, and a few other cars had arrived. Summer was the real time for drive-in movies, but some people seemed to feel that any season was appropriate for such an outing. Ben and Eve took things a bit further; for them it was a place to make love, make a baby, propose marriage....

The previews came on, and then the movie itself. It was strange to watch shapes flickering on the large screen without any sound to go along, but Ben hadn't bothered with the speaker tonight. When he and Eve came to the drive-in, they didn't pay any attention to the movie.

Eve felt a jolt and gave a slight gasp.

"Anything wrong?" Ben asked immediately, and she realized that both of them were on alert when it came to this pregnancy.

"The baby moved," she said in wonderment. "I'm always caught by surprise when that happens."

Ben placed his hand over her abdomen.

"I feel it, too," he said excitedly. "Just a quiver of movement, but it's there."

They waited for the baby to kick again, and only gradually did Eve remember she was still wearing Ben's ring. In no manner did she consider herself engaged to him, but she didn't have the heart to take it off. She left it right where it was, snugly fitted on the third finger of her left hand, glinting against the darkness of this cool April night.

AT LAST BEN HAD a reason to use his computer. He placed the keyboard in front of him and began typing in the prospectus for a new business venture: Lawrence Consultants, Incorporated. He liked the sound of that. Simple, but authoritative.

It was an idea that had been nudging at him for some time now. He knew he wanted to remain a corporate lawyer, but he needed a fresh direction. He liked the possibility of working with small businesses, helping them to get off the ground and expand. If he could interest a few other lawyers in a partnership, he might just have something.

The venture would need to be based in Albuquerque, near potential clients, and that was the only drawback to his plan. He'd moved here to be with his kids. How could he relocate to Albuquerque? He'd already discovered that an hour and a half each way was one hell of a commute.

Ben tapped a few more keys, considering. All right, he definitely needed partners. One of them could be in charge of the main office in Albuquerque, while Ben could work out of Cobb. He'd get a lot of use from his fax machine, that was for sure. Still, with some major juggling and compromise, it could be done. It wouldn't be a perfect solution, but he'd be working again. And he'd be near his kids, whatever that was worth.

Ben read over what he'd typed, then printed it out. This whole business idea was still only on paper, but it gave him a sense of purpose he'd been missing. He just wished he felt this positive about his relationship with his children. He was trying as hard as he could to be the best father possible, but all three of them continued to resist him— even Matthew.

It almost seemed as if each one of his kids were locked in a separate world, forbidding communication from the outside: Kate having sex at such an early age, refusing to gauge the consequences; Matthew still doggedly harboring the belief that someday Rachael and Ben would reunite; once-intrepid Jenny beginning to shrink inside herself. Maybe his kids needed a psychologist, not a dad.

Discouragement washed over Ben whenever he thought about his kids. All in all, there probably couldn't be a worse time for him to ask Eve to marry him; his personal life was more a disaster than ever. Yet somehow that didn't seem to matter. He loved Eve. Hell, he was crazy about her—crazy in love, when it came right down to it.

The corny phrase pleased him and lightened his mood. For seven days in a row, he'd been proposing to Eve. He'd started out at the drive-in theater and gone on from there. His strategy consisted of sheer repetition. Sooner or later, he figured he'd wear Eve down with his persistence. And so far she'd given him one encouraging sign, at least. She hadn't taken off his engagement ring since the night he'd slipped it onto her finger. In his more positive moments, he told himself that he and Eve were actually engaged. Didn't the ring prove it?

Now the outer door of his office swung open and in marched Josephine Scott. She was back to sporting the hat that looked like an overturned bowl of fruit, but she'd added a new touch to her ensemble—pristine white cotton gloves. She'd never dressed up quite this much before, and it made Ben wary.

"Josephine. What can I do for you?"

She arranged herself importantly in the chair in front of his desk. "It's a disgrace, Benjamin. You're still spending every night at Miss Kearny's house! Don't think I don't see."

"It's a good thing I have you to keep track of me, Josie."

"Don't get smart. I'm here to negotiate."

Ben gave her his version of an encouraging smile. "Have you decided to drop your suit against Eve's cat?"

Josie sat very straight, her back not even touching the chair. "You offered me a job, Benjamin. I've decided to accept your offer, provided certain conditions are met."

Lord, he'd almost forgotten. He'd been so relieved when she'd turned him down, he'd never thought about her changing her mind.

"What would those conditions be?" he asked, managing to sound neutral.

Josie pursed her thin lips, as if considering her words carefully before speaking. "I know what you're up to, Benjamin. You want to give me a job where I'll be buried behind a pile of books somewhere. Research, you call it. Busy work, *I* call it. You're just throwing me an old bone—and hoping the old bag of bones will snatch it up and be quiet for once." Josie grinned mirthlessly at her own humor. Ben had to admit she'd pegged his intentions.

"In spite of that, you still want the job?" he asked.

"I want a real job. You need a secretary, Benjamin. Someone to answer the telephone, take dictation, organize the place." Josie's gaze focused on his file cabinets, as if she couldn't wait to root around inside them. She sounded like someone who'd seen too many of those 1940s movies where the snappy secretary manages the office and everyone in it. Ben winced at the thought.

"Let's be realistic," he said. "How long has it been since you worked?"

"Benjamin, I was a secretary at Duke City Insurance for thirty years. I only stopped because they made me retire. I know the job."

He pictured a younger Josie, terrorizing an entire office staff and relishing every minute of it. She must have felt a real letdown when she'd been forced into retirement. Obviously she hadn't known what to do with all her free time except peer out her window at the rest of the world. She must be at least seventy years old now, not the age where she could just go out and expect to find another job, particularly in this backwater town.

Ben had actually begun to feel sorry for Josie. She sat there with such pride, a shriveled ill-tempered old lady. Only a flicker of her eyes now and then indicated she'd just made a bid for something important to her. Damn. He was really turning into a soft touch.

He pushed the phone toward her and lifted the receiver. "Show me your telephone style," he said. "Pretend someone called, and you're answering on behalf of Lawrence Consultants, Incorporated."

"What type of silly game is this?"

"Just do it, Josie. This is a job interview I'm conducting here, you know."

She pursed her lips again, but at last she addressed the receiver. "Good morning," she growled. "Lawrence Consultants, Incorporated. How may I help you?"

"Not bad. But could you make it sound like you don't want to bite the caller's head off?"

Josephine plunked the phone receiver back into place. "You made me an offer, and I'm accepting it. You hire me as your secretary, and I'll drop all charges against Miss Kearny."

"Do you know how to use a computer, Josie?"

"Certainly not. A dependable typewriter was good enough for me."

Ben envisioned her presiding over an ornate old-fashioned typewriter. With her straw hat and white gloves, she belonged in a Norman Rockwell painting, not a modern office.

But she wanted the job, that much was clear. She wanted it a lot. She clutched the purse in her lap, trying to look unconcerned while she waited for Ben's answer. Ben wondered how many times Josephine had actually gone after something she wanted, instead of merely peering out her window. Well, she was going after this now, and that counted for something.

"You start Monday morning," he said. "But I can only use you part-time, at least until business picks up."

Josephine gave him a feisty glance. "You're losing me as a client, Benjamin. You'd better get right to work finding another." On her way out the door, she turned to glance at him again, the tuft of flowers on her hat bobbing a little. "And you really ought to marry Miss Kearny, Ben. Marry her before that baby pops out."

"Josie, that's one piece of advice I wish I could take. Believe me."

CHAPTER TWENTY-ONE

THE STRONGEST BEVERAGE they served at the Rio Diner was coffee that tasted as if it had been boiled for nine hours. Ben settled for a cup, anyway, opening a menu as he waited for his ex-wife to appear.

It was Monday, and Rachael had asked to meet him for lunch. She arrived a few minutes late, as if to prove to Ben that meeting him was an inconvenience, even though lately she'd been the one who suggested all their encounters. He'd been trying to pull back from her a little, showing her that he couldn't be involved in her problems beyond the ones that had to do with his children.

Rachael ordered the tomato soup. Ben ordered a cheeseburger, allowed Rachael to have her say on the perils of red meat and then turned the subject to Kate.

"I'm more concerned about her than ever," he said. "She's so withdrawn."

"Part of that's to be expected. Think about it, Ben. That Flanders boy hasn't even tried to call her once. Her heart's broken."

"Let's not get too melodramatic about it."

"Well, it's the truth," Rachael said. "Everything's so much more intense when you're a teenager. She thought she was in love with David, and maybe she really was."

"Great. And she blames us for keeping him away."

Rachael stared broodingly at the jar of sugar on the table. "Deep down, she blames David for not loving her. And she blames herself for not being lovable enough."

"Kate's only fifteen," he said. "Let's keep this in perspective, all right? It's not the love story of the century."

"I think you could be closer to Kate if you'd take her problems a little more seriously."

"I take it damn seriously that my daughter had sex," he muttered. "And I take it seriously that she's retreated into that shell of hers. She's not even talking to Eve anymore."

"Kate is *my* daughter. She doesn't need Eve Kearny." Rachael paused as the waitress put their dishes down on the table with a clatter, then started in again.

"You know, Ben, you just have to realize that Eve is never going to fit into our lives. You keep trying to make her fit, but it doesn't work. Even Kate can see that. It's a good thing she's stopped confiding in that woman. It never led to anything good."

Rachael's condescending tone irritated the hell out of Ben. "I've asked Eve to marry me," he said. "Of course she's part of my life. Hell, she *is* my life."

Rachael picked up her spoon, only to set it down again. She stared at Ben. "You make it sound as if you put Eve before your own children."

"In a way, I have to do that. The kids need to know that Eve and I are united, and that nothing can come between us." Even as he spoke, he acknowledged to himself that he and Eve were having problems on that score. They still weren't a real couple yet. But it was a mistake to share too much of this with Rachael, who continued to stare at him as if he'd personally betrayed her.

"I can't believe you're saying any of this. You came all the way to New Mexico to be near the kids, and now you're telling me that Eve Kearny comes first. What happened to all your devotion to fatherhood?''

"That hasn't changed. I'm just as committed as ever to being a father.''

"For your *new* child, perhaps,'' Rachael said bitterly. "When it comes to our children...from the beginning, you've never given them what they truly needed.''

The food in front of them grew cold. Ben knew that Rachael was referring to herself as much as to the kids. She was accusing him of never being the husband she'd needed. He wondered if anyone could be the husband Rachael needed—a man perpetually willing to cosset her through her moods.

Ben stared out the window. There were no decorations up today; with Easter already past, the diner seemed to have run out of holidays for the moment. It made Ben feel dissatisfied.

"I think I should tell you something,'' Rachael said, her voice oddly clipped. "It's very possible Phil and I will be getting a divorce. We're already talking about a separation.''

He swiveled his head back toward Rachael; she had his full attention now. "Isn't there something you can do to work things out?''

"I don't know why you should act so concerned. You've never liked Phil.''

"Maybe not, but I've always wanted you to be happy with him,'' Ben said gruffly. "I've wanted the kids to be happy. Do you realize what a disruption this will be for them? They had to go through our divorce, and now this.''

"The children will be better off,'' Rachael asserted. "Phil and I aren't happy, and the kids know it.''

Ben studied his ex-wife closely. This was one of those times when she seemed unnaturally calm. That disturbed him, and so did her words. He'd never pictured Rachael and Phil separating. Surely that wasn't the solution.

"Rachael, have you considered going to see a marriage counselor? You and Phil, hell, you have a lot of things in common. You both like small towns, and..." He couldn't think of anything else, but he was trying. He experienced an unfamiliar flash of sympathy for Phil, the bachelor who'd gone back East and found more than he'd bargained for in a bride.

"I'm not so sure I do like small towns anymore," Rachael said. "The truth is, I've idealized them all my life. When you actually live in one, the reality is quite different. I'm seriously considering moving back to Boston with the kids. It will be too awkward to stay here and keep bumping into Phil."

Ben felt stunned. Rachael seemed to be measuring the effect of her words; she gazed at him with an expression that could almost be called gloating.

"You see, Ben, you should have stayed in Boston all along. But it's not too late for you to go back, too."

"It is too late," he said, struggling to control his anger. "I have a real life here now. I'm starting a business. Hell, I've even hired a secretary." Never mind that his business existed only on paper and that his secretary was a cranky seventy-year-old woman guaranteed to make him miserable. Never mind any of that. "The most important thing of all is my relationship with Eve. I'm committed to her, and that's exactly what I want."

"So you can stay here with her. Fine. I just know that *I* made a mistake when I married Phil Marcus. I'm going to reverse it. If you were smart, Ben, you wouldn't make a mistake of your own."

"What I have with Eve isn't a mistake," he said quietly. "Maybe what you have with Phil isn't one, either. Give him another chance."

"That's right—I forgot. You think *you're* some almighty marriage counselor. But stick to lawyering, Ben. There's nothing you can do about this." She gazed at him triumphantly. "If I take the children back to Boston—there's nothing you can do."

IT BEGAN as a deceptively ordinary visit to the doctor's office. Eve was well into her sixth month now, and the doctor proclaimed cheerfully that everything was fine.

"Continue staying off your feet as much as possible," Dr. Cole told her. "Otherwise, I think we're looking at the home stretch here."

As usual, none of this reassured Eve in the least. She felt like someone walking a tightrope high above the ground, no safety net to catch her. So far, so good, but one false move, one misstep, and she'd go plummeting downward.

As Eve and Ben headed home in his Jeep, she gazed at the mesa spread out before her, where scrubby piñon trees had managed to take root in parched earth. Far beyond she could see in striking contrast a lush stand of cottonwoods that flourished along the Rio Grande. She felt parched herself, the luxuriousness of the river valley seeming only a mirage. Why couldn't she believe Dr. Cole? And why couldn't she believe Ben's own reassurances that everything would be fine from now on?

She thought about the time she'd just spent with Ben at the doctor's office. She thought about his way of quietly, efficiently taking charge of things, his commanding presence that garnered respect from doctor and nurse alike. Ben had involved himself in this pregnancy—that was the thing. He was always asking questions about it, trying to figure it out. Trying to be a part of it, as much as possible.

The last time around, with Ted, it hadn't been that way. Her ex-husband had withdrawn from the pregnancy even before its tragic end. Ted had never accompanied her to the doctor, had never asked questions. He'd never comforted Eve when she'd needed it most.

At last Eve understood. After the divorce, she'd seen Ted only through the confused, blurred images of her own grief and heartache. Her vision had been distorted. But today, for the first time, she dared to see her ex-husband clearly. Sitting here beside Ben, she had the courage to examine her memories of Ted with a cold calculating eye. She compared her ex-husband to Ben and found him lacking in every respect.

"Damn Ted," she said all at once. "Damn him. Do you know something? He married again only a few months after our divorce was final. His wife got pregnant right away, and now they have a daughter who's almost a year and a half old. What did he need to do—prove that he could reproduce, after all? Did he need to prove that I hadn't completely threatened his masculinity? Damn him!" Suddenly there was nothing cool about her memories. The words burned in her throat, but she couldn't keep them bottled up any longer.

Ben seemed to sense the momentousness of this occasion. It was, after all, the first time she'd ever complained about her ex-husband to him, and she was throwing in a few curses for good measure. He pulled off the highway, killing the engine, then he turned to Eve, taking her hand.

"Your ex-husband is a jerk," he said, using one of his favorite descriptions. "But he's gone. He's out of your life. I'm the one who's here, honey. I'm here."

Eve gazed straight ahead, unseeing, lost in the pain of her past. "I tried to keep Ted," she said, her voice shaking out of control. "I even bargained with him. I told him we'd adopt. But I could tell he already saw the marriage as over. It was almost like he was planning ahead—planning how he'd dump me and find someone who could bear his children. He didn't really see me after the miscarriages. He didn't want to see me. He had a picture of the perfect family, and I didn't fit into it anymore. Damn him."

She knew the rage seizing her couldn't be good for her baby, but how did she stop it? It was too powerful a force, and it was possessing her, finally having its say.

"Ted didn't try at all," she went on, her voice cracking. "He didn't even try! He had to find a new wife. One who wasn't defective."

Ben maneuvered around the gearshift knob until he could hold her. "Forget about him. He's gone. He's out of your life. Marry me, Eve."

"Yes."

"What?" He sounded disbelieving, as if he'd asked her so many times he couldn't understand any answer but no.

She said it again, her throat raw from too many unshed tears. "Yes. I want to marry you. No matter what happens, I want our baby to have a proper mother and father. And...I love you. Most of all, I love you. I'm still so frightened, Ben, but I love you." A different force possessed her now, her love for Ben, sweeping away the rage. "I need you," she said. "Oh, how I need you."

Ben looked at her gravely. "You'll marry me, even though my life's more a mess than ever? Even though my ex-wife is threatening to yank my kids all the way back to Boston?''

"Yes. Yes, I want to marry you. Because you love me even though I'm—''

"Don't say it," he told her fiercely, his hands tangling in her hair as he tilted her face up to his. "You're the most whole woman I know, Eveline Kearny. I will be with you no matter what happens. I'll be with you forever. Can you believe that?''

"Yes," she whispered. The word seemed to come automatically to her now. Somewhere, underneath her fears, she felt the first stirrings of a fragile happiness. Surely this was a sensation that would be good for her baby: the happiness of accepting Ben at last.

"Kiss me, Eve."

The New Mexico sky arched over the Jeep, a blue washed by sunlight. And Eve kissed Ben—her lover, her husband-to-be. In his arms, she almost forgot to be afraid. Almost, but not quite.

BEN STOOD at the top of the ladder and surveyed his handiwork. He'd hammered in the last nail, and now a brand-new basketball hoop that took pride of place over the driveway of his house. The netting was still tangled, and he smoothed it out.

"How does it look?" he called down to Matthew.

"Okay," his son answered listlessly. Ben knew he'd waited too long to put up the hoop, but now that he'd actually gone ahead and done it, he'd hoped for a little enthusiasm.

"Come on, I'll challenge you to a game," he said as he climbed down the ladder.

Matthew nudged the basketball with the toe of his sneaker.

"What's gonna happen if we move back to Boston?" he asked.

"Your mom's just considering that as one alternative. She might very well decide to stay here in New Mexico." Silently Ben cursed Rachael. At least she could have kept this quiet until she actually made a decision; all three of the kids had been through enough turmoil.

"But what if we move?" Matt insisted. "When will we get to see you, Dad?"

Ben picked up the basketball and took a shot at the hoop. He missed, grabbed the ball and tried again. This time the ball went through the netting with a satisfying "whoosh."

"I'll tell you the truth, Matt. I can't be a long-distance father. If your mom goes through with this, then I'll go through with it, too. I'll move right back to Boston with the rest of you guys." Ben felt gratified to see the relief on his son's face. A second later, though, he wasn't quite so gratified.

"That means you and Mom can live together again," Matthew announced confidently.

Ben set down the ball and led his son over to the porch steps. He waited until Matthew was seated beside him. "I think I'd better explain a few things," he said. "Matt, your mother and I aren't getting back together again, not under any circumstances. I'm going to marry Eve in only a few weeks. You know that."

Matthew leaned over and fiddled with his shoelaces. "You're not married yet," he mumbled.

"It's going to happen. Eve's not such a bad person, by the way. In fact, I think she's pretty special."

"She's okay," Matthew said in a guarded tone. Ben was afraid that it would take his kids a while to accept Eve as their stepmother. Maybe a long while. But the important thing was knowing he and Eve were a real couple now at last.

"I'll always be your father, Matt," he said earnestly. "Even if Eve and I had to travel all the way around the world to be near you, we'd do it."

"But you'll have a new baby." Matthew seemed to be in the process of unraveling his shoelace. These days, there was a certain gawkiness to Matthew. He looked as if he was starting a growth spurt, and his limbs didn't know what to do with themselves yet.

Ben felt an intense surge of tenderness for his son, but was uncertain how to share it. Lately Matthew had been trying very hard to act "manly," and he didn't take kindly to demonstrations of affection.

"So you'll have a baby sister or brother," Ben said. "That won't change how I feel about you, just like having Kate and Jenny around doesn't change my feelings. I have enough for everyone. That's how love is, Matt. It's sort of like a balloon that keeps expanding and expanding—"

"Dad," Matthew objected, his expression pained now. He scrambled up from the steps and ran with the ball, shoelaces flying. Ben watched him pound up the driveway and leap toward the basket. The ball went in, clean and decisive.

So much for a heart-to-heart between father and son. Nonetheless, Ben noted a few encouraging signs. Matthew seemed crestfallen, but not distraught at being reminded that his parents were never getting back together again. Also, he finally seemed to approve of the basketball hoop.

Ben joined him for a vigorous game of one-on-one.

BEN'S ENCOUNTER with his oldest daughter later that week didn't go quite as well.

"I don't see why we have to do this," Kate muttered in protest as Ben led her through the cattails and marsh grasses along the bank of the Rio Grande. "It's stupid."

"This is a special place," he answered. "You never know what you'll see. Cranes, mallards, snow geese, red-winged blackbirds, yellow-breasted chats." Actually, the cranes had all flown back north by now. Ben wished Eve could have seen them, but she'd been staying off her feet, just as the doctor had ordered. She'd been the one to suggest that he bring Kate here, instead, hoping that a different setting might help Ben get closer to his daughter.

Now Kate tramped along behind him, deliberately refusing to walk by his side. It was a gentle spring day, the cottonwoods budding and a breeze stirring the water. The river was higher than usual, and Ben had come to realize that it ebbed and flowed with its own tides. He was becoming very familiar with the Rio Grande valley. Its beauty might be subtle, but he'd learned to see it all around him—a beauty that, perhaps, rivaled even the beauty of Boston.

He wished he hadn't reminded himself of Boston. These days he didn't like thinking about the city that had once seemed so exciting. For one thing, Rachael still talked incessantly about taking the kids back there. She had turned Boston into a weapon, and she used it on Ben whenever possible.

She wanted power over him, that much was evident. As the day of his wedding to Eve drew near, Rachael tried to exert more pressure. Her most obvious method consisted of marshaling the children to her side, promising them that their lives would all be wonderful again once they returned to Massachusetts. Five-year-old Jenny believed her mother's promises and chattered enthusiastically about "going home." Matthew remained ambivalent. And Kate . . . could anyone fathom what Kate thought?

It couldn't hurt to ask. Ben stopped walking and turned to his daughter. "Do you want to go back to Boston, Katie? I know, I know, I'm not supposed to call you that. But it's a fair question."

She stuffed her hands into the pockets of her denim jacket and stared at the far edge of the river. "Everybody's in such an uproar," she muttered. "Just the way Mom wants. She even has Phil jumping. He keeps asking her not to leave. It's pathetic."

"I see. I didn't realize Phil was so affected by all this. He must really love your mother."

Kate gave him a scornful glance. "Don't get your hopes up. They still fight a lot, and Mom still says she's leaving. Now that you've pumped me for information, Dad, can we just go somewhere else? I hate this place."

"I didn't bring you here to pump you for information," he said patiently. "But you haven't answered my question yet. Do you want to return to Boston?"

"Sure. Anything to get out of this stupid town." She sounded flippant, but she couldn't entirely disguise the hurt in her voice. She was probably thinking about David Flanders—the boy who'd stopped hanging around her as soon as he couldn't get what he wanted anymore.

Ben tucked his hands into his own pockets and gazed out over the shimmering water. "The guy isn't worth it, Kate. Don't waste too much time feeling bad about him."

She hunched her shoulders. "*Please,* Dad," she said with exaggerated politeness. "Let's just talk about something else."

He had plenty to say, and he was fairly certain his daughter didn't want to hear any of it. But she was out of luck in that regard.

"I remember the day you were born," he mused. "I'd never been so scared or excited in my life. The first time I held you, Lord, you wailed at me. But after a while you actually settled down and fell asleep in my arms. I promised myself right then that no matter how much it scared me to be a father, I'd protect you and keep you safe forever. I haven't done too good a job of that, I'm afraid."

Kate dipped her head forward, the curtain of hair falling in front of her face. But at least she seemed to be listening, and he went on.

"Katie—Kate, you're damn perceptive when it comes to writing stories about people. So pretend you're writing a story about me. Picture a man who doesn't know a whole lot about fatherhood, but who loves his daughter, anyway. He loves her very much, more than he knows how to tell her. So of course he wants her to be happy and well. Maybe he goes overboard. A lot of the time he refuses to accept that she needs to make her own decisions. You see, he's still imagining her as that baby he held in his arms, the baby he promised to keep safe. He's being unrealistic, no doubt about it, but maybe you can understand why he feels the way he does. Maybe, deep down, you wouldn't want him to feel any other way." He paused, "Well...what do you think?" His rather convoluted speech had made him oddly nervous.

She kept her head bent. Perhaps she hoped that if she didn't look at him, he would vanish, and this awkward conversation would be over. Ben felt more frustrated than ever. What else could he say to his daughter, his firstborn? He'd just confessed his well-intentioned bumblings as a parent. What more could he offer her?

But then she raised her head and flicked her hair back from her face. She gave him a sardonic perusal. "Your story's a little rough, but it has possibilities," she remarked dryly. "That's what Eve would say, anyway."

It was enough. Ben put his arm around his daughter—his prickly, sarcastic, independent daughter. She didn't move any closer to him, but neither did she move away. As they stood together on the marshy ground at the very edge of the river, he understood that parenthood would be a messy concern all the rest of his life. He'd never be perfect at it, and he'd never get it nailed down. He'd always be grappling with its problems, one way or another. But for now, he had been given this one moment of peace with his oldest daughter. The breeze rippled around them, and a majestic hawk wheeled overhead, gliding on a current of air. Sunlight glinted on the water.

Yes, it was enough.

CHAPTER TWENTY-TWO

SILAS T. COBB had outlived two wives. He'd wooed each of them in turn with promises of paradise. But instead of paradise, each wife had known only hardship and disappointment in the New Mexico desert. At last he, too, died, leaving behind not his dreamed-for utopia, but a scruffy little town struggling for survival on the banks of the Rio Grande. Even so, Eve found herself wanting to believe in her own private paradise in Cobb. Was she foolish to hope that it would all work out? Could she truly believe that in little over a week, she'd have a husband she loved with all her soul, and after that the baby she yearned for so desperately?

Eve's heart brimmed with too many emotions: longing, fear, the stubborn beginnings of happiness. Setting down her pen, she flexed her fingers. Who would have imagined she'd be suffering from writer's cramp these days? But Professor Halford had graciously agreed to reduce her teaching load so that she could spend more time resting, and so she had little to do except read, write about Silas—and plan her wedding.

Together she and Ben had made up innumerable lists of tasks to be accomplished, aided in their execution by Eve's friend Angela from the college. Help came also from another surprising quarter: cantankerous Josie Scott herself, who seemed to enjoy hounding the florist, the baker and even the reverend.

Now Eve set aside her notepad and tried to shift the pillows into a more comfortable position. Oscar blinked at her from the foot of the sofa, silently protesting the disruption.

"So, I'm going a little stir-crazy, what of it?" she told him. The only way she managed to cope was to take one day at a time. Every morning she promised herself that all she had to do was make it until nighttime. Reaching the end of each day was a triumph, another twenty-four hours that she'd kept her baby safe inside her.

The days were slowly adding up. Miraculously she was in her seventh month and now the end was in sight. She'd never carried a baby this far along before.

So why was she afraid to believe that she'd make it all the way? This pregnancy was different than the others. It had to be different!

At the sound of a key turning in the front door, Oscar dived under the sofa. And then Ben came striding into the living room, carrying his perennial energy, a quality all the more vibrant when compared to her own. He kissed her, bringing with him the scent of the outdoors—fresh, woodsy, brisk. She knew he'd spent some time at his office and then gone for a run. She envied his freedom of movement, her own limbs feeling heavy and unused.

"How's the work going on old Silas?" he asked, his hand lingering against her cheek.

"Just fine. How's the work going in spite of old Josie?" They smiled at each other.

"Josephine has a new project," Ben announced. "Now that she's organized my files, my desk, even my briefcase, she's taken to knitting at the reception desk. I think she's making a baby blanket for us, although she won't admit it. It's an awesome-looking thing, yards and yards of bright yellow yarn."

"That's sweet of her."

"Sweet and Josie—not exactly synonyms."

"Ben, you really went beyond the call of duty when you hired her."

"She surprises me. She can type a mean streak on that old clunker of a typewriter. Besides, I'm almost getting used to her," he admitted with a wry grin. "When business is low, I always have someone available to spar with."

Eve knew, however, that business was picking up. Ben had established contact with an attorney in Albuquerque who was very interested in joining Ben's consultancy for small businesses. With a partner, Ben would be able to move in exactly the direction he wished—if he managed to stay in New Mexico.

"Any more word on Rachael's plans?" she asked anxiously.

Ben's grin faded. "She won't let up speculating about what she's going to do, but she won't put any of us out of our misery by actually making a decision, either. It's strange. Only a few months ago I never would've believed that I'd rather stay in Cobb than return to Boston. But that's the way it is. This is my home now."

"I guess I'm surprised to find myself feeling the same way," Eve murmured. "A few months ago, this town still felt temporary to me. Now, well, I can't imagine leaving Cobb Community. Professor Halford has gone to so much trouble, making sure all my classes are covered, reassuring me that I can arrange any schedule necessary. I actually want that job, Ben."

"I wish I could tell you what's going to happen."

"We'll move to Boston if we need to. We'll work it out." She tried to sound reassuring, but she knew that Ben's ex-wife was a volatile person. She also knew that

Rachael was still in love with Ben. Rachael's difficult behavior only confirmed it.

Ben leaned over to kiss Eve again, his mouth demanding on hers. Every touch between them was potent now. Denied more intense physical contact for the time being, they had to make do. Ben, fortunately, could be very inventive. His lips traced a path of desire down her throat, along her collarbone, over the swell of her breasts. When he lifted his head again, Eve's pulses were racing, and a honeyed heat drifted through her veins.

"Ben," her voice wobbled precariously. "It's been too long for us. Too long without making love."

His eyes were very dark as he sat beside her and drew her into his arms. "I'm making love to you right now," he murmured. "Just use your imagination."

When they broke apart again, Eve's heartbeat had accelerated beyond the danger point, and it took a great effort to pull herself back to reality.

"I could kiss you all night," Ben said, his voice husky. "But I promised Kate I'd prepare the way for her. She wants to come visit you, even though she's afraid you don't want to see her."

"Of course I want to see her!" Eve exclaimed. "I've really missed having her drop by. Doesn't she realize that?"

"I've given her all your messages. And now at last she wants to talk to you. Why not take it from there?"

After dinner, Ben drove Kate over to Eve's and dropped her off. Kate stood in the doorway to the living room, hovering, as usual. For all her bravado, Kate was undeniably insecure.

"Come in," Eve urged.

Kate sidled into the room and immediately paid a great deal of attention to Oscar. The cat, usually so disdainful of visitors, actually allowed Kate to scratch his stomach.

"I keep wondering why you haven't been to see me, Kate. Are you still angry because I told your parents about David? Or is it the fact that I'm marrying your father?"

Kate scrunched herself over the back of the sofa, tickling one of Oscar's ears. The cat purred serenely.

"Maybe I just needed some time to myself," Kate mumbled after a few seconds.

"Maybe. But I thought we were friends."

"You can't be my friend. You'll be my stepmother." Kate's gaze strayed in horrified fascination to Eve's stomach. "And you're having my dad's kid. It's too bizarre."

"Having a baby isn't bizarre," Eve protested with more asperity than she'd intended. "It's something that can happen when you've been sexually active. Kate, you should realize that."

"Great. It's time for the sex-education lecture. Don't you and my dad ever quit? You're the ones who got caught, not me. I mean, you don't see *me* having a baby!"

"Thank God for that," Eve said fervently. "All right, look. I'm the first to admit that adults don't always make rational, well-thought-out decisions. But you know something? Your father's the right person for me. And I'm beginning to realize my ex-husband wasn't the right person at all, just like David wasn't the one for you. Kate, whether you're fifteen or thirty, having someone break your heart hurts terribly. But it makes you stronger, and it makes you ready for the right person when he does come along. And if he takes a long time to show up, so much the better. There isn't any rush. Part of me is very glad I didn't meet your father until now. This is our time."

Kate focused all her attention on the cat, refusing to look at Eve as she spoke. "You might as well just say it straight out. You're still lecturing. You're saying I shouldn't jump into bed with the next guy who comes along. Don't you think I'm smart enough to know that?"

Eve smiled ruefully. "You do have a way with words. And I guess I should give you more credit. Just work with me on this. I'm somewhere between a friend and a stepmother, and it's all new to me."

Kate didn't answer. Still avoiding Eve's gaze, she rubbed Oscar's head. The Siamese purred loudly.

At last Kate glanced up. "My dad said . . . he said you wanted me to be your maid of honor."

"I'm hoping very much you'll say yes."

Kate seemed to consider the proposition carefully. Finally she nodded. "Okay. I'll do it. Except for one thing. I won't wear some stupid, frilly dress. That's not my style."

Eve smiled again. Kate had just offered her some measure of acceptance, and it meant a great deal to her. She felt a surge of affection for Ben's daughter. She had so much love to give now. It encompassed Ben, his children and the baby she carried. It encompassed all of them.

"Your own style is fine with me, Kate," she said softly. "It's just fine."

THE DAY OF THE WEDDING dawned in chaos. First of all, Ben had to deal with the out-of-town guests crammed into his house: Eve's parents, his own mother, his brother, Steven, Steven's wife and Steven's two rowdy kids.

Ben had a theory about people. As far as he was concerned, human beings could be divided into two groups— those who were capable of functioning in a crisis and those who weren't. He liked to think of himself as be-

longing to the first group. On this warm Sunday morning
in May, however, his house was filled with people who
definitely belonged in the latter category.

Take Eve's parents, for example. They were an amia-
ble pair, but they'd seemed flustered since arriving in town
last evening and confronting the actual fact of their
daughter's pregnancy. Eve had already informed them of
her unusual circumstances over the phone, but obviously
they hadn't been prepared for the physical reality. They'd
wandered around Eve's small house, trying to be helpful
but only making Eve uncomfortable. At last Ben had
bundled the two of them off to his own house. Now they
drifted around aimlessly, uttering vague comments about
not being able to locate their toothbrushes and perturbed
comments about their daughter being so obviously pregnant on her wedding day.

And then there was Ben's mother, padding through the
house in her slippers and robe, telling anyone who'd listen that her other son, Steven, would never have been
party to such an unconventional wedding. Steven and his
wife, Judy, had locked themselves in one of the guest
rooms, taking a vacation from their two exuberant sons,
ages four and six. Already the kids had strewn half a box
of cereal on the kitchen floor and overturned a carton of
milk.

"All right, that's it," Ben announced grimly at last.
"Josh, Steven, Jr.—clean up the mess you've made.
Pronto! And Mother—no more comments about Eve's
pregnancy. I'm damn glad she's having this baby, and so
is she. Her worst nightmare was that she wouldn't be
walking pregnant down the aisle. So be happy for her. Got
it?"

Steven might be the favored son, but Anne Lawrence
knew when her other son meant business.

"Of course, dear," she said promptly. "A new grand-child. Imagine that! I'm thrilled."

Eve's parents fell into line, too.

"We only want what's best for Evie," said her mother.

"Our first grandchild, you see," her father added distractedly. "We hadn't dared to hope that this time... Poor Evie."

Ben felt an unexpected sympathy for his new in-laws. He understood now that they'd been covering up their concern for Eve. They didn't appear to be the most involved parents in the world, but clearly they loved their only daughter.

After his nephews had suitably mopped up the kitchen, Ben sent them outside to play basketball. Then he climbed the stairs to put on his tuxedo. He smiled wryly. At least his house was now truly a home, the remodeling finished, the guest rooms hastily outfitted with beds and bureaus. All he had to do at this point was retain his sanity until the relatives packed their bags and left. After that he could bring his bride home—his wonderfully pregnant bride.

At the thought of Eve, Ben's step lightened. Nothing mattered today except that he was marrying the woman he loved. Sometimes he still couldn't believe she'd actually said yes. But he could also tell that at last she'd started to trust in his constancy. Slowly and cautiously she'd let him into her heart.

Ben himself had forgotten caution by now. All he wanted was to say, "I do." If his bride were more mobile, he would have insisted on a speedy elopement. Just the two of them... well, just the three of them. Ben grinned and took the rest of the stairs two at a time.

Somehow Ben managed to shepherd his various relatives to the church on schedule. Soon afterward, Eve arrived with the assistance of her friend Angela. She lumbered to a bench in the church courtyard and immediately sat down. The doctor had given permission for the wedding to proceed as long as Eve stayed off her feet as much as possible, and she was following his instructions meticulously.

Lord, she was beautiful, her red hair swept up beneath a delicate lace veil that floated on the breeze, her body draped in folds of white silk. A local seamstress had fashioned Eve's unusual maternity wedding gown, and it suited her. Ben liked the low scooped neckline. But Dr. Duellno Kearny was so lovely that any gown would have suited her today. Ben gazed at her, almost awed by the fierce emotions she inspired in him. He desired her with an intensity fanned by their months of abstinence, and he knew that when at last he made love to her again, the intensity would only grow and deepen. He felt other desires, too: the need to protect Eve, for all her stubborn independence, and the need to cherish her as he had cherished no other woman. Simply and completely, he loved her.

Sitting beside her on the bench, he took both her hands in his. The air was filled with the sweet heavy scent of the honeysuckle and lavender trailing over the adobe wall next to them, and for a moment they seemed lost in their own private garden. Eve trembled under his touch.

"Nervous?" he asked.

"A little. No—a lot."

"Do you believe in me, Eve? Do you honestly know how happy we're going to be together? I want you to realize that before we walk down the aisle."

She gazed at him, her eyes a blue as clear and bright as the sky above. "I do realize it," she whispered, her fingers tightening on his. "Just be with me, and I'll always believe it."

"You won't be able to get rid of me, love. Not now, not ever." As far as he was concerned, the minister could perform the ceremony right this second. Unfortunately wedding protocol had to be observed. The guests had to be seated, and all the rest of it.

"Ben, your children just arrived," Eve said, motioning toward the front of the church. "Rachael brought them."

"I understood Phil was going to drop them off. Rachael swore the last thing she wanted to do was come here today."

"Well, we did invite her," Eve reminded him. "I suppose you should go talk to her."

Ben's children were soon occupied with their two mischievous cousins, and Rachael stood by herself. Ben went over to her. "Hello. I didn't expect to see you this morning."

"Hello, Ben." Her tone was a little too flippant. "I decided I couldn't possibly miss the occasion. After all, how often does a woman get to attend her ex-husband's wedding? It's truly a cause to celebrate." She stared at him, her features tensed. "Please allow me to congratulate the groom," she said. And then she lifted her face to his and kissed him full on the mouth. It was a bold kiss, with a hint of desperation to it.

Ben pulled away, and turned to seek out Eve. She remained seated on her bench, surrounded by well-wishers, yet she was gazing straight at Ben and Rachael with a startled expression. The last thing Ben wanted was for Eve to have any more worries; that kiss couldn't have reassured her.

He turned back to his ex-wife. "You know, Rachael," he said quietly, "I'm not what you need. Maybe I never was, and I'm sorry for that. But are things so wrong with Phil that you can't fix them? According to Kate, the guy's been making a fool of himself, trying to convince you to stay with him."

Rachael gave a brittle laugh. "I'm the one who's made a fool of myself. I let you go, Ben. And now look at you! The perfect father, the perfect family man... the perfect husband."

"I'm not the perfect anything. And maybe Phil isn't perfect, either, but you married him for a reason."

"You're standing up for Phil?" she scoffed.

"Yeah, I guess I am. The guy eats your egg-free omelets, doesn't he? He complains, but he eats them." Ben could tell Rachael wasn't in the mood for any light-hearted comments, but he could no longer placate her. He'd already paid his debt of guilt for not being the best husband or the best father. It was time to stop paying and to go on with his life. Rachael had to go on, too.

"We'll always be the parents of three kids," he said to her now. "We did something good together, producing those children of ours. But we're not together anymore. I'm with Eve, and you're with Phil."

"How convenient you make it all sound," Rachael said, her voice still brittle. "You need it to be convenient, don't you, Ben? I'm a problem for you, and you want a tidy solution."

"I'm learning to live with a little mess in my life," he stated dryly. "But this isn't about me, Rachael. Stop trying to use me to avoid your problems with Phil."

He saw anger flicker across her face, and then it was gone. Now her expression turned pensive, even forlorn, and he realized that she was doing what she'd done for years—trying to play on his sympathies, trying to get him to draw her out. He'd succumbed to this tactic of hers too often.

"Go home to Phil," he said. "And let me give you some advice, Rachael. Be straight with the guy. Don't expect him to guess everything you're thinking or feeling. Just be straight with him."

Anger hardened Rachael's features again. "I believe I won't stay for your wedding. I was there the first time around—quite enough for me." It was a scathing speech, but Ben could handle it. He preferred to be scorned rather than idealized by his ex-wife.

Rachael hurried out through the low wooden gate in the adobe wall. As soon as she had gone, Ben returned to Eve. Now several of her students milled around her, and he wasn't able to speak freely. He could only kneel beside the bench, taking her hand and pressing it reassuringly.

"It's okay," he told her. "It's all okay."

She smiled at him, her face luminous, as befitted a bride. "Yes," she said, pressing his hand in return. And, hearing that one unquestioning word she'd spoken, Ben knew she truly trusted him at last.

Everything was definitely going to be okay.

CHAPTER TWENTY-THREE

THE MUSIC BEGAN: Mendelssohn's "Wedding March," its sonorous tones mellowed by the string quartet that rendered it so gracefully from an alcove near the front of the church. It sounded more like a minuet than a march, fitting Eve's mood as she sat concealed in the foyer and watched her wedding begin. She felt ebullient and lighthearted in spite of the heaviness of her body. All her nervousness had vanished, and if she had her choice, she would have danced up the aisle to Ben's waiting arms.

From this angle, she could see him standing beside Steven, the best man, and Matthew, the ring bearer. His profile was strong and decisive, but still those quizzical lines radiated from the corners of his eyes. They bespoke his ability to examine life and see all its absurdity and charm. Ben was a man who knew how to laugh at himself, if need be. He was also sexy, romantic, energetic, and more than a bit dictatorial. Eve loved him totally, even the dictatorial part.

Sitting here in the solemn dimness of the foyer, she didn't feel solemn at all. She felt buoyed by her love and by the knowledge that marrying Ben was the most necessary thing she would ever do. She lifted her hand to caress the diamond pendant hanging around her neck. Another diamond sparkled on her finger, fitted snugly there.

The wedding continued, all according to plan. Five-year-old Jenny began her journey down the aisle, an expression of deep concentration on her little face as she scattered petals from her flower basket. Her blond hair fell in ripples to her shoulders, and she wore a pretty dress with pink ruffles. Jenny—the image of a storybook child.

But Eve knew from Ben about Jenny's endearing quirks: her penchant for toy trucks rather than dolls, her insistence that everything in her bedroom be ordered just so before she could turn off the light and go to sleep, her fascination with anything mechanical. Of all Ben's children, Jenny was the one who approached Eve with the most wariness; it would no doubt take Eve a long while to show Jenny that she didn't intend to usurp her mother's place.

Now Kate strode down the aisle, dark hair draped over her cheeks, a bouquet of dahlias clutched in her hands. Eve herself had chosen this particular flower for Kate. The blooms were showy and dramatic, but the white petals were softly tinted in rose. That was Kate all right, a mixture of drama and vulnerability.

Kate had acquiesced to the bouquet, even while allowing no advice on her clothes. She wore a short narrow denim skirt, black tights, granny boots and a cream silk blouse with billowing sleeves. As far as Eve was concerned, it was the perfect wedding attire—absolutely unique, just like Kate herself.

And now it was Eve's turn. The music swelled, much as she herself swelled with the life inside her. On her father's arm, she moved in slow stately steps down the short aisle, carrying her own bouquet of forget-me-nots and white violets.

Ben looked incredibly handsome as she approached him, his tall, broad-shouldered frame emphasized by his elegant tuxedo. He gazed only at Eve, his eyes dark.

Eve's father relinquished her to Ben and she leaned against him, allowing him to support her with his strength. She smiled up into his face. At last the moment had come to exchange their vows, here in this sun-browned adobe church amid a motley cluster of guests: irascible Josie Scott, a beaming Professor Halford, a misty-eyed Angela, a cluster of other teachers and students from Cobb Community and as many curious townspeople as would fit in the pews.

This church was one of Silas T. Cobb's few architectural legacies, modeled after the grace and simplicity of the ancient Spanish missions of New Mexico. The altar was fashioned of plain unvarnished oak, and the floor of uneven brick, the only extravagance the stained-glass windows that lined the nave.

Now sunlight streamed in through the glass, transformed into beams of gold and ruby and turquoise. The last refrain of music faded away, and Reverend Marquez began. He'd been instructed to keep the ceremony short and to the point so that Eve could sit down again as soon as possible.

"Do you, Benjamin Robert Lawrence, take this woman..."

"Yes," Ben said firmly.

"Do you, Eveline Marie Kearny, take this man..."

"Yes!"

Before Eve knew it, young Matthew solemnly held out a velvet cushion to her and Ben. Matching wedding bands gleamed on the cushion. Eve's hands shook so much that she almost dropped Ben's ring before she slipped it on his finger. His own hands were remarkably steady as he slid on her wedding ring.

"I now pronounce you husband and wife." Reverend Marquez took a deep breath. "You may now kiss the bride."

Eve's husband bent his head to kiss her. His lips were firm against hers, promising secret delights when at last they could be alone. But Eve savored this kiss, this moment, as the gold and ruby beams of light shimmered around her, and the lilting music of the violins and cello filled the air.

She and Ben turned to make their trip back down the aisle, and it was then that the pain ripped through her belly—a pain so sudden and severe that she bent over with a moan. She would have fallen had her new husband not reached out his arms to catch her.

"Ben," she gasped, all her happiness vanished in the dreadful reality confronting her.

"Ben," she cried again, even as the pain tore through her. "Oh, Ben, it's the baby. Something's wrong. The baby!"

THE AMBULANCE rocketed down the highway toward Albuquerque, lights flashing, siren blaring. Eve writhed on a stretcher, her immobility gripping her in agony. She longed to run from the pain, to outdistance it somehow. But she couldn't get up, or escape.

Through a haze of tears, she gazed at Ben as he crouched over her. His features were drawn stiff and white.

"Hold on, honey," he kept murmuring. "Just hold on."

Eve still wore her wedding gown, but now it was drenched with perspiration. She clasped her hands around her stomach, sobbing out her terror to Ben, trying to make the terror into something she could understand.

"Oh, God, it was never like this the first two times. Never. I can't predict the pain...can't...dammit to hell! This isn't a contraction. It just...just won't let up..."

She tried to ride the pain by talking through it, but her words were like so many matchsticks tossed into a roaring furnace. The pain burned her up, consumed her relentlessly. She felt Ben grip her shoulder, and even that was agony. She tried to twist away from him.

"Oh, God..."

A medical technician leaned over her, slipping a blood-pressure cuff around her arm. "It's true you're progressing quite rapidly through labor, but please try to remain calm," he said. "We're fully equipped to deliver your baby, should the need arise."

At least now Eve had a new focus for all the terror and anger throbbing inside her. She wanted nothing more than to reach up and throttle the technician. He sounded so damn calm, as if delivering premature babies was something he did every day.

Miraculously, the pain gave her a short reprieve. At last she could turn to Ben, rocking a little on the stretcher as the ambulance catapulted forward.

"If only I'd done something different," she said in misery. "The wedding. It was wrong of me to want the wedding."

"The doctor said it would be fine. You followed all his instructions." As usual, Ben reverted to logic, marshaling facts to prove his case. Yet, in spite of all his reassurance, Ben's face was ashen, his expression haggard as he bent over to caress Eve's damp cheek. "You're not to blame for this, darling. You're not to blame for any of it."

Pain assailed her again, and now she was cold. It was as if she'd been knocked off her feet by a tidal wave of pain, and she was drowning in it. She'd taken enough Lamaze classes to know what to do next, but knowing didn't help her. Her breath came raggedly, all rhythm destroyed. The tears streamed down her face, drenching her.

She was trembling uncontrollably by the time the ambulance reached the hospital in Albuquerque. Still trapped on this stretcher, a modern bed of torture, she was rushed down a corridor. Ben jogged alongside, his face so drawn in torment that Eve almost forgot her own anguish.

"It'll be all right," she said, struggling to tell him. "It'll be all right."

"Hey, I'm the one who's supposed to be comforting you," he said with a bleak smile as they reached the delivery room.

After that, Eve felt as if her entire body was being hurled against a wall of pain. She'd heard friends of hers complain in excruciating detail about labors that prolonged endlessly: eighteen, twenty-four, thirty-six hours... but now she knew that one of those endless labors was far preferable to this accelerated madness. If only it had come on more slowly, given her time to adjust... given her baby time....

Confusing images swam in front of her: metal poles jutting up like more devices of torture, Ben's face hovering above her, grooved with worry. And then Dr. Cole's oddly boyish features under his wavy head of silver hair.

"It's okay, Eve," the doctor said. "Try to relax."

"What did I do?" she gasped. "What did I do wrong?"

"Listen to me," the doctor said. "You did nothing wrong. Do you understand? Now I want you to push, Eve... push!"

If everything else had happened too quickly, then the pushing itself was endless. Now Eve had to hurl herself purposely against the wall of pain, over and over at the doctor's command. She gritted her teeth and clenched her jaw until her head pounded with the effort. Ben gripped her from behind, supporting her back.

"You can do it," he said. "Honey, you can do it."

"One more time, Eve," Dr. Cole joined in. "Give it all you have."

She wanted to scream at both of them. Dammit, they acted as if they were football coaches, and she was the receiver running for a touchdown. Her entire body felt as if it would burst open. But if she *could* push, just one more time...

"My God, it's a baby," Ben said in a tone of wonder, his voice catching.

"It's a boy," added the doctor.

Eve swiped away a film of tears to behold her child, but everything was happening too quickly again. She saw only a glimpse of tiny limbs before her son was whisked away from her. Something was terribly wrong. This was the moment when the lusty cry of a newborn should fill the room. But no cry came.

"Respiratory distress," Eve heard someone mutter, and that was all. They took her baby from her, and left her only with empty, aching arms.

THE NURSE KEPT UP a cheerful patter as she helped arrange Eve in the hospital bed. "A sponge bath is so refreshing, isn't it? You're good as new, truly you are. I'll fold your wedding gown and leave it right here. It's so romantic, you know, the way you came straight from your wedding to deliver your baby. We'll be talking about it for months to come. And you mustn't be concerned about the baby, really you mustn't. They're doing everything they can for him. He'll be fine, I'm sure of it...."

Eve didn't think she could tolerate another second of this nurse. Every inch of her body throbbed and hurt; it had been only a short while since the birth and she was certainly not as good as new. But she could have withstood that if only they'd allowed her to hold her baby. She prayed silently, despairingly, as the nurse cranked back her bed. *Please, please let my baby be all right. Please...*

At last the nurse left, and Ben came into the room.

"Is there any word yet?" she asked, her breath coming on a sob. "Any word at all?"

"Nothing yet. I'm sorry." He sank into a chair beside her bed, wearily bowing his head.

"Dearest..." Eve smoothed her hand through his hair. It was damp with perspiration, as if he had shared every second of her physical ordeal with her. "We have to keep believing our baby will live," she whispered. "We have to keep hoping and praying."

"I'd do anything to keep this from happening to you again," Ben said in a muffled voice. "Evie, I can't believe there was ever a time when I didn't want this child."

She smiled faintly at his use of her childhood nickname; he'd definitely been spending time around her parents. Now the two of them remained in silence for a long while, sharing their torment.

Eve had believed she could never face such a moment again. And yet she was doing it somehow, confronting her worst nightmare. She ached with grief and longing, yet still she was facing this moment with a courage she'd never known she possessed. Perhaps the courage came from Ben. Perhaps he was the one who made her strong at last.

He lifted his head and gazed at her with red-rimmed eyes. "Eve, I love you, no matter what happens. Please believe that."

She ran her fingers through his hair again. "You can banish Ted's ghost," she said softly. "I know I'm with you, not him. You won't leave me. After all, I tried so hard to get rid of you before, and you just wouldn't give up on me."

Ben kissed her palm, then held her hand against his face. "Eve," he said gently, "I know you've wanted to avoid... you've wanted to avoid thinking about a name for our baby."

All through the pregnancy, it had been one of her superstitions. She'd feared that if she gave in to the temptation to consider a name for her child, something would go wrong.

And now, indeed, something had gone very wrong. Her baby was fighting for his life somewhere in this hospital. But even though she felt her heart would break—that it had already broken—she faced this nightmare of hers squarely. Gone were all her self-recriminations, her useless superstitions. What she had left was a powerful unshakable love for her husband and for the child they had created together.

"I want to call him William," she said, her voice surprisingly firm. "I've always liked that name. What do you think of William Robert Lawrence?"

"I like it. I like it very much." Ben's voice was heavy with emotion, but he smiled at her. "William Lawrence it is."

Dr. Cole walked into the room looking drained, his boyish features seeming to have aged. Ben and Eve faced him together, gripping hands.

"Your son's a fighter," the doctor said, managing a tired grin. "He gave us a big scare for a while there, but he's going to be just fine. He's going to make it. Congratulations, folks. You're a family now."

EPILOGUE

EVE STRETCHED LAZILY in her husband's arms and kissed him one more time. It was barely dawn, but already they'd made love. With an active two-year-old in the house, they'd discovered that the early morning hours were one of the few times they had for uninterrupted togetherness.

Now Ben kissed the hollow between Eve's breasts, her diamond pendant nestling there. He often teased her for wearing it so often, but she had to admit she still clung to certain superstitions. This pendant, as much as her engagement and wedding rings, seemed to symbolize the love she and Ben had forged together. And so she wore the pendant for good luck—and to celebrate her good fortune. She'd been married more than two years now, and she was more enthralled than ever with her husband.

"Happy, darling?" Ben murmured.

She ran her fingers over his skin, reveling in the masculine swirl of hair across his broad chest. "Very happy," she answered. She glanced over at the nightstand, where they'd placed an advance copy of her biography of Silas T. Cobb. The book had arrived in the mail yesterday, and they'd been celebrating ever since.

"I can't believe I'm finally a published author," she said. "Of course, it won't win me any awards in the academic world...."

"Don't put down your accomplishment," Ben said. "It's something to be proud of. Not to mention that the publisher wants to see your next manuscript."

Eve was currently researching an obscure nineteenth-century writer hardly anyone had heard of. She liked obscure subjects, just as she liked dusty little towns like Cobb, New Mexico. It had been quite a relief when Ben's ex-wife had finally made the decision to stay in her second marriage—and therefore stay in Cobb. Rachael and Phil had somewhat of a volatile relationship, but they were still together.

"Mommy, Pop," came a demanding little voice from the nursery.

Laughing ruefully, Eve pulled on the nightshirt Ben had so seductively unbuttoned a short while earlier. She grabbed her robe, tied the belt and then went down the hall to greet her child. Bending over, she swept young William Robert Lawrence into her arms and gave him a big hug.

"Good morning, pumpkin," she greeted him.

"Not a pumpkin," Will answered seriously. He allowed the hug for a moment, and then struggled for freedom. Already Will showed an independent streak that his parents found exhausting. It seemed they were always chasing him down as he ran off confidently to explore the world.

Eve watched with a smile as Ben entered the room and gave Will a big hug, too. Will had inherited his mother's bright red hair and his father's dark eyes. And even at two, he seemed to possess Ben's love for logic, as well a Eve's fascination with books. He liked playing with puzzles and having countless stories read to him. With his vivid sense of curiosity, this made for an unbeatable—if tiring—combination.

Eve, Ben and Will all trooped downstairs for breakfast. Oscar was perched on the kitchen counter again, and Eve had to shoo him off. The cat gave Ben an offended stare, as if blaming him for the indignity. Oscar still didn't trust this relocation; perhaps he missed harassing Josie's chickens. To console him, Eve opened a can of gourmet chicken-and-liver cat food. After a few suspicious sniffs, Oscar started nibbling.

Eve set out milk and cereal on the table. She still wasn't much of a cook, and neither was Ben. They had so many other things to keep them occupied: four children to juggle between them, Eve's part-time teaching schedule at Cobb Community, her research and writing, Ben's flourishing consulting firm. It seemed there was always a small business in Albuquerque or one of the surrounding towns that needed the expert advice of a corporate lawyer. Of course, Ben had two partners now. Sharing his workload allowed him plenty of time for family.

"Are you going into Albuquerque today?" Eve asked as she poured milk over Will's granola.

"Yep," Ben answered. "But first I have to stop by the office and try to convince Josie not to toss her computer into the garbage bin."

Eve and Ben exchanged a wry glance. Josie's difficult personality hadn't changed one iota during the past few years. But Josie was a fixture at Lawrence Consultants now, and although she'd never admit it, the job meant a lot to her, Ben and Eve knew.

"How's your day shaping up?" Ben asked as he poured himself some cereal.

"Busy. The baby-sitter's agreed to keep Will an extra hour so Kate can come by and see me at school. She wants to discuss her college applications." Eve smiled again. Eighteen-year-old Kate had given them numerous sleepless nights during the past three years, but she seemed to be coming into her own. She was as dramatic as ever, and just as independent as her little brother Will. But she knew that she wanted to go to college and that she would major in English. Kate dreamed of being a novelist, and Eve had no doubt her stepdaughter possessed the talent and determination to accomplish that dream.

Meanwhile, fourteen-year-old Matthew was deep in the throes of adolescence, and eight-year-old Jenny was still adjusting to the realities of having a little brother. All in all, it was a tumultuous life. Eve knew there would always be worries and joys, and more worries. She couldn't envision it any other way. Perhaps she didn't have the perfect family, but it was close enough.

Surveying her son and her husband with satisfaction, Eve's reverie was interrupted by a soft murmuring from outside the window.

"The cranes," Ben said. "They're starting to head back north again."

He and Eve went to stand at the window, where a graceful V of sandhill cranes floated high across their field of vision. The guttural cries of the birds traveled through the morning air.

"I always hate to see them leave," Ben said, putting his arm around his wife.

Eve placed her own arm around Ben. "They'll be back," she reminded him. "They always come back. They know, Cobb, New Mexico is the place to be."

He tilted her chin and kissed her. "With you, Eve . . . *that's* the place to be." His voice was husky.

Eve kissed him back with all the love in her heart. And then together they went to chase after their son, who had scrambled down from his high chair to embark on yet another adventure of exploration.

HARLEQUIN SUPERROMANCE®

WHERE ARE THEY NOW?

It's sixteen years since the CLASS OF '78 graduated from Berkeley School for Girls. On that day, four young women, four close friends, stood on the brink of adulthood and dreamed about the directions their lives might take. None could know what lay ahead....

Now it's time to catch up with Sandra, Laurel, Meg and Kim. Each woman's story is told in Harlequin Superromance's new miniseries, THE CLASS OF '78.

> ALESSANDRA & THE ARCHANGEL
> by Judith Arnold (Sept. 1994)
> LAUREL & THE LAWMAN
> by Lynn Erickson (Oct. 1994)
> MEG & THE MYSTERY MAN
> by Elise Title (Nov. 1994)
> KIM & THE COWBOY
> by Margot Dalton (Dec. 1994)

**Look for these titles by some of
Harlequin Superromance's favorite authors,
wherever Harlequin books are sold.**

MILLION DOLLAR SWEEPSTAKES (III)

SWP-H994

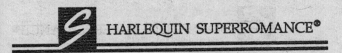

HARLEQUIN SUPERROMANCE®

Superromance Showcase is proud to present
award-winning author

Karen Young

The Promise, the last book in the O'Connor Trilogy, is the
story that started it all.

At last you get to meet Kathleen Collins and Patrick O'Connor
in the first flush of youth and passion. Their panoramic story
will take you from the shores of Ireland to New York to
Savannah. Separated by tragedy, each goes on to forge a new
life. But nothing can keep them apart forever—not even
Caroline Ferguson, whose father makes sure she gets
everything she wants....

The Promise. A story so special, it had to be showcased.

Look for *The Promise* this September, wherever
Harlequin Superromance books are sold.

SHOW1

HARLEQUIN SUPERROMANCE®

He's sexy, he's single...and he's a father!
Can any woman resist?

Jake Winslow's sure to touch your heart.
He's Harlequin Superromance's newest FAMILY MAN.

JAKE'S PROMISE by Helen Conrad
Jake Winslow is back for one reason: he wants his son.
After his wife's death, it seemed best to allow the baby's
grandparents to care for him. But Kenny's older now, and
everyone knows a boy's place is with his father. Everyone,
that is, except Kenny's aunt, who has her own reasons
for wanting to keep father and son apart....

Watch for JAKE'S PROMISE by Helen Conrad.
Available in October, wherever Harlequin Superromance
books are sold.

This September, discover the fun of falling in love with...

love and laughter

Harlequin is pleased to bring you this exciting new collection of three original short stories by bestselling authors!

ELISE TITLE
BARBARA BRETTON
LASS SMALL

LOVE AND LAUGHTER—sexy, romantic, fun stories guaranteed to tickle your funny bone and fuel your fantasies!

Available in September wherever
Harlequin books are sold.

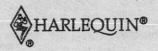
HARLEQUIN®

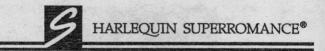

HARLEQUIN SUPERROMANCE®

The O'Connor Trilogy
by award-winning author KAREN YOUNG

**Meet the hard-living, hard-loving O'Connors
in this unforgettable saga**

Roses and Rain is the story of journalist Shannon O'Connor. She has many astonishing gifts, but it takes a near-death experience and the love of hard-bitten cop Nick Dalton to show her all she can be. July 1994

Shadows in the Mist is Ryan's story. Wounded in his very soul, he retreats to a secluded island to heal, only to be followed by two women. One wants his death, the other his love.
August 1994

The Promise is the story that started it all, a story so powerful and dramatic that it is our first featured Superromance Showcase. Laugh and cry with Patrick and Kathleen as they overcome seemingly insurmountable obstacles and forge their own destiny in a new land. September 1994

**Harlequin Superromance,
wherever Harlequin books are sold.**

MIRA™™

The brightest star in women's fiction!

This October, reach for the stars and watch all your dreams come true with **MIRA BOOKS**.

HEATHER GRAHAM POZZESSERE
Slow Burn in October
An enthralling tale of murder and passion set against the dark and glittering world of Miami.

SANDRA BROWN
The Devil's Own in November
She made a deal with the devil...but she didn't bargain on losing her heart.

BARBARA BRETTON
Tomorrow & Always in November
Unlikely lovers from very different worlds... They had to cross time to find one another.

PENNY JORDAN
For Better For Worse in December
Three couples, three dreams—can they rekindle the love and passion that first brought them together?

The sky has no limit with **MIRA BOOKS**.

HARLEQUIN®

Don't miss these Harlequin favorites by some of our most
distinguished authors!
And now you can receive a discount by ordering two or more titles!

HT #25525	THE PERFECT HUSBAND by Kristine Rolofson	$2.99	☐
HT #25554	LOVERS' SECRETS by Glenda Sanders	$2.99	☐
HP #11577	THE STONE PRINCESS by Robyn Donald	$2.99	☐
HP #11554	SECRET ADMIRER by Susan Napier	$2.99	☐
HR #03277	THE LADY AND THE TOMCAT by Bethany Campbell	$2.99	☐
HR #03283	FOREIGN AFFAIR by Eva Rutland	$2.99	☐
HS #70529	KEEPING CHRISTMAS by Marisa Carroll	$3.39	☐
HS #70578	THE LAST BUCCANEER by Lynn Erickson	$3.50	☐
HI #22256	THRICE FAMILIAR by Caroline Burnes	$2.99	☐
HI #22290	PRESUMED GUILTY by Tess Gerritsen	$3.50	☐
HAR #16496	OH, YOU BEAUTIFUL DOLL by Judith Arnold	$3.50	☐
HAR #16510	WED AGAIN by Elda Minger	$3.50	☐
HH #28719	RACHEL by Lynda Trent	$3.99	☐
HH #28795	PIECES OF SKY by Marianne Willman	$3.99	☐

Harlequin Promotional Titles

#97122	LINGERING SHADOWS by Penny Jordan	$5.99	☐
	(limited quantities available on certain titles)		

	AMOUNT	$
DEDUCT:	**10% DISCOUNT FOR 2+ BOOKS**	$
	POSTAGE & HANDLING	$
	($1.00 for one book, 50¢ for each additional)	
	APPLICABLE TAXES*	$_____
	TOTAL PAYABLE	$_____
	(check or money order—please do not send cash)	

To order, complete this form and send it, along with a check or money order for the
total above, payable to Harlequin Books, to: **In the U.S.:** 3010 Walden Avenue,
P.O. Box 9047, Buffalo, NY 14269-9047; **In Canada:** P.O. Box 613, Fort Erie, Ontario,
L2A 5X3.

Name: _____

Address:_____City: _____

State/Prov.: _____ Zip/Postal Code: _____

*New York residents remit applicable sales taxes.
Canadian residents remit applicable GST and provincial taxes..